D0275340

EAST FORTUNE

EAST FORTUNE

James Runcie

NEWCASTLE UPON TYNE
CITY LIBRARIES

Class No.

Acc. No.
4 560353
Issued

WINDSOR
PARAGON

First published 2009
by Bloomsbury
This Large Print edition published 2009
by BBC Audiobooks Ltd
by arrangement with
Bloomsbury Publishing Plc

Hardcover ISBN: 978 1 408 43045 3
Softcover   ISBN: 978 1 408 43046 0

Copyright © 2009 by James Runcie

The moral right of the author has been asserted

All rights reserved.

British Library Cataloguing in Publication Data available

NEWCASTLE UPON TYNE
CITY LIBRARIES

Class No.
F

Acc. No.
C4 590353

Issued

Printed and bound in Great Britain by
CPI Antony Rowe, Chippenham and Eastbourne

For Marilyn

*Love depends
On habit quite as much as the wild ways
Of passion. Gently does it, as the rain
In time wears through the very hardest stone.*

Lucretius: *Book IV, De Rerum Natura*

FRIDAY 6 MAY 2005

CHAPTER ONE

Jack Henderson was trying to live as calmly as possible. He seldom left home, drew little attention to himself, and took few risks in what he considered to be a hazardous world. His was a life of disciplined withdrawal; without pain or disturbance.

It was two in the morning on the night of the General Election. Jack was driving home from Edinburgh. He could see the last of the city lights recede against a spray of summer rain. Traffic moved away from junctions and roundabouts with entitled confidence. This was how driving should be, he thought, with fewer vehicles and everyone knowing where they were going.

He noticed a figure ahead and in the distance. It was a man standing as if his car had broken down. Perhaps he was waiting to hitch a lift.

Jack quickened the speed of the windscreen wipers; brushing away the rain. He noticed that the figure was younger than he had first thought, a student perhaps, staring into the windows of each passing car.

Jack kept his speed steady.

The figure stepped out into the road. He stretched his arms out and his legs apart, making an X, palms facing the windscreen, the hands with a slight tremor that Jack only remembered later. His face had a questioning look that asked: Why are you doing this to me?

Jack noticed that the sleeves on the man's shirt were too short and that his hair was longer than he had first thought. The figure did not seem to be part of the world.

Now the face was up against the windscreen, the flesh ruddy and sudden in the darkness.

Jack felt the weight of the collision.

The face contracted and fell away.

Initially Jack hoped that he had made a mistake. Perhaps he had been dreaming. Perhaps the moment of impact had been a bump in the road, a speed restriction, a dog or a fox.

But other cars were coming towards him in the opposite direction and they were already slowing. Hazard lights flashed behind him.

Jack could see a shape on the ground in the rear-view mirror, a shadow in the darkness, clothing in the middle of the road.

He pulled over and turned off the ignition.

He knew, even then, that this was a last moment of normality before everything would have to change. If he could just arrest this moment, stop time, then everything might yet be all right.

But it was not all right.

He opened the door. There was a surge of noise, braking, people shouting.

Jack could see the silhouette of another man jumping out and slowing cars down.

Now there were lights all around him, people gesticulating, running, stopping and staring.

Jack walked over to the body in the road. Already there was too much blood. The head was pulped on the right side. The legs were splayed away. Nobody lies twisted like that, Jack thought; nobody bleeds like that and survives.

He looked at the head and at the blood; even in the darkness it gleamed a dark crimson: clotted.

4

He tried to work out the man's age. He could see that he was too old to be a student, somewhere between twenty-five and thirty. He wondered how soon his parents would know and if he had a girlfriend.

Jack knew that he would never forget this. It would be a hinge in his life, like the birth of his daughters or the time the woman who became his wife said that yes, she loved him, she would always love him and she would marry him; or the time when that same woman said that although she still loved him the fact was she couldn't live with him any more, she just couldn't. He had never understood what she had wanted out of life. He had never nurtured her.

Nurtured. Even then Jack had thought it a strange word to use.

Now this.

He knew he should concentrate on nothing but the body in the road; a young man who could almost have been a son, a boy, lying in a ripped corduroy jacket, blood draining through his T-shirt: a moment out of the night, the light rain falling, the wood beyond.

Before this Jack had been an ordinary man driving home. He had withdrawn from the world to avoid just such disasters, and yet here it was in front of him, lying in the road: abrupt catastrophe.

He tried to think when he had first seen the figure in the distance. If only he had decided to accelerate before the boy stepped out.

What was he doing walking so far out of town? You never saw people walking around near the A1, you just didn't. You only saw them in the daytime, families who had gone for walks or picnics or men

5

and women whose cars had broken down; never at night.

And why had the boy chosen Jack's car? Why not the previous Mitsubishi or the next Nissan Micra? Why this moment of conjunction when there was no one else on the road?

Jack tried to think of the length of time everything had taken before this moment: how he had been watching the election results come in with his daughter; how they had shared supper together and he had left far later than he intended before realising that he had to find an all-night petrol station. Even the fact that he had allowed a car out at a crossing, or that he had let someone clean his windscreen for a pound at a red light must have made a difference. Any later and the boy might have thrown himself under another car. Any earlier and he might not have been there at all.

There had been little traffic when he had started out on his journey but now there was nothing but cars, vans and lorries. Jack could see a police vehicle approaching.

A man stopped his car alongside, putting on the hazard lights. He had thrown a packet of biscuits on to the back seat. He must have been trying to open them when the accident happened.

Accident.

Another man in a brown linen suit and open-toed sandals was standing in front of the dying boy, for he was dying, Jack knew that, waving traffic away. The man was hopping from one foot to the other. Perhaps he was trying not to get the blood on his socks.

Someone else had stopped: a fat man with a

comb-over getting out of a car and sweating, leaving a black Labrador in the back seat and his wife too scared to get out. She was holding a little boy in a yellow fireman's hat.

'He fair threw himself at you,' the man was saying. 'There was nothing you could do . . . I saw it happen . . . I'll say so . . . you'll need a witness.'

He took his shirt off to staunch the blood.

A woman got out of a yellow Nova and put a mohair rug over the boy in the road.

'Poor wee lamb,' she said.

Jack looked at the rug because he didn't want to look at the boy's face. What kind of tartan was it? he thought. It was one of the less familiar clans.

What could he do to undo it all, this moment?

'I'm a nurse,' the woman was saying. 'We have to stop the bleeding.' She started stroking the boy's head, pressing at the blood with her husband's shirt, watching the life die away. 'Have you called an ambulance?'

Jack felt for his mobile phone but couldn't remember the number. It was different on a mobile phone, wasn't it? He could see other people doing it for him. The boy began to cough in the road.

Jack couldn't look at the face or the rug any more. He began to concentrate on the boy's shoes. They were polished brown brogues. They seemed almost too clean for the rest of his clothes.

People were always speeding on this road, the woman was saying, there've been complaints, local campaigns; drivers speed up as they leave the city, hope you weren't speeding.

Her husband was stopping all the other cars, gesturing to the ambulance to come through.

7

Jack heard the paramedics talking about a *triage category one*.

A policeman started asking him questions. Was Jack the driver of the car and would he like to step aside? He had spots on his neck and silver numbers on the shoulder of his uniform that made Jack think of Sudoku. Perhaps all the policeman's numbers added up to forty-five.

He appeared to be talking about a digital breathalyser. Now the metal grates were between Jack's teeth and he was asked to blow through a plastic tube into the small hand-held device. The policeman was telling Jack that it used an electrochemical fuel cell as a sensor. If the reading was under the legal limit of 0.05, the driver was normally free to leave, although obviously this wouldn't apply under these circumstances.

As Jack waited for the result he could see a policewoman taking statements from the witnesses, writing by hand in the light of the cars. It was taking her for ever. He thought how much better it would be if the policewoman knew shorthand. He could almost hear his mother's voice: *Don't they teach them anything these days?*

He did not know how he could avoid telling her what had happened. His mother would try to console him, he knew, but there would also be a silent judgement, a feeling of disappointment; the sense that Jack could probably have avoided the whole thing if only he had been more aware.

He wanted to speak, to explain himself, apologise even now to the boy who was being lifted into the ambulance; but the policeman said, 'Better no say anything at this stage, sir.'

Jack was driven away from the scene, back past

8

the hospital and into Edinburgh.

There were fewer people in the streets of the city. A girl in a white T-shirt was taking off her shoes to run barefoot and catch up with her friends; a homeless man in a sheepskin coat was holding out a beaten paper cup from McDonald's.

A sheepskin coat? Jack thought. In the summer?

At the police station the chairs in the fluorescent room reminded Jack of school. He was offered a mug of tea. He never normally took sugar but now he asked for three spoons. He could do with a blanket too and then he remembered the rug covering the boy. Would the woman have taken it back, or would she have abandoned it? Perhaps it would be evidence?

The clock read twenty-seven minutes past three. For a brief moment Jack felt he was in an airport. There was the same consistent light.

He worried how much he would have to explain. Perhaps he would spend the night in the cells, await trial, and never leave?

The policewoman who prepared to take his statement had short blonde hair and pale-blue eyes. They were the colour of speedwell, Jack decided. She had a soft voice with a hint of Fife in it. When had she decided to be a policewoman? He looked at her fingers for rings. Not married. Or did she take her jewellery off when she was on duty?

Yes, he was called Jack Henderson and it was his car. No, he hadn't been drinking. Yes, he'd already been breathalysed. They should have known that. Why did they keep asking? Were they trying to catch him out? The boy had stepped out right in front of him. There was nothing he could have

9

done. Surely they knew that?

Jack had always been scared of accidents and chance collisions, of bicycles and drunks, people holding kebabs and takeaways and cans of Tennent's Extra, staggering, being sick, a drunken Scotland shouting through the Saturday-night traffic.

And he had always been anxious about driving. He preferred trains and buses but what could he do, living in the countryside where there were only three or four buses a day, and not earning enough for perpetual taxis?

He told the policewoman that he'd always been frightened of accidents. He wanted to say, 'In fact I've always been scared, full stop.' That was why he had withdrawn from the world in the first place: fear of accidents, fear of life.

'A *cautious* driver then?' the policewoman asked.

'A *careful* driver. There is a difference.' He didn't mean to sound pedantic.

She asked him whether he had ever had any convictions in the past and when his car had last been serviced. It was clear that Jack was yet to escape blame but he could not think how he could have done anything differently.

'The boy stepped out in front of me,' he said. 'There was nothing I could do. I know he saw me.'

Jack waited for the transcription of his statement. He could hear typing on a keyboard from the next room, a man shouting, 'What the fuck's it got to do with youse, you bastards?' A woman hushing, 'Calm down, Jim.'

'Don't you start telling me to fucking calm down.'

Jack looked at the clock and then at a duty officer, who appeared to be doing a crossword. A mute television in the corner was showing the election results. *LAB HOLD EDINBURGH NORTH AND LEITH.* The policewoman drummed her fingers.

'Don't do that,' Jack wanted to say, halfway between a parent and a husband.

She smiled briefly and turned away, embarrassed. She had probably gone over her shift and was into overtime. She needed the money, Jack thought. He guessed that she would rather be at home, anywhere other than here with some middle-aged bloke who'd just topped a stranger. Perhaps they had a name for the victims, like train drivers after their first 'one under'. Jack remembered reading that the most popular time for train suicide was eleven in the morning; so two o'clock in the middle of a summer night was perhaps a bit out of the ordinary. The eleven o'clockers. They got up and decided. It was like going to work.

Had the boy chosen him deliberately? Had he checked for single male drivers, avoiding families, old people and young lovers? Perhaps he had thought that a single middle-aged man would be able to cope better; and in a reassuring Mondeo Estate too, not some nippy little hatchback or convertible: sprightly enough for speed yet still sufficiently heavy to do the job. How much had he planned it—the volume of traffic, the weight of cars, the best position to ensure maximum impact? Had he chosen this stretch of road on purpose, just after the speed cameras where people always tended to accelerate away—or had it been an

11

impetuous, random decision, a piece of chance or accident that had brought them together?

Perhaps the boy had thought nothing at all and just walked out, on substances, drugs or drink? Or perhaps he was calmly rational, fearing neither pain nor consequence?

Jack asked the policewoman when he could go home.

'We're just about done.' She was not prepared to treat him as she might have done before the accident. 'All you have to do is sign the statement and you're free to go.'

'Now?'

'We'll call a taxi,' the policewoman said. 'You do have money? It's quite a way to North Berwick.'

'What about the boy?'

A bit of softness appeared in her face.

'You can phone in the morning.'

The taxi smelled of cigarettes and Magic Tree. Jack sat in the back and looked at the tightly gelled grey curls of the driver as he talked about the problems at Hearts football club.

'We might as well move the whole shebang to Lithuania,' he said.

The sky was lighter now. It didn't really matter what happened to him any more, Jack thought. He was no longer in control of his life.

The driver began to talk about the election and the Prime Minister having sex five times a night.

'What's wrong with doing it once properly? That's what I always say.'

Jack tried to think of the last time he had slept with Maggie. It must have been three years ago. He had hoped that they could reach some kind of mutual understanding, beyond passion, but he had

12

been wrong.

'It's because he's going to lose the war. That's what I think,' the taxi driver was saying. 'He has to make up for it with sex.'

He drove with one hand and kept turning round to see if Jack was all right. Jack guessed that the policewoman had tipped him off. 'You watch him,' she must have said.

He asked the driver to take a different route so they didn't have to pass the scene of the accident.

'Are you sure? This is the way. The A198.'

'There was an incident earlier.'

Incident.

'Cleared up now. They radioed. It'll take ages to go cross-country.'

'Please.'

'You're throwing your money away.'

'I don't care about the money.'

'You want me to go by all the windy back roads?'

'If you can.'

The taxi driver began to talk about Edinburgh's new traffic measures, which took everyone round the houses, and picking up the stag parties and hen nights (women were the worst, you wouldnae think it but they were). The streets were like the bottom of a baby's pram, he said, *all piss and puke*.

Jack arrived home. The house was too big for him now that the family had left. He looked out at the long-redundant swing, and at the photographs of the children in silver frames: his two daughters against a celestial-blue studio backdrop.

He lived in a villa of red sandstone with flagstone floors and a large family kitchen. He had bought it when it was falling apart and he had been restoring it over twenty years. He had not worried

13

then about coastal erosion or global warming; all he had wanted was a house on a cliff and a view out into infinite possibility. It would never be as grand as his parents' house but he had wanted to provide the kind of childhood environment he had known himself, a constant sense of home, a place of refuge.

He opened the door to the larder and looked at foodstuffs past their sell-by date, left over from a time when his wife had prepared all the food. There were items he didn't have a clue what to do with: baking parchment, liquid glucose syrup, dissolving gelatine, organic hemp oil. At the back he could see a Highland Spring bottle with a Post-it note Sellotaped over the label. *HOLY WATER. DO NOT THROW AWAY*. Maggie was a Catholic. There had been tension within his family about her from the start.

He turned on the television. Jeremy Paxman was arguing with George Galloway. 'Are you proud of having got rid of one of the very few black women in Parliament?' Although the debate was feisty it did not seem to have any relevance to anything in Jack's life at all. Nothing mattered except the boy in the road.

He made a pot of peppermint tea and took it outside. He sat on the garden swing in the dark, rocking himself backwards and forwards, like one of his two daughters, Annie and Kirsty, ten years previously. He thought of the alternative routes he could have taken on the road home: any other decision that would have spared him this.

He tried to think again if it might have been his fault, if there was anything he could have done to avoid the accident. He hoped the boy had given some kind of warning or left a note. He should have asked.

He finished his tea and returned to the house. He stopped outside the bathroom and read the framed poem on the wall outside.

> *I have a child; so fair*
> *As golden flowers is she,*
> *My Cleis, all my care.*
> *I'd not give her away*
> *For Lydia's wide sway*
> *Nor lands men long to see.*

Maggie had given it to him on Annie's first birthday. Now Jack walked into the family room, passing once loved objects that were no longer needed. There was his grandfather's wax stamp and his Morse code key, the frayed lampshade he had never replaced, the Greek amphora Kirsty had made at a pottery class when she was thirteen.

Through the window he could see the mist of summer rain, lit by the garden light, dripping in quick repetition from the slates of the roof into the gutters, bouncing off the down pipe and the satellite dish, falling through the blossom and the leaves, resting on the ferns and the climbing hydrangea: everything Maggie had planted to make the garden theirs.

Jack tried to recall good things in his life; the luck and the happiness he had known that might explain this balancing act of fate, this nemesis: Fortuna, a sudden reacquaintance with death.

That morning he had felt hopeful. He had sat in the garden and seen a blackbird gathering moss from the roof. He had watched a bumblebee bounce against the kitchen window and heard the cry of swifts newly returned.

Yes, he thought, he had been quite happy despite the withdrawal from his family. This was what the ancients had been after, an untroubled, solitary existence, away from all the fever and the fret.

Rain fell on his face as dawn began to break.

*   *   *

The next morning the police phoned to say that the boy had died. His parents lived in Edinburgh's New Town. They had one other son: Allan.

They would let him know about the funeral.

Jack tried to concentrate on his work.

He thought perhaps he should do something on the myth of Iphis, who hanged himself when Anaxerete did not return his affection. How many in the classical world had died or killed themselves for love?

Perhaps he would make his students study the description of the moment of death in Lucretius: the departure of the spirit as smoke floating in the air.

Quod genus est Bacchi cum flos evanuit. Just as happens when the bouquet of wine has vanished . . .

Could his students think of a better word than 'bouquet'?

Aut cum spiritus unguenti suavis diffugit in auras. Or when the sweet breath of ointment has dispersed into the air . . .

Couldn't they do better than 'ointment' or 'unguent'? Why couldn't they be bold and use 'perfume' or 'fragrance', and make the fact of

16

death nothing more than the fragrance of a passing woman?

Aut aliquo cum iam sucus de corpore cessit. Or when the flavour has passed from a substance . . .

Wasn't there a better way of translating this to make death more sensual, more pleasing, evanescent?

Jack could not concentrate. He decided to write to the boy's parents. He had to say something and writing it down would clarify his thinking. Then he could begin to come to terms with what had happened.

He made himself another cup of tea, and tidied up the kitchen, thinking of what he might write. He looked out his best fountain pen and filled it with ink. Each time he started he could not quite think how to phrase the letter.

Dear Mr and Mrs Crawford,
*   I wanted to write to say how sorry I am that the accident happened.*

Was 'accident' the right word? How else could he describe it? 'Incident'? That made him sound like a policeman. 'Event'? It was a bit more than an 'event'. He remembered reading articles in the Sunday papers telling him never to apologise or admit responsibility at the scene. It meant that he couldn't say what he really felt. He crossed out what he had written, drew out a fresh piece of paper, and began again.

I am sorry about all that has happened. It must have been a terrible shock.
Was that good enough? It seemed so bald.

17

'Shock'. Surely he could do better than this? And was it a 'shock' in any case? Perhaps there had been signs, warnings, previous attempts? He could not assume anything at all.

It must be awful to lose a child in this way.

Would the parents still see their son as a child? Jack didn't regard his daughters as 'children' any more. Perhaps he should say 'son'? Or would that imply that to lose a son was worse than losing a daughter?

I wanted to let you know that, if there is anything I can do, or if you would like to talk about what happened, I would be happy to do so.

'Happy'? Glad? Would he really be 'happy'? Perhaps he should say 'prepared'. *I would be prepared to do so*. But was that friendly enough? How could he strike a balance between concern and distance?

He had never had to write a letter of condolence to a stranger before. It was different with friends. He had learned to suggest that the deceased were still with them, even if not in any bodily form. We carry them with us into the rest of our lives, to the last extremity, *tempus in ultimum*. We hear their voices. We can recall them at any time. They live within us.

But he could hardly say all this to a couple he had never met.

Jack decided to write what he could, correcting as he went. Then he would write the whole letter

18

out again, a fair copy.

It took him over an hour and he decided to post it straight away. Then there would be no time to change his mind or refine it further. The job would be done.

Writing the letter taught Jack to keep busy. When he lost concentration, and had forgotten what he was doing, he snapped back to realise that all he was thinking about was the figure in the road.

So he looked for distraction: organising the timetable for next term, marking essays and dissertations, setting up extra seminars for the students who had fallen behind, anything to avoid thinking about Sandy Crawford.

Jack tried to picture the long fetch of the boy's life: what kind of family he must have come from and how he had come to be separated from its security.

How bad did life have to become for a man to be so determined to throw it all away?

*   *   *

Without his car, Jack travelled by bus to the university. It was slower but simpler. He did not have to concentrate and it gave him more time to think about all that had happened. He did not know whether he would have to tell his colleagues or what they might say behind his back. Perhaps they would think he had not been concentrating or that he was drunk; not that he ever drank that much.

On the bus Jack sat behind a woman who was complaining that she shouldn't have to pay for a

19

TV licence because she only had a small television, and besides, she only watched opera. The girl opposite looked like an art student. She was lettering a phrase into a new notebook: *I HARDLY EVEN KNOW YOU*. And then at the bottom of the page: *CAN'T YOU SEE?*

Out in the streets the wind hit him for the first time; the early-summer air of a city that never stayed warm for long. He stopped at a florist in Nicholson Street. The floor was crowded with wedding sprays and funeral wreaths. White chrysanthemums spelled out the word 'Elaine'.

He chose four bunches of white freesias and asked for them to be sent to the boy's home.

A film crew was shooting a period drama near by. Two men with cans of lager started a football chant every time the first assistant called 'Action!' demanding £20 to go away.

> *Twenty quid, twenty quid, twenty quid!*
> *Twenty quid, twenty quid, twenty qui-id,*
> *Twenty quid, twenty quid, twenty quid,*
> *Twenty QUI-ID, twen-ty quid.*

He took the lift to his office in George Square and tried to keep to his routine: Roman authors in translation on Tuesdays, Latin every Wednesday, philosophy and set texts on Thursdays. He had organised his timetable so that even in term time he had a four-day weekend.

Jack knew that he had to try to stay calm, not letting the death affect him, but it returned with every passing police car, each ambulance siren, and with the sight of every solitary male figure waiting to cross the road in the distance. These were his daily reminders, *ne obliviscaris*: do not forget.

A few days later, amidst the bills and the junk mail on the doormat, he found a handwritten letter.

Dear Mr Henderson,
    Thank you for your letter and the flowers. The funeral will be held next Thursday 19 May at Greyfriars Kirk at midday. If you would like to come you would be welcome. We appreciate your letter at this difficult time.
    Yours sincerely,
Peter and Iona Crawford

He wondered if people would know who he was at the funeral and how many people he might have to tell. He could already imagine them pointing him out.

That's him.

Perhaps he could stand at the back without anyone noticing. But he would have to meet the parents; he would have to say something.

He wished Maggie was still with him or that he could persuade her to come. He could hardly ask one of the girls; Annie was travelling, Kirsty had her exams, and besides, then he would have to explain everything.

He did not want to worry them. He did not want to be blamed or face any kind of confrontation. That was why he had withdrawn in the first place, he reminded himself. Now, it seemed, he had failed even at that.

       *   *   *

Jack had forgotten that he had promised to go with his parents to a concert in the Queen's Hall. His mother called to remind him.

'I noticed that you didn't write it down when I mentioned it.'

'I've had a lot on.'

'More than usual?'

'No, it's not that.' He wasn't going to tell her on the telephone.

It was a concert of motets and madrigals. Jack had to pretend to like the music more than he did. He saw himself as more of a blood-and-thunder man: Beethoven. Mahler. Wagner.

'They are a very good group of Americans,' his father was saying as they entered the Hall.

The audience was mostly retired. The spaces around the seats were cluttered with walking sticks, shopping and handbags. Jack caught himself wondering how often the people left their homes and how many more concerts they would be able to attend before they died.

The music consisted of love songs and laments; for lost love, lost youth, and lost opportunity. Perhaps, Jack thought, Sandy Crawford had been driven to distraction, and then death, by love. He began to imagine talking to a girl, or perhaps a boy, at the funeral: the survivor, the punished, the left behind.

As he listened to the music Jack thought of his friends who had never reached old age, struck down by breast cancer, AIDS and accident: Katy, Peter, Jan; now this boy. It was another marker in his life. A stop.

A woman with long dark hair stepped forward

22

and began to sing how cruel and inexorable fate had coloured her sweet life. Jack knew that it was unhealthy to think that she was speaking directly to him when the words were random acts of coincidence. They could hardly have been *meant* but the music was saying what he could not.

He knew he should tell his parents what had happened and how he felt; that this recent disruption meant that he could not think of anything else. But how would he begin and how could they hope to understand?

Perhaps, Jack thought, it would be better to protect them from the news. They were old. They had seen enough disappointments. And Jack had surely lived long enough not to be a child to his parents any more; not to need mothering or fathering or for anyone to tell him that everything was going to be all right. In any case everything was not going to be all right. No one was going to kiss this better.

He tried to concentrate on the music. The singer was coming to the end of another lament. She was begging her lover to deign to remember all that they had shared. She could never forget him.

Si vous pri, que de moi vous voelle remenbrer,
Car je vous porroie oublier.

He returned home to discover that Maggie had telephoned. Jack worried that she was phoning about one of the girls, or money, or an unspecified anxiety he could do nothing to allay, but when he returned the call it appeared that she just wanted a chat.

'What are you doing next Thursday? I'm going

to be in Edinburgh. I've got a meeting at the Botanics.' Her tone was surprisingly cheerful. 'I don't suppose you're free?'

'I'm afraid not.'

'What are you doing?'

'Nothing. A long-standing engagement. A seminar.' He could hardly tell her it was a funeral.

'Can't you change it?'

'No. Why? Is it urgent?'

'You normally can.'

'Well, I can't change this.'

'What is it? Are you all right? Has something happened?'

She had always been able to tell what he was thinking in the past but Jack would not confess.

'No. Nothing has happened.'

'Are you sure?'

'Of course I'm sure. And I have to be away in the afternoon.'

'Oh well, another time. I'm glad you're going out. That's something.'

'I don't stay in all day, you know. I still have a job.'

'I know. But I don't want you spending too much time on your own. You know how you get . . .'

Jack was sure his wife had noticed the anxiety but he was prepared to say anything, however inadequate, rather than tell her what had happened.

*   *   *

He had been to enough funerals and was more familiar than he wanted to be with readings about people stepping out into the next room, or

24

footsteps that had been with us all along. But death had never been his direct responsibility before.

The Minister spoke about the inevitability of human pain. He argued that suffering could make people strong, and that Sandy's death had been a kind of sacrifice. He had been a bright young man who had been unable to cope in the real world. The Minister talked about the delight of Sandy's jokes and his curiosity about the world before the loss of self-worth, the gradual closing; his silencing from all those around him.

They sang a hymn: 'Jerusalem the Golden'. A man stood up and told the congregation that he had not only been Sandy's brother but also his best friend. He read the lyrics of a song Sandy had written:

> *All the things we've said*
> *All the life we've led*
> *Everything we've shared*
> *Everything we've known*
>
> *All the times we've loved*
> *All the times we've fought*
> *Everything we've shared*
> *Everything we've known*
>
> *Forgive me, forgive me,*
> *I hadn't thought, I hadn't known*
> *A life by myself, a whole life alone*

Allan Crawford talked about Sandy as thoughtful and kind but also troubled by the carelessness of everyday life. He had seen poverty and injustice and he wanted to fight and change it and he had tried to do too much of it on his own. He couldn't understand why people didn't think as he thought.

As he spoke Jack looked at a woman in the front row. It was either a relation or Sandy's girlfriend. Her hair was dark and swept back, severe more than sober, and she was wearing a black summer dress. It was as if she was no longer part of the world. Her eyes were dulled but not red. Jack wondered if she was on medication.

He thought of the suicides he knew from history; the urging on to silence when death became a need, a desire beyond all other: behaviour that could not be redirected, a silencing.

After the blessing the congregation left to the sound of 'American Pie'.

This will be the day that I die.

There was a wake at the house in Drummond Place. Jack had said that he didn't want to trouble them but Sandy's father had insisted that he come. It was like a summer party with white wine and elderflower cordial; cucumber and smoked salmon sandwiches; strawberries and chocolate cake.

The house was filled with floral displays from friends: white lilies, white orchids, white roses. There were bereavement cards on the mantelpiece and side tables: impressionist paintings, Constable skies; images of permanence and good taste.

In the hall were large collages of family photographs behind sheets of plastic: the mother with her boys on the beach, family groups in church cloisters, mountains they had climbed, sites where they had camped.

The inner doors of the house had been

26

removed, ready to be stripped for another round of DIY. There were sample doorknobs and taps for the bathrooms amidst the flowers, the condolence cards and the golfing memorabilia.

'Would you like a drink, Mr Henderson?'

'Jack. Please call me Jack. That would be kind.'

Iona Crawford showed him school photos of her son in a navy windcheater on the top of a mountain, a Munro probably, smiling with his thumbs up. Perhaps she had moved it to make it more prominent. Jack wondered if Sandy had been the favourite.

'He loved mountains. Until he thought he had better things to do. If he'd stuck with mountains . . . Still . . . We can't change anything now . . .'

Jack studied the photographs for longer than was necessary. It was easier than speech.

'We'd had a bit of trouble with him before, over Highers,' Peter Crawford said. 'He'd even seen the doctor and got the medication but none of us were ever expecting anything serious. Hypomania, they called it. I thought that sounded bad, but the doctor said it was only a mild form and that rest, a bit of exercise and mountain air would do him good.'

'What did you do?'

'We went to Skye, climbed the Cuillins. It was the best time we had together. But then, after a couple of years at uni, it all started to go wrong. Perhaps we expected too much of him. He said he was tired, he couldn't write essays any more. Then he took to his bed. Nothing we could say would get him out of there. He was listless. He said that he had lost his sense of taste and found eating exhausting. His brother thought he was just "being a student" and that it was only a bit of attention-seeking. I wanted to tell him to pull himself together but Iona kept saying if a child is called attention-seeking it's because they want attention.'

'I've always thought that,' his wife said.

'So we made sure we looked after him, brought him food. We left it on trays outside the door, but it was no use. He didn't want to recover. He believed that, if nothing moved, if he could just keep everything still, then he could survive in that state for ever. No one would notice. Every time we went in to see him he pretended he wasn't there. For a time he only moved when we were out of the house.

'Then Krystyna came. At first I didn't think she could deal with it all. But she turned the whole thing round. And I was grateful to her. Sandy was always calmer when she was with him. But then he must have collapsed again; just when we thought he was getting better. It doesn't seem fair.'

'I miss him so much,' said Iona. 'I thought if I could only keep him at home he would be safe. But you can't hold on to your children for ever, can you?'

'I suppose not,' said Jack.

Sandy's mother was beginning to cry.

'I'm sorry. Please excuse me. It was good of you to come.'

Jack walked out into the garden, and saw the girl from the front row at the funeral. Her skin seemed whiter than it had been in the kirk; her hair even darker. The only colour other than black was a touch of pale-grey eye shadow and a silver bangle on her arm. She was smoking.

'I am sorry,' she said, putting out her cigarette.

'It is not allowed in the house.' She spoke with an Eastern European accent and looked as if she would rather be anywhere other than standing in this garden; this city; this country.

'I'm sure they wouldn't mind.'

'I think they do. Even today.' She looked at Jack as if she could not understand why he was talking to her. Then she guessed. 'You are the man?'

'Yes.'

'I am Krystyna.'

'I'm Jack.'

She nodded.

'I should say I am sorry. For you. For what happened.'

'I don't think . . .'

'Because . . . you know . . . I am . . . I was . . . the girlfriend . . .'

'I understand.'

'You have been told about me?'

'Only a little.'

Jack did not know how to continue.

'Where are you from?' he asked. They could have been at a drinks party.

'Poland. Kraków.'

'Your English is very good.'

'I have been here for three years. And I learned before I came.'

'Are you a student?'

'No. I have a job. One day I'd like to study more. But now, of course, everything has stopped.'

'I can imagine.'

'I did not expect this.'

'No. I don't suppose we can ever prepare for something like this.'

The sun was in Krystyna's eyes. She moved into

partial shadow.

'Did you see him walk out?' she asked.

'Yes . . .'

'Was it clear? That he wanted to do this?'

Jack remembered the night again.

'It seemed so. But I keep thinking I should have swerved.'

'He would have done the same,' said Krystyna. 'Like in football. They go the same way. Sandy did it in the streets all the time. It was always an accident. But he kept doing it. If someone was walking towards him and stepped out of his way, Sandy would move in the same direction. It was so confusing.'

Jack wanted to ask how long Krystyna had known him and if she had seen the body. He could not picture what the undertakers might have done to such a battered head, or to the chest, to make the corpse look at rest. He remembered the policewoman telling him that Sandy had died, and that no one since then had used the word 'dead'. He had 'gone', or 'passed over', he was 'no longer with them'. But he didn't seem to be dead.

'You were brave,' Jack said. 'In the service.'

'You saw me?'

'I didn't mean to stare. I thought you might have been his sister.'

'No.' Krystyna smiled. 'He did not have a sister . . .'

'Yes. The police told me. I remember now. I'm sorry.'

'I could feel people were looking at me the whole time. I did not know what to do.'

'I suppose you just have to get through it,' said Jack. 'You cannot do anything else.'

'Yes, it is like that.'

'I am very sorry.'

'We should have known,' said Krystyna. 'All of us. We should have stopped it happening. We didn't have enough patience. None of us did.'

'You mustn't be hard on yourself.'

'No,' said Krystyna. 'That is where you are wrong, I must be hard on myself.'

'I understand,' said Jack.

'Really?' Krystyna's tone was brittle, as if she was ungrateful for Jack's sympathy. 'I do not think you do,' she said. 'I do not think you can understand at all.'

Jack stepped away, preparing to leave.

'I'm sorry.'

Krystyna leaned forward, swaying slightly. For a second Jack thought she was about to faint. He wondered if he was going to have to catch her, explain what had happened, be responsible once more.

Krystyna held up her hand, apologising with her body before she said any words.

'I am sorry. That was not polite. I did not mean to be rude. I only mean that we cannot understand what it is like for each other. I cannot understand what it is like for you.'

'You can imagine.'

'I can try to imagine. It must have been horrible. To drive that car; for all of this to happen.'

'I keep remembering it,' Jack said, 'and then I keep trying to forget it. Perhaps it is the same with you.'

'Yes, sometimes . . .'

'I cannot know,' Jack said. 'Neither of us can. I cannot know what it has been like for you at all.'

31

'No. Perhaps we are the same.'

'We try to understand . . .'

'And then we understand that we cannot understand,' said Krystyna. 'I'm sorry, I must go. I must see other people.'

Krystyna walked away. Jack looked at her and beyond her; at the sawflies on the roses and at the haar drifting in from the sea.

*   *   *

He knew that it was ridiculous to want to see her again. He tried to tell himself that he should forget Krystyna altogether, but he wandered round the Polish areas of Edinburgh, hoping that it would seem accidental if they met.

He looked at buses pulling away, crowded with people starting or finishing their days, men and women who simply got on with the sheer business of living.

Jack wished he could feel part of it all but how was he supposed to stop thinking about the night, the boy in the road and the light rain falling?

He looked in Polish cafés, delis and restaurants. He tried to keep on the move, maintaining the illusion of knowing where he was going. He realised that it might take weeks to find Krystyna.

He finally saw her in a queue for a bus at the top of Easter Road. She was with a group of friends but stepped away as soon as she saw him.

'It is you,' she said.

Jack asked Krystyna if they could talk. They might both find it helpful, he said. He wasn't sure. But he thought he should offer. He wanted to do something to acknowledge what had happened. He realised that, because of his nervousness, he was saying too much, speaking too fast. Perhaps they could go for a drink.

'I am not sure this is a good plan. I am not sure it would be good for us to talk about it.'

'I keep thinking about it,' Jack said, avoiding the truth of *I keep thinking about you*.

She looked at him and he thought that he could detect pity.

'All right,' she said, 'if it is polite . . .'

'You don't have to.'

'I could maybe see you Thursday. If you like.'

They met in a pub on Leith Walk. A group of students were discussing what they took to be some of the great mysteries of life: why twenty-four-hour shops had locks on their doors when they were open all the time, what was the best thing before sliced bread, and how did Danish pastries, English muffins, French fries and Scotch eggs come to be named?

Jack asked for a vodka and tonic and a pint of lager. He knew that he was too old for all this. Even when he was at his smartest, in slimming black, his older daughter told him that he looked like a minister who had seen better days.

Krystyna had found a table in the garden under a large green umbrella. A barbecue was starting up. Jack remembered when they had last had one at home. Annie's friends had come round and used a vocabulary that he could only partly understand. They told stories about their racist grandparents counting the number of black television presenters and used incomprehensible phrases such as 'buff', 'scran', 'bang-off' and 'allow that!'.

A group of Krystyna's friends called over—

33

'*Częôść!*'

'Would you like to join them?' Jack asked.

'I do not think so.'

'I hope you're not embarrassed to be seen with me.'

'They probably think you are a friend of my father.'

Best get that out of the way, Jack thought.

'Don't look so worried,' Krystyna said.

'I'm sorry,' Jack said. 'I don't normally do this. I tend to avoid my students.'

'I am not a student. It is fine.'

Jack could see that Krystyna was being brave, putting in her defences, lest he ask her too many direct questions.

'Thank you for seeing me,' he said.

Krystyna lit a cigarette.

'I do not know what you want.'

'To talk . . .'

'What do you want to speak about?'

'It's hard.'

'Of course it is hard.'

'There is so much to say but I cannot sort out my thoughts,' Jack said.

'You are worried about asking too much?'

'Yes, that's right.'

'It's OK.'

'I'm not sure that it is.'

Jack wanted to know how much Krystyna blamed him for what had happened. Perhaps another driver would have avoided Sandy, or only wounded him.

'Do you think about it all the time?' he asked.

'Of course.' Krystyna took a sip of her drink.

Jack wondered if she was hoping that the action

alone would fill the silence.

All he wanted was to find out if she thought as he did; that they had been involved in an event that no one else could understand. They were responsible and yet they were also victims; forced to stop their lives without knowing how they could recover or continue.

'Normally I know what to say,' said Jack, 'but I can't find the right words at all.'

'We have time,' said Krystyna.

'I hope so.'

Jack noticed the birthmark on the inside of her upper arm, just above her left elbow. It was like a splash of dark-brown paint or a smear of chocolate. On her engagement finger was an amber ring.

'Do you have enough people to talk to?' he asked. 'About what happened?'

'I have friends. They are mostly Polish. I know I have to be strong.'

'What about your family?'

'My mother is dead. I have not told my father. He is too far away. He did not know about Sandy. *Jednakże*, he does not like failure.'

'It's not failure.'

She pushed away a strand of her hair.

'I see Allan: his brother. Other people do their best but I think they are a little bit embarrassed. Why did you want me to come here?'

'To see if there was anything I could do to help.'

'To understand?' she asked.

'I don't know. Perhaps one can never understand these things. Was there any warning?'

'So many. But I did not believe Sandy.'

'You can't blame yourself.'

35

'I can. Trust me.'

'Then I'm sorry,' said Jack.

Krystyna began to tell her story.

'Before, Sandy came to see me all the time. He did not stop. Even when I asked him. He said he wanted to check that I was real, that I had a place in the world, and that he was not making me up. If he could see me then he knew that I was real.

' "Sometimes," he told me, "I am not sure we are alive at all."

'He said it was like being in a coma or a dream, because he could not do anything about the world. Nothing he did made any difference. It did not matter what he said or did. The world ignored him.

'I did not know what to do. Then the policewoman came with a note in her hands. I saw Sandy's writing and a strange word I did not know, *weary—even the weariest river finds somewhere safe to sea*. I did not understand what he meant.'

'I wanted to go to the inquest,' said Jack. 'But it didn't seem right.'

'The policewoman gave me the note. "We will need you at the hospital," she said. "When you've had a moment." I did not know what she meant when she said "moment". What is a moment? How long is a "moment"? The last time I had been in a hospital was when my mother died. Then she said, "You might like to bring a friend."

'I did not know who to call or what to do. I do not know how you do things in this country. I had no idea. So I called his brother.'

Jack remembered Allan in the middle of the wake, drinking from a can of beer with a girlfriend in a silver dress. His suit had looked too small for him.

Krystyna was still speaking.

'He had this blackness, Sandy kept telling me. It was always there, over his shoulder, behind him. He said he sometimes felt he was being followed by his own illness. The only way he could stop it was to lie down. I could not understand. "You can't be followed if you're lying down," he said.

'Then I was in hospital myself, lying down, next to his body. I kept my eyes open and on the light in the ceiling. I was thinking that I was going to be there for ever, everything had stopped, and there was no escape from anything. Just the end. And melancholy—is that the right word?'

'Grief.'

'Ah yes, grief.'

'I'm sorry,' Jack said. 'I didn't mean to go into all this.'

'I think you did.'

Krystyna looked down at her empty glass and lit another cigarette. Jack offered her a second drink and returned to the darkness of the bar. The students waiting in front of him were talking about great nights out, the end of exams, weekends away in Dublin.

'You must not be upset with yourself,' Krystyna said when he returned. 'It was an accident. Nobody blames you, I promise.'

'I know . . . well . . . no . . . I don't know.'

'You were in the wrong place. That is all. It cannot be your fault.'

'I can't help thinking about it. I worry you'll blame me, that you are angry with me, that you think I could have avoided him.'

'I don't. I am angry with Sandy. I am angry with myself. I do not have any anger left for you.'

37

'Can you think about anything else?'

'We cannot help what we think.'

'I'd like to see you again,' Jack said.

Krystyna was surprised; almost amused.

'Why?'

'If you need help; or if you want to talk to someone.'

'*To jest los . . .*'

'I'm sorry?'

'It is fate.'

'What will you do now?'

'Go on. What else can I do?'

'I thought you might like to go home—have some time away?'

'I don't know what "home" is any more. If I have a home it is here.' Krystyna stood up. 'I am sorry. I have not been polite.' Then she stopped, opened her bag and tore a page out of a notebook. 'Here is my phone number. In case you want it. I must go now. I have to work.'

She held out her hand so that Jack could shake it: a formal farewell.

'It was nice to meet you,' she said, speaking as if it was a phrase she was remembering from her first English lesson. 'I hope we meet again.'

'I hope so too.'

Jack stayed on in the pub and went over everything they had said. He tried to think how he might have expressed himself better or encouraged Krystyna to stay longer. Perhaps she had left so abruptly because she was upset and she did not want to show him.

He walked back to his office, past the skateboarders in George Square and the chaplaincy centre that offered consolation to 'all

38

faiths and none'. It was a student world of kebab shops and cafés (*Haggis samosas are back!*), of second-hand bookshops, bookmakers and poundsavers. Jack could not imagine what Krystyna made of it all or how she could ever feel at ease in such a city.

He gathered up the exam papers he had to mark and took the bus home, out through the south of Edinburgh, following the road he had taken the night Sandy had died. The roadside hedges were thickening in the warm rain; spindle and blackthorn, blackberry and crab apple, woodland ghosts with yellow rapeseed behind. The bluebells were dying now.

He could see the noticeboards out of the window: *Two miles, thirteen fatalities in three years. One mile, six fatalities.* Jack wanted someone to stop, to recognise what had happened to him. It could be a stranger, anyone who would allow him to feel less solitary.

He walked back from the bus stop past the willow scrub by the river, the banks deteriorating, vegetation halting the flow. It looked clogged and stagnant.

That night he listened to the sea rise and fall in the distance. He thought how long it might take Krystyna to recover and how selfish love could be when removed abruptly and without warning; the punishment involved.

He could not stop thinking about her: the sound of loss in her voice, the distance between them as she spoke. He looked out into the garden to see the first of the wisteria coming into bloom, the promise of summer.

CHAPTER TWO

Krystyna was twenty-seven. She had come to Edinburgh to earn money, to improve her English, and to be with her friend Eva who was working as a dental technician. They lived in a two-bedroom flat on a main road above a Thai restaurant.

When she had earned enough money Krystyna planned to go back to university, to do an MA or an MPhil. She wanted to study what it had been like to leave her country in the past. She would research the experience of Polish émigrés who had come to live in Scotland during the Second World War; Jews leaving the ghettos, the airmen of 309 Squadron, the students at the Polish Medical School; all those who had been forced to reinvent themselves while still retaining a sense of their original nationality. It was a story of blood and belonging.

Perhaps this was the reason she had been so willing to see Jack. Because he worked at the university she hoped that he might help her.

She earned most of her money as a contract cleaner, driving round Edinburgh with her friend Myra, letting herself in to houses in Merchiston and Morningside, taking it in turns to do the wet work and the dry work, sometimes annoyed at the washing up left in the kitchen, the piles of ironing and the extensive bottles left over from parties: all the careless remains of wealth. So much money seemed to have been spent on so much *stuff*.

Sometimes she and Myra would laugh at the possessions that littered houses which were already too full; at model railways, doll's houses, and dying bonsai trees; at plasma television screens and gym equipment that showed no sign of ever being used.

Each time they drove out on their cleaning run Krystyna thought of Sandy. She looked at the cars and tried to think how he had decided to step out into traffic. Jack said that he had appeared calm, determined. Krystyna could not remember Sandy ever being like that.

At night she dreamed of standing in the road instead of him, the car coming towards her. She shuddered at the impact, the falling away. She could almost feel herself losing consciousness. At other times she would be driving the car itself, heading towards Sandy, deliberately killing him, unable to do anything to stop it.

They had been with each other for just over a year. Krystyna had been attracted to Sandy's curiosity, his enthusiasm for all that was new. He wasn't going to be tied down to a single job or career path. He would earn money as a sous-chef or he would work for a polling company, saving enough for the next round of travel to a place where he could live cheaply, Sri Lanka or Taiwan, spending six months working and then giving it all up to see what happened.

He would work and talk through the night, hardly sleeping until the inevitable collapse would come and he would take to his bed for days, even weeks, lying in the darkness, hardly eating, preparing himself for the next manic assault on life.

He kept saying that he only wanted to be with Krystyna, and after a while neither of them appeared to be spending any time with anyone else.

'Where are you going?' he would say. 'Why do you need to see Fergus? Why are you having a drink with Magda? Why can't we just have a night in?'

'We always have nights in,' Krystyna said. 'It is all we do.'

'And what's wrong with that?'

When she questioned him his tone became threatening. Didn't she understand that they had something more valuable than friendship? It was absurd to spend time with other people when they could be with each other.

He phoned her every day and then all the time. Krystyna began to dread seeing him. She tried to be as gentle as she could but the kinder she was the greater advantage he took.

Krystyna suggested he should see a doctor.

'I'm fine. I'm in love. That's all. There's nothing wrong with me.'

'But, Sandy . . .'

'What's wrong? Isn't this perfect?'

'No, Sandy, it is not . . .'

'Don't you like it? What more can I do? I love you. I want to be with you. What's wrong with that?'

'It is too much.'

'How can love be too much?'

'I do not know.'

'You don't like it?'

'Sometimes I do not know if I can breathe. Sometimes I think I have to get away from this. You cannot see that?'

Sandy was pouring sugar into his coffee. He held the spoon in midair, letting the white grains fall.

The rest of the room was still. Nothing seemed to be moving except for the falling sugar. He kept putting more and more into his cup.

'Stop it,' Krystyna said. 'Enough. You do not need to do this.'

'I can do what I want.'

The coffee and the sugar began to spill into the saucer.

'I think we should stop,' Krystyna said.

'You don't mean it,' Sandy replied.

'I do. I am sorry.'

'My life is nothing without you.'

'That is not true.'

'How do you know what I feel? You don't know the effect you have on people.'

'You exaggerate.'

'All I want is you.'

Krystyna had taken such care to avoid a confrontation.

'It isn't right,' she said. 'I can't be everything you need all of the time. In the end you'll be disappointed. I won't be able to live up to what you want. I am not right.'

'But what if I think you are?'

'I can see you think that,' Krystyna said, 'but you have to believe me. This is not good for either of us.'

'I think you're wrong,' Sandy said.

'I am sure you do. But what you think does not make it right.'

'Doesn't it?'

'No, it does not.'

'I can't believe you're saying this.'

'I am sorry.'

'You'll miss me,' he said.

'I know.'

'And you'll regret it.'

'Yes, Sandy, I know I will.'

He picked up a knife from the block by the sink and stabbed it into the breadboard.

'And if you don't I'll make you regret it.'

'Don't . . .'

He walked out, down the stairs and into the street. Krystyna thought about opening the window and calling down, already worried, telling him to come back, but she could not stand it any more.

That had been three weeks ago.

Now, after his death, his *suicide*, Krystyna was determined not to take all the blame. His death even made her angry and she took out her frustration on all the objects that confronted her: kitchen sinks, taps, strainers and stainless-steel drainers. She wiped down hobs and oven doors, marble worktops and kitchen tables. She concentrated her aggression on white surfaces and dark floors, on stairs and banisters, rubbing away the detritus of privileged lives until her hands hurt.

Sometimes she even said his name as she polished, *Alexander Jamie Crawford*, whispering the words, 'I hate you, I hate you.'

'Slow down,' Myra said. 'You'll exhaust yourself.'

'It is all right.'

'There'll be nothing left to clean.'

The suicide was melodramatic selfishness, Krystyna decided; ingratitude for all the time they had been together. She had shown such patience and had been rewarded with death and guilt.

She had to find more work. In fact she wanted to do nothing but work. She would work so hard that perhaps she never needed to think again.

*   *   *

She became depressed and feverish. She was sick. Then she missed her period.

She began to panic. *Cholera jasna*.

She couldn't be pregnant. She just couldn't.

She decided to say nothing even though she kept vomiting in the mornings and taking to her bed as soon as she came home from work. Eva asked if she was all right and suggested that they went away together to forget about all that had happened. They could even go back to Poland.

Krystyna thought of her friends and the abortions they had had. It was why she had always been so careful. She couldn't ever see herself going through with such a thing and she was angry with herself and with Sandy all over again. It must have been the last time they had slept together, when she had just stopped taking the pill and had only agreed out of tiredness and nostalgia. How stupid could she have been? Why couldn't it have happened when they were happy and free, when they had experienced all the early stages of discovering each other, when trust was absolute and everything had been an adventure?

She checked for the symptoms of pregnancy on the Internet, knowing that she had virtually all of them, and picked up a test in the chemist. She looked at the instructions on the back of the packet and saw that she wouldn't have to wait more than a minute for an accurate result. Anyway she already knew. She bloody knew.

How could Sandy have done this to her? How

could she have let it happen?

She drank down a full glass of water. Then she looked in the kitchen for a container. There was a measuring jug, the glass bowl they used for beating eggs and the china basin for the apple cakes they cooked to remind them of home.

Krystyna wished her mother was still alive. She wouldn't tell her father or her brothers. *O mój Boże*.

None of the containers were appropriate or hygienic. For a moment she wanted to smash them on the floor. *Skurczybyk*.

She opted for the transparency of the glass. She carried the bowl into the bathroom and set it down at the foot of the chair. Then she went into the bedroom and took off her trainers, her socks, her jeans and her pants.

She returned to the bathroom and sat down on the chair. She read the instructions again:

1. Remove the test from the airtight package.
2. Holding the strip vertically, carefully dip it into the specimen. Do not immerse the strip past the max line.
3. Remove the strip after four to five seconds and lay the strip flat on a clean, dry, non-absorbent surface.

She had forgotten to prepare the surface. She thought of kitchen towelling but realised that would confuse the test paper. She brought a white side plate back from the kitchen and sat down once more.

Gówno.

She picked up the bowl and peed into it. Her

46

urine was the colour of straw. She did not know if that was good or bad or whether it mattered.

She pulled out the test strip from the packet and lowered it into the bowl. She wondered if her thoughts could have any effect on the outcome. Could she will the colour bands not to appear?

And if they did not appear would she be relieved or disappointed?

The test result took as long as Sandy must have taken to die. She wondered what he would say if he could see her now. Not that she would have let him.

She put the strip on the plate, poured the bowl into the toilet, and rinsed it in the sink. Then she dressed and washed her hands, drying them on a towel that was still damp from Eva's morning bath. It never did dry properly. That was another thing that annoyed her.

What am I doing here? Krystyna thought. Why?

She stood looking at the piece of paper. The control and the test lines had both begun to colour the pale pink of baby clothes. '*Cholera jasna,*' she said.

She walked back into her bedroom and lay down on the bed.

It was a hot afternoon and she wanted it to be dark but she was too pre occupied to get up and close the curtains. She would just look at the sky and the tenement block opposite.

The test was positive.

Gówno, gówno, gówno.

Perhaps it was all some sick test of fate to find out how strong she was. She decided not to see a doctor. What would be the point? *She knew*.

Out in the streets of Edinburgh the only people

47

Krystyna noticed were mothers with children. They were lifting prams and buggies on to buses, squeezing into the lift of the St James's Centre, strapping their babies into backs of cars whose stickers warned other drivers to take care: *Princess on Board, Proud Mum, Dad's Princess*. She couldn't move without noticing that a lot of people had had a lot of sex: *Baby Under Construction, It Started With a Kiss, I Love My Bump*.

'Fuck off,' Krystyna wanted to say. '*Spierdalajcie*.'

The kids themselves were dropping their dummies and small toys all over Edinburgh, crying out for food, wriggling to escape their confined spaces. Elder children threw tantrums on the floors of bookshops, or raced ahead towards traffic, or stood in the middle of a shopping centre refusing to go home. In the supermarkets mothers loaded their trolleys with nappies, toilet paper, kitchen rolls, baby powder, bottles and sterilising equipment. Krystyna did not think she had ever seen so many children. Did the world need another child? Would she really have to go through all this?

She took long baths at night. She kept topping up the hot water, letting it spread across her belly.

How soon would she start to show and what should she expect? A swollen stomach, tender breasts, discomfort, backache. She thought of the clothes she would have to wear, smocks and skirts with elasticised waists and accommodating tops. There would be so much to buy: cribs and mobiles and nappies and food, and she would have to work even more hours to support the two of them. At least as a cleaner she could take the baby with her.

She realised that she was imagining she had a

child already. It was easier than the alternative.

She stepped out of the bath and began to towel herself dry, more aggressively than she had intended.

She tried to picture the future, alternating the days on which she imagined she had a son, Adam, or a daughter, Carolina, and the days on which she had no child at all. But on those days she missed her previous conceptions, her Adam, or her Carolina. It was as if they had already been born, had lived and were lost to her.

The days on which she imagined having a child became more common, easier to live with, although she worried how much it would inherit from Sandy, especially if the child was a boy.

How much would he look like him? Would he be a permanent reminder of all that had happened, or would he be an act of grace, a kind of redemption?

*   *   *

She saw Jack again. He had sought her out of guilt. She worried that at some point she would have to make it clear that it was only ever going to be a friendship. She didn't want any misunderstanding. But neither did she want to make any assumptions or be rude.

They climbed Calton Hill. It was Krystyna's nearest walk and she had been up most weekends when she was with Sandy. Going on her own, and now with Jack, was a means of reclaiming it for herself.

It was a hot, dry day, which made the climb seem steeper. Already Krystyna thought how much more difficult it was going to be if she maintained her pregnancy.

After they had reached the top they looked down towards Princes Street and out to the silhouette of the Old Town. It was a view that made the city seem more European than it did on the ground. The Castle reminded Krystyna of Prague, even of Kraków. They sat on the steps of the National Monument.

'It's a long time since I've been here,' said Jack. 'It must be ten years . . .'

'And who were you with when you came?'

'I think I was on my own.'

Krystyna looked at him.

'You know I don't know anything about you. Where do you live? What do you do? What about your family?'

'Nothing very interesting. I'm a senior lecturer in Classics. I tend to work most of the time: teaching, translating. I don't seem to do much else.'

'Have you always lived here?'

'More or less.'

'You were born here?'

'Yes.'

'So it is your home? You belong?'

'Yes, I suppose I do.'

Krystyna noticed that Jack had not talked about his family.

'What is it like to be Scottish? Tell me.'

'It's probably just as hard to explain what it's like to be Polish. I don't know.'

'What about your childhood?'

'It seems so long ago now.'

'Tell me.'

'You really want to know?'

'Of course.'

Jack began to tell her about the parental home in East Lothian, the countryside that surrounded it; memories of his brothers.

'How many do you have?'

'Two. I'm the middle child.'

'The peaccmaker.'

'That's what they say—neither the responsible eldest nor the favourite youngest. What about you?'

'The second,' said Krystyna. 'I have an elder brother.'

'Ah . . . so you are your father's favourite?'

'Not since I left. I would not be his servant. He thought I was ungrateful. Wc do not get on well.'

'I am sorry.'

'Did you have a happy childhood?'

'Sometimes I think it was too happy,' said Jack.

'Is there such a thing?'

'Now I am the one being ungrateful.'

'It is unbelievable,' said Krystyna. 'Being too happy . . .'

'It was quite idyllic, I suppose—a house in the country; a mother and father who loved each other. It meant there was nothing to rebel against. You spend your life trying to live up to the standards and expectations your parents have given you.'

'That does not sound hard.'

'I'm not complaining.'

'It sounds very, I am not sure of the word, is it "privileged"?'

'It's traditional. I'm sure you've seen a traditional Scottish country home.'

'Only the ones I clean.'

51

'This is different.'

'A country house. I cannot imagine it . . .'

'Come and see it, if you like.'

'No. It would not be right.'

'Why not? I've got to go there in a couple of weeks. My father does these amateur theatricals.'

'I do not understand.'

'It started off as something for the grandchildren to make them appreciate Shakespeare; you know, get them when they're young, like the Church, but mostly it succeeded in putting them off. But we do it because my father takes it so seriously and we don't want to disappoint him.'

'It is always Shakespeare?'

'Every summer.'

'It must take a lot of time.'

'My father is retired. Why don't you come?'

'I cannot do that. What would everyone say? What about your wife? Or your children?'

He looked surprised, as if he had already told her about them.

'Oh they don't come, I'm afraid. I don't have a wife any more.'

'I am sorry. I did not know.'

'No, that's all right.'

'She died?'

'No. She left. The girls are away. University, travelling, you know the kind of thing. Come to the play. Be my guest . . .'

'I do not think so, Jack.'

It was the first time she had said his name. It sounded strange, more familiar than she had intended. It surprised her. Perhaps she had said it out of pity after he had mentioned his wife.

52

'You should come. Honestly,' Jack continued, 'there's something charming about it. I think that's why we still do it. You could even be in it, if you like. We're always stuck for numbers.'

'What about the audience?'

'It's just the family. When you're not in a scene you just sit down and watch. It's very informal.'

'Do you have costumes?'

'Of course. And then there's a bit of a dinner party. It's like a shooting party, except with Shakespeare instead of guns. Why don't you come?'

'I have not been invited.'

'I'm inviting you.'

'I would not know what to say.'

'You don't have to say anything. The lines are all written down for you.'

'It would be crazy.'

'Yes. But that's the point. You could return to Edinburgh and tell your friends how mad it is.'

Krystyna was surprised by his enthusiasm. Talking about the eccentricity of his family had given Jack a confidence she had not seen before. It made it harder for her to say no; and besides, the event sounded so odd, so British, that she thought she might even enjoy it. It was like a secret piece of tourism, revealed only to the few.

'What is the house like?' she asked.

'It's very beautiful,' Jack said. 'It explains everything.'

'Everything?'

'Well, almost everything,' Jack replied, and then appeared to stop himself. 'I don't think I've ever said that before.'

Krystyna tried to think what it could be like: a

country house, a *dacha*, a home; perhaps it would be a place where no one could reach her, a retreat from all that had happened and all that was about to happen; a kind of sanctuary.

And what else would she do? She could not think of any alternative other than remaining in her room and staring, without thinking, at the walls.

'What do you say?' Jack asked.

'All right,' Krystyna replied. 'Why not?'

She began to walk ahead of him, down the hill and back into the city. She would be nervous on the day, she knew, but at that moment she had a feeling of recklessness, of light.

CHAPTER THREE

Jack's parental home was situated on the outskirts of East Fortune in the grounds of a large farm that had first belonged to his great-grandmother. The house was of pale-grey sandstone, the pitched roof was clad with Dutch pantiles, and the six chimneys that protruded from it had been symmetrically arranged to frame the crescent-shaped exterior. Bought at the turn of the twentieth century, the building had dominated family life. Each descendant had been told of the importance of passing the house on in a better condition than when they had inherited it. The gravel front was weeded and raked each day, the walled garden was tended every week, and a man came to clean the sash windows, inside and out, at the beginning of every month.

The building was situated in a low valley, but the outlook was open and wide, with views from the hills behind the house that stretched out to the Firth of Forth and the North Sea. The sight of the coast was both an end and a beginning: the edge of adventure.

Jack's mother Elizabeth had been born and brought up in the house, marrying Ian Henderson at the age of twenty-five and providing him with three boys: Angus, Jack and Douglas. In return, her husband was expected to earn enough money to keep the place going and sustain the traditions to which Elizabeth had been accustomed: talk to factors and land agents, pay the bills, and provide a steady sense of home for their sons.

It was a house of privilege and expectation. This was not a family that tolerated failure. If tasks were to be undertaken, no matter how trivial, they had to be performed well.

Ian Henderson had already given the family his *Julius Caesar* and his *King Lear*. He had educated them, somewhat against their will, in English history through his unique interpretations of *Richard II*, *Henry IV* and even *Henry V* (although at the age of sixty-nine this had been something of a stretch). Now he had chosen comedy, and even risked ridicule, by taking on the part of Malvolio in *Twelfth Night*. Angus had been signed up for Orsino, Jack was going to be Feste, and Douglas, Sir Toby Belch.

Their father had phoned each son in turn and asked, 'You will learn your lines, won't you?'

His three boys had replied, as they did every year, that they would do their best without intending to do anything of the kind.

55

Angus had been persuaded to arrive early to help erect the set. As the tallest and the broadest of the three brothers he was always called in first to help with any manual labour. His father told him that he had 'farmer's hands'.

The set was a series of painted hardboard flats that could be clamped together to make a castle on the back lawn. They had used them a few years previously for the History Plays and now they were brought out every summer. Ian had decreed that, whether it was history, comedy, or tragedy, most Shakespeare plays needed battlements.

He was wearing a threadbare Viyella shirt and a pair of faded red corduroys. He hadn't bothered to dress properly because he was planning to go through his costumes later that morning. In fact he was still wearing his slippers; a twenty-year-old pair of Church's with one heel down. He had hinted that someone might like to give him a new pair for his birthday but guessed that his family probably thought he was too old to get the wear out of them.

He asked Angus to carry out the stage weights. They were heavier than he had remembered. So much of Ian's life now consisted of conserving his energy and making sure that he wasn't surprised or caught out by old age. He had to concentrate harder on tasks that he had previously taken for granted. He wasn't sure his children realised what an effort his life had become, but then, he flattered himself, it was probably because he disguised it so well.

'You know Jack's bringing a friend?' he said as he watched Angus move the flats into position.

'Male or female?'

'Female.'

'You don't think . . .'

'We'd better not ask. She's Polish, apparently.'

'How did he meet her? Jack hardly ever goes out.'

'She's called Krystyna.'

'Sounds very exotic. How old is she?'

'I didn't like to ask,' said Ian. 'Jack's been quite moody recently.'

'He's always moody.'

'I thought Krystyna could be the Captain.'

'Are you sure that's wise?' Angus lifted another panel and asked his father to hold it steady while he weighed it down. 'Bit of a baptism of fire, coming to the family play.'

'Well, she can see us warts and all.'

'You'd have thought she might have better things to do.'

'Oh I don't know. A day in the countryside, a spot of Shakespeare . . .'

'Was it your idea to ask her?'

'Jack volunteered. He said that it would make up for his girls not coming, and besides, he said that she'd been having a hard time. Apparently she needs cheering up.'

'I can't see Jack cheering anyone up.'

'Now, now.'

'And he's playing Feste, for God's sake. All that gloomy singing . . .'

'It will be an adventure for her.'

'I thought Jack had renounced the world to concentrate on his work?'

'Apparently not . . .'

'And I'd have thought he would be a bit out of practice with the ladies.'

57

'Well, we'll just have to see, won't we?'

Ian had never examined his sons' relationships closely. Angus and Tessa were fine in themselves; but Douglas and Emma found it impossible to conceal their difficulties and for Jack to break his near-monastic existence with this new girl was very odd. He only hoped that his son wasn't about to make a fool of himself.

'And here's Sir Toby!' he called when Douglas got out of his car. 'And the lovely Viola. Have you learned your lines?'

Douglas sighed. His father could think of nothing but his bloody play. He had no idea how busy their lives were, how tense their journey from Glasgow had been, and what an effort it had been to persuade Emma to come in the first place.

'Not quite, Father.'

'That means you haven't learned them at all.' He wished his children would make more of an effort.

'I'm sure we'll muddle through,' said Emma, stepping forward to kiss Ian on the cheek.

'Muddle through? That's hardly the spirit. I'm relying on you. You're the professional, after all.'

'Well, Ian, I'll see what I can do.' It was so demeaning for a proper actress to do am. dram. The rest of the family kept putting the stress of the verse in the wrong places. Every year Emma wanted to take over and tell them all how to speak it properly.

Douglas put in his case for the defence.

'There are a lot of lines, Father. And we've been very busy. Any chance of a drink?'

'It's only just gone midday.'

'Well, that's all right then.' Douglas walked off

58

towards the kitchen.

'It's amazing you lot get any work done at all.'

'It's the artistic temperament,' said Emma. 'At least that's what my husband calls it . . .'

Ian had once had such high expectations of his boys. He knew that it was wrong to show disappointment but there were times when he could not help it. Angus had given up his rugby and done well enough as a fund manager, but Jack could have been a professor if he'd put his mind to it; and for Douglas to abandon law and fritter away his intelligence by working in television was a complete waste of his ability: everyone thought so.

'You're here,' said Elizabeth. 'Home at last.'

'We're not late,' Douglas replied. He leaned over the kitchen table to kiss his mother on both cheeks. He knew that both of his brothers kissed her on the lips but he had never thought it appropriate.

'Mind your cardigan in the sauce,' she said.

'Bugger . . .'

Emma handed him a piece of kitchen towel and then kissed her mother-in-law.

Douglas dabbed at his clothes.

'The colour almost matches,' he said. 'Perhaps they should market it. Apple, jade, grass, and now pesto . . .'

'Your mother's playing Fabian,' Ian announced.

'I'm going to play him as a very elderly retainer who could have a heart attack at any moment; someone who's been kept on but is absolutely useless. Would you like a drink?'

Douglas was already fetching glasses down from the kitchen cupboard.

'That's why we're here, Mother.'

'Oh dear. I rather hoped that you were here to see me.'

'Where is everyone?' Emma asked. There weren't enough of the family in evidence for a performance.

'Angus is just seeing to the stage and Tessa's getting a few last-minute props. Imogen and Sarah are coming but Gavin has cried off. He is in London, I suppose, but I wish he'd been able to come. You know how important it is for Ian and he had him down to play Sebastian. Jack's girls are both away. At least the Macleans are coming with *their* children but it's been quite a struggle to make up the numbers.'

Ian opened some sparkling wine.

'Jack may not be bringing the girls but he's coming with a new girlfriend instead. At least I think she's a girlfriend.'

'Isn't that intriguing?' said Elizabeth.

Douglas was not so sure.

'It doesn't sound very likely.'

'You never know,' said Emma. 'Your brother can be quite charming when he wants to be.'

'Do you think so?'

'You know, the hermit academic . . . mysteriously wise . . .'

'We mustn't say anything,' Elizabeth said. 'You remember how he used to hate people making any assumptions about his love life.'

'He's lucky to have a love life at all,' said Ian.

'Most of the time he only meets students,' Douglas said. 'Perhaps it's one of them.'

'I just hope everyone is polite to her,' said Elizabeth. 'We don't want a scene.'

'Oh you've no need to worry on that score, my

darling,' said Ian. 'We're hardly going to say anything tactless . . .'

'But it would be good to tease him, don't you think?' Douglas asked. 'Just for a bit?'

'Don't,' said Emma. 'Don't even start.'

*　　　*　　　*

At the railway station Elizabeth Henderson was welcoming but guarded, shaking Krystyna's hand and offering her a seat in the front of the Range Rover.

'No, it's all right,' Krystyna said. 'I'll go in the back. I know you have not seen your son for a long time.'

Elizabeth was impressed by her guest's politeness.

'I suppose he does have longer legs. As long as you don't mind . . .'

'Of course not.'

'We could have taken a taxi, Mother.'

'That's far too extravagant.'

'They're much cheaper than you think.'

'Nonsense.' Elizabeth had been brought up to believe that you should only take a taxi if you were either pregnant or over eighty.

Sometimes she wished everything could return to the time when her children were young, when there was enough hope and confidence to believe that each of her sons could become anything he wanted. But that was the time before compromise, before all the complications involved in growing up and finding partners and earning money.

'How is everyone?' Jack asked. He knew that if he kept asking questions there would be less time to satisfy his mother's curiosity about Krystyna.

Elizabeth told them about Ian's preparations for the play and how invaluable Angus had been (they were so grateful he had come early) and that Tessa had found the most beautiful dress imaginable.

'She'll make the most marvellous widow.'

Krystyna tried to remember the family pairings: Angus and Tessa, Douglas and Emma, Jack and . . .? She realised that she still did not know his wife's name.

They drove out of town, passing craft centres and caravan parks, barn conversions and new-build developments. Then they turned off the main road and followed the old drovers' way, over river and burn, the fields divided by drystane dykes.

As they bumped over a cattle grid and veered on to even more rugged terrain, Krystyna wondered how big a house it would be and whether it was a mistake to have come.

'Are you all right in the back, Krystyna?'

'I am fine, Mrs Henderson.'

'You must call me Elizabeth; everybody does, even the doctor, which I find rather disconcerting.'

They turned into a narrow drive. A Jack Russell ran out to greet them followed by a slow-moving Labrador. Jack collected the suitcases.

'You won't leave me alone, will you?' Krystyna asked as they entered the hall.

'Ah Jack,' his father called. 'Come and get your clown outfit.' He walked towards them and extended his hand. 'You must be Krystyna?'

'I hope it is OK for me to come.'

'You've saved the day,' Ian said, giving her the firmest handshake she had ever received. 'We didn't have enough people for all the parts. Jack's daughters have rather let us down.'

'They're busy, Father.'

'They came last year . . .'

Both girls had sworn that they would never be in the play again.

'Come into the snug,' said Ian. 'We are laying out all the costumes there.'

The room was filled with swathes of material that stretched back through generations of family history: velvet smoking jackets, old dress shirts, taffeta gowns cast off from long-forgotten balls.

'I only hope it doesn't rain,' said Ian. 'But I suppose it might be appropriate: the wind and the rain. Have you learned your lines, Jack?'

'I know the songs.'

'Is that all?'

'You're lucky to get that.'

'I do sometimes worry what you do all day. Elizabeth has looked out this sailor's suit for you, Krystyna. I do hope it fits. Are you all right about being the Sea Captain?'

'I hope my English is good.'

'It's probably better than ours. Anyway, it's all written down for you. And we're not up to professional standards. Except for Emma: Douglas's wife. We all have to admire her. That's the only rule.'

'No, you don't,' said Emma, coming into the room. 'We all have to admire you, Ian.'

'I wouldn't say that.'

Jack smiled.

'No, you wouldn't say it, Father. But you'd like it to be the case.'

'I just want everyone to be happy.'

Jack turned to Krystyna.

'Father takes it all very seriously.'

'What a beautiful house,' she said out loud, amazed that the family had dedicated a whole room to dressing up.

'We nearly lost it in the Lloyd's fiasco,' Ian explained. 'Fortunately, Angus is rather good with money and so after some rather deft manoeuvres we were able to survive. Close thing, though. Terrible business, asbestos . . .' He was tying a series of gartered laces across his legs. 'Do you think these will do?' he asked. 'I think I'd prefer leather. Perhaps I could do something with a dog lead?'

Krystyna was shown into a side room, where she could change into her costume—white trousers, a wide leather belt from the 1980s, and a heavy brocaded jacket with epaulettes. She looked at herself in the mirror and smiled. She knew that she was crazy to be here, but at least she didn't have to think about her life any more.

Ian Henderson laid out his staging plans on the dining-room table. He had drawn a grid with maps and diagrams for each character telling them where to move and when. Emma was shown that, when she was to perform her first great soliloquy, 'I left no ring with her, what means this lady?', she was to move across from C1 to C3 and then diagonally across to D3.

'I think I'll just feel my way,' she said. 'You know, the usual upstage centre to downstage centre thing.'

'Oh well,' said Ian. 'I suppose that I had better leave it to the professionals.'

Emma knew that he didn't really mean it. This production was the manifestation not of life as it was lived but of how Ian wanted it to be. If his family would only just do as he said, moving from A1 to B1 to C1 in real life, then everyone would be happier.

During the rehearsals he stood in the centre of the lawn and outlined his plans for the performance. Some people would enter 'from the beehives', others would come in 'from the west side of the ha-ha'. Those who weren't required in any given scene were expected to form the audience. There was a drinks table at the back of the auditorium and they were going to have an interval during which people could have a swim if they were too hot. Supper would be on the terrace afterwards.

A confident couple in Tudor dress arrived with two small girls in tow. They were the Maclean family and had come down from Perthshire. They apologised for being late. They had been held up in traffic.

This was not considered a sufficient excuse.

Ian had the adults down to play Maria and Aguecheek and they had missed their rehearsal slot.

'You should have left earlier,' he complained. 'You know how bad it can get on the bridge.'

'Jacqueline was finishing her illustrations. You know what it's like, Ian.'

'I'm glad to say that I don't.'

The Maclean daughters were dressed in paisley dresses and wore their blonde curls in ringlets. They were called Sophie and Jasmine and had been fairies in the previous year's production of *A Midsummer Night's Dream*.

'Come *along* everyone,' Ian called out. 'The

curtain will rise in fifteen minutes.'

'Where is the curtain?' Krystyna asked.

'In his head,' said Emma. 'It's all in his head.'

'Are the musicians *ready*?' Ian called out.

The musicians in question turned out to be the Maclean girls. The four-year-old had her recorder; the six-year-old was proficient on the violin. Angus had already taken them to one side to prepare the opening.

'Talented children make me sick,' Emma said. 'They think they can do it all without any training. I suppose we had better brace ourselves. My first line's quite near the top.'

Jack appeared with a white face and a clown's hat. He was carrying a jester's stick, and waved it at Krystyna.

'I'm sorry about this. I really am,' he said.

'Here comes Sir Toby,' Douglas called, swaggering with a fake pot belly, carrying a half-emptied bottle of wine. 'Now for a bit of wenching. Where's the lovely Mrs Maclean?'

'He'll be drunk by four o'clock,' Emma told Krystyna. 'As long as he doesn't try to sober up with a swim.'

'Are you two all right?' Jack asked.

'What does it look like?'

Tessa emerged from the house dressed in black with a veil.

'Do you think I look suitably miserable?' she asked.

'You're supposed to be in mourning,' Ian said. 'Not on your way to a ball.'

Tessa had not met Krystyna and came over to introduce herself.

'It's very brave of you to come, you know.'

66

'It is fine. I had nothing to do.'

'I'm sure that's not true.'

Tessa had tied back her faded auburn hair to reveal a pale freckled face that had once been open but now appeared hesitant and guarded. Krystyna could tell, almost immediately, that something must have happened to her in the past.

Then she noticed Tessa's left arm through the black gauze of her dress. Livid burn scars mottled and puckered the flesh. Tessa noticed the look and Krystyna felt embarrassed. She wished Jack had told her more about his family.

'You look very elegant in the sailor jacket,' said Tessa. 'Are you one of Jack's students?'

'No.'

'I'm sorry?'

'No, I mean I am older than I look, I think. I am twenty-seven.'

'I see. But how did you meet?'

Krystyna had not prepared her answer.

'In a pub.'

'Jack—in a pub? That's more his brother's line . . .'

'He is a good man.'

'I know.'

'But we are friends. You understand?'

'Of course. But nobody minds.'

'I think I mind,' said Krystyna. 'I don't want people thinking it is more.'

'Your secret's safe with me.'

'It's not a secret . . .'

'*Beginners, please*,' Ian called. 'The stage is set. The musicians are ready. Strike up, pipers!'

Emma walked over and took Krystyna by the arm.

'Come with me. We're on in a minute.' She took her to a wooded area at the back of the stage. 'Have you got your script?'

'I learned it.'

'You've *learned* it?'

'Jack said I should try. So I did. As a surprise.'

'Well, you'll be the most popular girl in town, I can tell you. Not that you weren't already . . .'

Those not in the opening scene took their seats and the play began. The Maclean girls played their music, Angus made his Orsino as foppish as he could but, as a large, bearded former rugby player, he was having difficulties.

Ian watched his family with proprietorial intensity, waiting for his first lines. It was going to be a long afternoon.

Emma strode down centre, looked around and declaimed: *What country, friends, is this?*

Krystyna answered: *This is Illyria, lady.*

And what should I do in Illyria? My brother, he is in Elysium, Perchance he is not drowned.

Krystyna was surprised when Emma spoke the words out loud, enunciating Viola's grief. Everything she had been unable to speak about herself was contained in the verse of the play. She had been trying to forget about Sandy but the thought of him came back, without warning, as if it had never been away. She felt the language of the play recede as the memory of him returned. She had not expected tears but now she could not speak without her voice fragmenting.

'Very good, Krystyna,' Ian shouted at the end of the scene. 'Very moving.'

Jack continued with Emma:

Good madonna, why mournest thou?

Good fool, for my brother's death.
I think his soul is in hell, madonna.
I know his soul is in heaven, fool.

He could see Krystyna lighting a cigarette as soon as her scene was over, hoping that no one would notice. Her hands were shaking. Jack had forgotten that the play contained such sadness. This was supposed to be a comedy, he thought, a festive celebration to while away the darkness of winter.

The two Maclean girls began to imitate the pompous way in which Ian Henderson walked, marching up and down with their heads high and their arms swinging, muttering in posh gruff English, 'Carry on,' 'Do keep up,' 'For goodness' sake,' their mouths full of marbles. Jack and Angus began to laugh as their father strove valiantly to hold on to his audience.

I will be proud, I will read politic authors, I will baffle Sir Toby, I will put off gross acquaintance, I will be point-device the very man . . . 'Will you stop arsing about over there . . .'

The children giggled in a frightened way. They turned to see where their mother was standing.

'Come on, darlings,' said Mrs Maclean. 'Let's go and play where he can't see you.'

'Thank you . . .' Ian resumed his performance: *I do not now fool myself, to let imagination jade me; for every reason excites to this, that my lady loves me.*

Mrs Maclean took her daughters round to the side of the house, where they could run around without disrupting the play. Then she returned to continue her performance.

Ian called out instructions in between scenes, determined that there should be no letting up, but the rest of his family had begun to flag. Elizabeth had fallen asleep under a parasol, Stewart Maclean was reading the Saturday papers, and Douglas was drinking his way through the part of Toby Belch. Only Emma and Tessa were taking the play seriously.

I prithee tell me what thou thinkst of me.
That you do think you are not what you are.
If I think so, I think the same of you.
Then think you right: I am not what I am.
I would you were as I would have you be . . .

Jack watched his father walking up and down backstage. He was going over his lines, anxious for his cue, determined not to make a mistake.

He wondered if he was the only one who had noticed him forgetting more than in previous years: his slow delivery and decline in energy. He had begun to take on the look of a man who was frightened of being caught out.

They reached the part where Feste had to drive Malvolio mad. Shakespearean comedy was crueller than Jack had remembered.

They have here propertied me, keep me in darkness, send ministers unto me, asses, and do all they can to face me out of my wits.

Krystyna lit another cigarette and walked across the lawn to see the view of the fields beyond the house. The heat had brought out the aroma of garlic in the country lanes and the air was heavy with summer. She watched the bees gather nectar and return to the hives. She remembered eating honey as a child, direct from an old teaspoon, and drinking ice-cold water from a metal cup. How old had she been at the time? Five? Seven?

She tried to think where the two little girls had

gone. No one was paying them any attention.

She walked round to the side of the house to see the Macleans' younger daughter reaching into the swimming pool. She had dropped an object into the water, something shiny like a mirror or a brooch, and Krystyna saw her topple forwards into the deep end.

It happened so quietly, with the light bright on the surface, that for a few seconds Krystyna thought that she was dreaming.

'Oh,' the other girl said. Then she looked at Krystyna. 'Jasmine's fallen in.'

The figure in the water was upside down and sinking to the bottom of the pool. Her dress billowed above her. The paisley darkened as it absorbed the water, spreading out over the surface, obscuring the girl's head.

Krystyna watched, intrigued at the pattern forming, the spread of the clothing and the weight of the material.

Then she woke up. She realised that she had to jump in and save the child.

She dropped her cigarette and dived from the side of the pool. She felt the cold of the water burst around her. I'm *pregnant*, she thought. What is this doing to my baby?

The costume from the play was heavier than she had anticipated, pulling her down to the bottom of the pool. She should have taken the jacket off but there had not been time.

Krystyna pushed herself forwards and turned on to her side. Then she reached out her right arm and felt for the girl's waist, pulling her along.

She stretched her left arm out wide, making half-strokes through the water, and used her legs

71

to kick them forwards. Krystyna was running out of breath but wanted to surface once she was back within her depth.

She felt the brightness of the day, the sun in her eyes. Then she could hear the child coughing, alive. No words, no call for mother, no tears.

Krystyna stood up and stumbled back through the water, turning Jasmine round, holding her against her chest, patting her on the back as she choked back to life.

'*Uspokój się proszę,*' Krystyna said. '*Spokojnie moje dziecko, już wszystko jest dobrze, cichutko.*' She was surprised how easily the motherly gestures came.

Jasmine's sister was standing where she had left her. No one else had seen them.

Krystyna held Jasmine at a slight distance and looked into her shocked white face. Then she swept the hair away from her eyes.

'Better now?' she asked.

Her own clothes felt heavy and cold. She sat down to rest on the edge of the pool and noticed that Jasmine had cut her ankle.

'Bracey gone,' Jasmine said. 'All wet.'

Krystyna took charge.

'Let's find towels?' She looked at Jasmine's sister. 'Do you know where they are?'

'Me show,' said the girl.

They walked back to the house, drying and changing in the scullery. Krystyna did not know whether she would say anything or if the incident would be kept as a secret between them. She tried not to think what it would have been like had she not decided to leave the play: the parental horror, the child floating, attempts at resuscitation,

72

the ambulance called, people standing, activity redundant, lives ruined.

'Good heavens,' cried Mrs Maclean when they returned. 'What's happened to Jasmine?'

'Jas-jas fell in the water . . .'

'Well, that was very silly of you, wasn't it, darling?' She looked at Krystyna but continued speaking to her daughter. 'And did the nice lady fish you out?'

'Lost bracey,' said the girl.

'Never mind, darling, we can buy you another one. Was it very frightening?'

'Cold now.'

'Let me see what we've got in the car.' Mrs Maclean picked up her daughter and smiled briefly at Krystyna before walking away. 'So kind of you,' she said. 'I hope you didn't get too wet.'

Krystyna realised that being foreign made her anonymous. The family and their friends were so settled that nothing unnerved them. She could not imagine what had given them such confidence or decide if it was all a façade. People could be so careless, she thought, so unaware of how quickly a life could change or be ruined.

*   *   *

The play was nearing its end. Jack was singing about the wind and the rain. Krystyna stood and listened. She could not see him as a little tiny boy at all. All she could see was sadness, a lost man who never would 'thrive by swaggering'.

He was looking out to a fixed point on the horizon. He was distant as he sang, far from his family. Krystyna thought it was the way she herself

73

might be when she could no longer concentrate on what people were saying to her.

A great while ago the world begun . . .

She thought of the last time she had seen a performance of Shakespeare at home. It had been a political production of *Hamlet*. They had gone as a family and her father had become annoyed when, towards the end of the play, they had stressed the folly of defending a patch of Poland against the army of Fortinbras. *It is already garrisoned.*

She could picture her mother before she was ill, gathering blackberries and redcurrants for jam, making sure the family could carry the fruits of summer into the colder months, wanting to please, doing all that she could to alleviate her husband's temper.

But that's all one, our play is done,
And we'll strive to please you every day.

A group of women began to lay a long table by the bay window. Elizabeth Henderson had said that it was so much more civilised to eat outdoors in the summer. She walked slowly along the dinner table, checking that the cutlery was properly aligned and that the seating arrangement conformed to the plan she had drawn up that morning.

The servants in the play had been friends from nearby villages. Now they became waiters at the table. One of them brought out six or seven garden flares and began staking them in the ground. When she lit them she found that they produced more flame than she had anticipated and one of the torches burst into light next to Tessa.

'Get that away from me!' she said.

'I'm sorry,' the girl stammered. 'The man said

74

they don't always light very well.'

'The man was wrong.'

'I'm sorry. I didn't know.'

Krystyna asked Jack what was happening.

'Tessa suffers from nerves.'

'Only nerves?'

'And she's scared of fire. Have you seen her arm?'

'I did not ask.'

'Don't.'

'I was not going to do that. I have manners.'

'And try not to smoke in front of her if you can avoid it.'

'I am sorry.'

'It's all right. I'll tell you later. It's just that she hates any kind of flame. But we don't talk about it. I'm sorry. I should have warned you.'

Now she had been told not to enquire any further, Krystyna wanted to know.

Perhaps this was what it would be like for her in the future. As soon as people knew that her boyfriend had committed suicide it would be all that they wanted to ask her about.

Perhaps her child would be a distraction. She imagined people either asking about the father or deliberately avoiding the subject.

Ian was pouring out more wine, calling people after the characters they had just played: the fair Olivia, good Cesario, more wine for Sir Toby.

He still had a piece of spinach stuck between his teeth but Krystyna did not tell him. He hoped that she had enjoyed the play.

'I was impressed. They all obey you. You have state control.'

'I suppose you know all about that.'

'I was only eleven years old when the Berlin Wall came down.'

'I was about forty when it went up. I suppose you've seen a lot of changes. Did you experience what it was like before?'

'A little; after martial law my father was still a Communist.'

'Really? I thought they all went into denial. I visited Prague in 1991 and they had all vanished: not a Communist in sight.'

'My father was a big Party member under Gierek.'

'Old school, then?'

'I am sorry?'

'A real Marxist?'

'Absolutely. After *Solidarność* he would walk into shops and denounce soap.'

'Soap?'

'And toothpaste. All capitalist decadence. What is wrong with state soap? What is wrong with state toothpaste?'

'They must have been rather surprised.'

'It was embarrassing. "How many toothpastes do you need?" he said. Only when my mother showed him Western make-up did he understand that capitalism had won. It was revolution by Max Factor.'

'What does he do?'

'He was the boss of a steel works outside Kraków. Now he is a civil servant. He is very political.'

'Are you?'

'My country is a mess. That is why we are all coming here.'

'I hear there's hardly a plumber left in Poland.

They're all in Britain.'

'We have Vietnamese. You have Poles. Maybe it will go on until all the poor countries are empty.'

Ian laughed.

'I love a bit of optimism. How did you meet Jack?'

Krystyna still did not know how to answer.

'It is a long story.'

'We have time.'

'I do not know him very well.'

'Well, he can be a bit shy; but he's a good egg.'

'Egg?'

'Sorry. Person. Should have done better, of course, but it's hard to recover when your wife walks out.'

'He does not talk about this.'

'Too busy with his books, probably. He was never that good with other people. But then university lecturers seldom are, don't you find? They don't get out enough.'

'Jack goes out, I think.'

'Only when you make him. He's very shy.'

'Do you think so?' Krystyna asked.

'Well, he always was as a child. Perhaps he's different now. Parents lose touch with their children eventually, don't they?'

'Not all the time. Your family seems very happy.'

'We do our best.' Ian paused for a moment, and then stood up, as if he had only just remembered what he had to do next. 'Thank you so much for being in the play. I can't tell you how much it means to us. It's so refreshing when new people come into our lives.'

'You are very kind.'

'No. You are the one being kind. I only hope you

enjoyed it.'

'I have never been to a play like this before.'

'It all went so quickly, didn't it? But then everything moves so much faster when you're older. Are you sure you don't want any port?'

'I'm fine.'

'Good girl. But I'm sure the others will. I should go and see to it all . . .' Ian made a half-hearted gesture with his hands and walked away.

Krystyna thought about her own father. He was so much more irate, worrying always about money and the need to earn a living, never at ease. She had not meant to talk about her family. At least no one seemed to know about Sandy.

It was late but the air was still warm, heavy with the prospect of a storm. Krystyna could see Jacqueline Maclean sitting on the edge of a grass bank with her two daughters, staring up into the sky, pointing out the stars before bedtime.

'It doesn't look like a plough at all, Mummy . . .'

'It is. Let me draw it in the air for you. Look.'

Elizabeth rose from the far end of the table. She was talking to Tessa.

'There's nothing sadder than the end of a meal, don't you think? And I do so hate the leftovers, the waste.'

'Don't let it upset you,' Tessa said.

'But if you've sown something from seed, watered it, nurtured it and watched it grow; if you harvested it, washed it, prepared it and served it, then it's very hurtful when people push it aside.'

Ian returned to the table to find Douglas pouring white wine into a glass that already contained the dregs of some red.

'It might as well be meths.'

78

'I do know the difference.'

'That quaffing and drinking will undo you.'

'I don't care.'

'Is everything all right?'

'Of course it is.'

Jack suggested that they went inside for their nightcap.

'I do not think so,' Krystyna said. 'I have had enough.'

'Come and sit with us for a bit,' he said. 'Wind down.'

The living room displayed paintings of the three sons and silhouette portraits of the grandchildren. There was a separate picture of Ian in all his regalia, and a full-length portrait of Elizabeth in a dark velvet ball gown and a string of pearls. It had been painted when she must have been at her most eligible, at the age of twenty or twenty-one, and it came from another age. Looking at it, Krystyna realised that Angus had married a woman with the same profile as his mother.

She overheard Douglas saying to Jack, 'How on earth did you meet her?'

Jack replied, 'It's not what you think.'

'What is it then?'

'I don't know.'

'But you're hoping to move things on a bit?'

'It's none of your business.'

'It is if you bring her here.'

'Don't tell me you're jealous?'

'Of course I'm not jealous.'

Angus sat at the piano and began to play a Chopin nocturne. The rest of the family was amused by the seriousness of his attempt, his head low over the keyboard. He was overemphasising the dynamics, his foot heavy on the pedal for sustained longueurs.

Krystyna rested her head on the sofa and tried not to fall asleep. The music reminded her of the lessons she had taken at school, trying to play scales and broken chords as quickly as possible, getting them out of the way so she could concentrate on her pieces. She had given up around the time of her first serious boyfriend: Radek. She asked herself what would have happened if she had stayed with him and what he was doing now. She certainly wouldn't have been sitting in a large country house on the outskirts of Edinburgh with people she hardly knew.

Jack came and stood beside her.

'Would you like me to show you to your room?'

'*Jestem zmęczona.*'

'Sorry?'

'I am tired.'

'Let me help you up.'

'No. I can do this.'

She rose from the sofa, walked slowly out into the hall and then rested her hand on the banister at the foot of the stairs. She wondered how many hands had worn the wood away from the handrail to such a smooth, unpolished finish.

Jack waited outside the door to her room, letting Krystyna open it for herself.

'No one will disturb you.'

'That is a pity,' she said dreamily, and then corrected herself. 'That was a joke.'

'I know.'

'Thank you for asking me. You are kind.'

'You're very welcome. They all love you.'

'I do not think so.'

80

'They do, believe me.'

Krystyna smiled, touched his shoulder and closed the door.

The room was filled with paintings of Italian hill towns, avenues of trees, a still life of lemons on a sky-blue plate; amateur efforts, Krystyna realised, executed on summer holidays long ago.

She sat on the high brass bed with its white counterpane of Indian cotton. It had been made up in the old-fashioned way with sheets and blankets rather than a duvet. Hospital corners. She realised that nothing in the house was new. The carpets and furniture, the fixtures and fittings had all come from previous generations.

Behind the rose-patterned curtains the window was open.

Krystyna lay back on the bed and tried to recall the events of the day, the journey out of Edinburgh, the play, and the little girl in the swimming pool. She tried to imagine which members of the family would call themselves happy, and if Ian had been satisfied with the performance. What would he be thinking now?

Outside the storm broke. Some days seemed endless, Krystyna thought, while others raced away.

She could still see Jack, in his jester's costume, singing: *But that's all one, our play is done . . .*

It was not love that she was feeling, she told herself, or even the beginnings of it. It was different, but it was a need, born from the sensation that so much remained unsaid between them. From now on, she thought, any time apart might seem a lessening, a missed chance, an occasion for regret.

81

She began to fall asleep, thinking that she had not known this feeling of safety for a long time. It was a house no one would ever want to leave. What would it be like just to stay here, she thought, in this home and this bed, and do nothing but attempt to recover and have her child, absenting herself from her own life and becoming part of a different family altogether?

*   *   *

Krystyna waited until she heard enough people downstairs before coming down to breakfast.

'Have whatever you want,' said Jack, when she walked into the kitchen. 'It's all laid out. Mother's had it ready for hours.'

'I wouldn't say hours.' Elizabeth was dressed in a navy-blue Sunday suit and had a hat waiting on the sideboard. 'Did you sleep well, Krystyna?'

'It was a very comfortable bed. Thank you.'

'Have some toast.' Elizabeth picked up her hat and began to inspect it. 'There's porridge too, of course.'

Krystyna smiled at the 'of course', and poured out some coffee.

Elizabeth turned to her next chore.

'I'm going to ask Douglas to take all the bottles to the recycling,' she announced. 'Perhaps he'll get the message that way.'

Emma was not convinced.

'With a hangover? He'll either take it as a challenge or feel guilty and drink more to forget.'

'That doesn't sound very charitable.'

'It wasn't meant to be.'

'Is he still in bed?'

82

'I suppose so. I told him we had to leave before lunch. I've got to meet someone about the next play I'm doing.'

'On a Sunday?'

'Right, *kirk*.' Ian was standing in the doorway. 'Everybody ready? Have you had breakfast, Krystyna?'

'I will just have coffee. And a cigarette. I will go outside for the cigarette.'

'That doesn't seem very substantial.'

'It is what I have always, Mr Henderson.'

'Ian, if you don't mind. We're friends now.'

Jack knew that his father was not one for waiting.

'It's all right,' he said. 'We'll catch up.'

'I don't suppose Douglas is anywhere to be seen?'

'What do you think?' said Emma.

Jack checked with Krystyna.

'Are you sure you're happy to come?'

'I like church,' she said.

She followed the rest of the family down the drive and out into the road. She looked at the shafts of sunlight through the trees and remembered walking with her grandmother when she was a girl. 'God's promises', she had called them.

The kirk was a stern and simple building decorated by the Ten Commandments and plaques commemorating the dead.

Jack hoped that Krystyna would not be reminded of the funeral. He had not asked her about her faith. He knew that she was Catholic, but did that mean that she believed suicides were denied salvation? If she could make Jack

83

responsible for the accident, or if he admitted some kind of responsibility, would this help Sandy on his way in the afterlife? Krystyna would surely not go as far as this, but Jack could not be sure. Still, he realised, he hardly knew her.

Elizabeth Henderson was certainly making an effort, showing Krystyna to the pew, making sure she had a hymn book, introducing her to the remaining regulars who kept the faith alive.

The first reading was taken from the Book of Genesis: Sarah laughing at the idea of having a son when her husband Abraham was a hundred years old. Jack wondered whether anyone had ever laughed in the kirk. It was such a solemn place.

Afterwards Ian took him aside. He wanted a word in private.

'I'm sure I can borrow my son for a minute. You'll be all right, won't you, Krystyna?' he asked. 'You will be with some of the most interesting women in Scotland.'

'Then I will try to be interesting.'

'I think you'll do rather more than that.'

Jack and his father turned left, away from the path, and walked to the end of the graveyard. Ian wanted more than a word. He had decided that it was time to choose his burial place.

'A bit early, isn't it, Father?'

'Not at all. But I can't talk to the others about this. They're too preoccupied.'

As a child the death of his parents had been the one thing that Jack could not imagine. Other people suffered the loss and yet he felt that his family was somehow immune, his father driving confidently to and from Edinburgh, his mother giving piano lessons and recitals for charity.

84

'I don't know what the hurry is,' Jack said to his father, trying to sound as normal as he could. 'I'm sure you'll bury us all.'

'Don't be ridiculous.' He spoke as if his son was six years old. 'I can't make up my mind about the exact spot but I'm not keen on cremation. I definitely want to be buried.'

'And here?'

Ian looked surprised. He couldn't accept that his son would doubt him or that anyone could think he might want anything different.

'Yes. Somewhere here. Definitely.'

Jack thought back to the services of his childhood: the smell of damp linen, old men singing tremulously, shrunken women in their best hats.

Hamish Watson, Fiona Johnson, Angus Nicholson.

'It seems smaller, don't you think?' his father was saying. 'It's positively cluttered.'

'I suppose people will keep dying,' said Jack.

He thought of Sandy, and of Krystyna.

'I'm in the departure lounge, of course,' his father would tell his friends on the telephone. 'Although there's a wee while before take-off . . . with luck, there might even be delays . . .'

Prostate cancer.

'How have you been feeling?' Jack asked.

'Not too bad,' Ian replied. 'The doctors insist on keeping me alive.'

'Are you taking all the medication?'

'Of course,' Ian replied. 'But I don't think it's doing any good. Johnny McIntosh has to take fourteen pills a day. Although anyone who takes so many can't be that ill.'

They stopped under an oak tree. Jack remembered his father's adage: two hundred years growing, two hundred years standing, two hundred years dying.

He looked back at the kirkyard with its sturdy tower, a Covenanter stronghold, *the graves of the martyrs, the peewees crying*.

'What about the stone?' he asked. 'What do you want it to say?'

'I can't decide.'

'What did your father have?'

'I think we just had his name and dates. We probably picked *In loving memory*. That's always a safe bet.'

'I think we have to do better than that.'

Ian was surprised by contradiction. He could still picture Jack as a boy in the back seat of his car on one of their days out, complaining that he always had to sit in the middle. He was the son who played his cricket defensively, who put too much sauce on his chips and who ate his ice cream so slowly that it melted down the cornet and over his hands before he had finished.

'I want it planned,' Ian continued, 'so that when the moment comes you all know what to do. I'd like to enjoy it.'

'You won't be there.'

'Oh I think you'll find that I will.'

They passed the graves of people Ian had known in the past: Billy McIntyre, the farm labourer; John Maltby, who ran the post office; Hamish Anderson, the session clerk.

The graves surrounded them, chronicling lives, disasters, and the accidents of war. They told of age and of love; of lives lived as bravely as fear and luck would allow.

Jack remembered Sandy's coffin being carried from the kirk to a private cremation. He wondered where the ashes had been scattered and if Krystyna had been back since.

Ian stopped by the headstone of Robert Little, the publican who had always greeted his father with a free dram at weekends.

'Do you really believe in the resurrection of the body?' Jack asked.

His father paused, surprised by the directness of the question.

'I believe in the promises of Christ.'

Jack remembered him reading the Lorimer translation into Scots soon after it was published.

> *Deith is swalliet up in victorie*
> *Whaur, than, O Deith, is thy victorie?*
> *Whaur, than, O Deith, is thy stang?*

This would be the moment to talk about what had happened, he thought; the boy in the road, the inevitable collision. As far as Jack knew, his father was the only other member of the family who had killed a man. It had been in the war and he had been sick as soon as he had realised what he'd done.

'I kept thinking of his sweetheart back at home.'

Jack could talk to him now. His father would surely understand and be sympathetic. But he did not know how to begin.

'I think here, don't you? Under the spreading yew . . .' Ian said.

The decision had been taken while Jack had been dreaming. The opportunity had passed.

87

'I'll ask the Minister.'

'It'll be a bit of a dig . . .'

'We'll manage,' said Jack, unable to imagine the day.

'It's a good spot.' Ian looked down to the river. 'The waters of life near by. Your mother will like it.'

Jack looked out at the view: the distant fields bordered by the drystane dykes, the thick fields under open azure skies. He tried to recall what it had been like when he was a small boy, with his father walking ahead down the lanes with the dogs, admonishing him to keep up, as the doves circled above the old doocot. He had taught his son the name of every field and stream: Peffer and Pilmuir Burn, Brownrigg and Binning Wood, Fourtoun Bank and Kilduff Hill.

They left the kirkyard and closed the gate. Jack felt the heat of the day beginning to rise. He tried to anticipate the next time he would come here, attempting to inoculate himself against the shock.

They walked back along a road that was dried and rutted with tractor tyres. Jack thought back to the walks they had shared in the past, when his father still displayed some of the army attitudes left over from the war: *If it moves, shoot it. If it doesn't, paint it*. He could smell the wild garlic under the trees.

He expected some kind of acknowledgement of the conversation they had just had but his father was already on to the next thing.

'I think I'll need my sunhat,' he said.

In the kitchen Elizabeth had been telling Krystyna about the history of the house and how her mother had stocked up on rations at the start

88

of the war.

'She was hopeless with measurements and ordered a ton of soap—the village lived on it for years.'

They looked up, surprised to be interrupted. Jack could smell roast lamb and hoped they might be able to stay on for lunch.

'I'm giving you a lift,' Elizabeth said. 'Krystyna needs to get back to Edinburgh. We've had such a lovely chat.'

'I told your mother what happened.'

'Oh,' said Jack.

He could not think what to say. If he had wanted his mother to know he would have told her himself.

'Why?' he asked

Elizabeth defended her guest.

'She had to talk to someone, don't you think? Of course I read about the accident in the papers but I never thought that it might have anything to do with you. Or with Krystyna, of course. Why didn't you tell me, Jack?'

'I didn't know where to start.'

'And why does everything have to be such a secret? You don't tell people things and then we're never prepared when the truth finally emerges . . .'

'Perhaps there were *reasons* why I didn't want anyone to know. I don't see why I have to tell everyone everything that happens to me . . .'

His mother looked over her glasses at her son.

'We're your *family*, Jack.'

'I'm sorry . . .'

'I could not pretend any more,' said Krystyna. 'I saw that you were not going to say anything. You cannot be alone.'

'I didn't want anyone to have to worry. I didn't want to have to talk about it . . .'

'It was very brave of Krystyna to tell me, don't you think?' Elizabeth asked.

'I can see that. But I didn't want it to become a big thing.'

'It is a big thing,' Elizabeth said. 'That's the point. I'm sorry if you're upset with us.'

'I'm not upset. I thought it was private.'

Krystyna tried to calm him.

'How can it be private? That is what a family is for. People know something is wrong even if they do not say.'

Jack wasn't sure he needed the lecture.

'I'm sorry, Mother.'

'That's all right.' Elizabeth rose from the table. 'I've told her all about you, of course.'

'That's all I need.'

'Don't worry. I haven't given away any *secrets*.'

'I didn't think there were any left to give away.'

He and Krystyna had specifically agreed not to say anything about the accident. It was typical of his mother to get the story out of her. Jack worried how soon the rest of his family would find out what had happened and how much more explaining he would have to do. He knew that there were limits to his mother's discretion.

Ian walked into the room.

'I hope you're both staying for lunch?' he asked.

'We have to go back,' said Krystyna. 'There is a Polish Mass at the cathedral.'

'But you've already been to church.'

'I must go once more. Your church does not count . . .'

'I see.' For the first time that weekend Ian was

silenced. 'Well, I do hope you'll come again,' he said.

'I would be honoured.'

'I'm not sure honoured is quite the right word.'

'I think it is.'

'Then I'm flattered. And thank you again for the play. It was very good to meet you, Krystyna. I'll remember every minute of it.'

'I am not sure about every minute.'

'Well, perhaps nearly every minute. Now I'm going to take a look at the roses and the bees.'

'I'll bring the car round,' said Elizabeth. She did not like goodbyes. They always took longer than expected.

When the actual moment of departure came something made Jack hesitate. He realised that he wanted to wait for his father to emerge from the house, to see him one more time.

'Come on, Jack,' his mother said. 'What are you waiting for? Get in.'

'Just a minute.'

He heard a sash window being raised, and he looked up to see Douglas framed above them, shielding his eyes against the brightness of the day. Angus and Tessa came out of the house to wave them off.

'Here we are,' Ian called. He stopped when he realised that all three of his sons were looking at him. 'What are you all waiting for?' He was almost irritated.

Jack smiled.

'Nothing, Father.'

Ian had taken off his jacket but was still wearing a tie. Dark-blue braces held up the trousers of his Sunday suit. He was brandishing an old pair of

91

secateurs and carrying a gardening trug. On his head was a floppy white sunhat that looked too big for him.

Elizabeth started up the car and a flock of starlings flew from the trees. The blossom had fallen with the morning breeze.

She tried to catch her husband's eye but he was already striding away from her. Soon the bees would leave the last of the lavender and the buddleia and travel further, seeking out the wild flowers that grew by the river; white bryony and charlock, dandelion and nettle.

Ian continued walking out into his garden, with his floppy hat and his secateurs, watched by his three sons and the women who were with them, intent on nothing more complicated than seeing to his bees and dead-heading a few roses.

He turned a corner, out of sight. He did not look back.

CHAPTER FOUR

From the train Douglas looked out at pallets burning in desolate factory yards, rusting track abandoned in the sidings, the distant Kent coastline.

He was on the early-morning Eurostar to Paris. A group of French girls were taking digital photos, laughing as they showed them to each other.

A man in a cheap suit was saying, 'OK, OK, but we can't guarantee the performance parameters of the fabric abrasion-wise.'

The woman across the corridor was telling her

companion that she wanted her daughter to become a dentist. It was a good ambition to have, a sensible career. 'You never see a poor dentist, do you?'

Douglas knew his parents would have preferred him to have a proper job; they would have been far prouder if he'd entered a sensible profession with prospects. He could have become a doctor, a lawyer, or something important in international finance rather than the murky world of television. He certainly wouldn't have been travelling in standard class.

He knew that he should not be on the train.

It was mad to see Julia.

He tried to justify the decision. He could hardly blame Emma. Their work took them away from each other and their sex life had dwindled but after two rounds of IVF that had been predictable. They could have worked harder at their marriage, been kinder, perhaps, and taken each other less for granted, but they had been so tired by all that had happened that neither of them had the energy or the will to resurrect or redefine the little they had left.

Douglas worked and drank and slept. He had lost touch with most of his friends (his schedule was so unpredictable he could never commit to any arrangements in advance) and he only saw people socially when his wife or his parents forced him to do something that he could find no excuse for avoiding.

He had met Julia in Vienna. She was working for the British Council; he was making a documentary. They had been out a couple of times, flirted and then kissed on the last night.

Julia was a few years younger and lived in London. Her husband was some kind of corporate lawyer but Douglas had not asked too many questions about him, or her two boys, just as he had skirted around the fact that he was married to Emma. He had kept it vague, half implying that they were separated. After the first betrayal the rest had followed.

They had exchanged phone numbers and told each other that it would be good to meet if they ever found themselves at a loss in a foreign city again. Then Julia sent him a text: *In Paris 2 July. Want to come?*

Douglas felt guilty as soon as he received it. He waited a few hours and replied: *Why not?*

At first he thought their meeting couldn't do any harm. They had settled on lunch rather than dinner. They did not know each other well and Douglas could treat the whole thing as just another flirtation. He had had enough of them in the past. But however much he told himself that such a meeting was normal, almost routine, he still felt the anticipation.

He tried to define why Julia was different from previous ambiguities. She was less available, less neurotic, and married with two sons. Douglas decided this made her safer (neither desperately single nor in need of a child) and at the same time more dangerous (they would both know the rules).

He wondered if his presence on the train was due to the fact that he had seen Jack and Krystyna together and had felt unexpectedly competitive. His brother had discovered a renewed sense of purpose. The despair of the abandoned husband had disappeared. Instead he had turned up at the family home with a girl who was falling out of her dress and was young enough to be his daughter. It was a form of showing off, Douglas decided, and now perhaps he wanted something of the same; a change, new energy, hope. He was not going to accept that his behaviour was attributable to something less justifiable such as lassitude, loneliness or the simple selfishness of a midlife crisis.

He had arranged to meet Julia at the Brasserie Lipp. Douglas had always liked it because it was where Hemingway had decided to write his longer stories, training for the race that would be a novel, trying to stay sound and good in his head. Douglas had once thought of becoming a writer himself but he did not have the patience. Early attempts had left him bored and frustrated, and besides, he drank too much already.

The brasserie had retained its art deco style, with ceramic tiles of palm and aspidistra and gas sconces above the coat hooks. Douglas was shown upstairs to a table next to an elderly couple who were eating their meal in silence. They had to be married to each other, he thought, to say so little. He only hoped that they did not speak English.

He sat with his back to the wall, looking out into the room. Already he worried that Julia would not think to come upstairs.

He ordered a sparkling water and tried to look as though he lunched in St-Germain every day. Although the other diners had dressed with an unstudied elegance Douglas had made an effort, buying a new white shirt, moleskin trousers and a pinstriped velvet jacket that he hoped would make him appear raffish. He'd even added a silk scarf in

95

honour of the encounter.

He was just about to take off the scarf when Julia arrived. She was wearing a dark-burgundy blouse, her blonde hair was swept behind her ears, and a pair of reading glasses hung from a chain around her neck. She appeared to have taken as much trouble as Douglas to look effortless.

He stood up and Julia turned her head at the last moment, forcing him to kiss her on the cheek rather than the lips.

'I hope I'm not late.'

'No, it's fine. I wanted to be first.'

Douglas knew that he should not have been so forward so soon. Perhaps Julia was simply avoiding smudging her lipstick but he would have to reclaim lost territory.

The couple at the next table looked up to assess the new arrival but Julia dismissed them with a firm *'Bonjour'*. She sat down and picked up the menu.

'Oh God, I can't read this,' she said. She put on her reading glasses. 'Another sign of ageing.'

'You look fantastic.'

She could sense Douglas staring at her as she read, and she spoke without looking up, concentrating on the menu.

'You're looking good yourself. Not sure about the scarf.'

'I've only just bought it.'

'The jacket's good.' She smiled. 'What shall we have?'

'I thought the pâté followed by the *daurade*,' Douglas said. Then he worried that he wasn't good with bones.

'Well, I'm going to have the beetroot salad,'

96

Julia announced, summoning the waiter, 'and then some steak. I see you're not having any wine.'

'Not yet.'

'I hope that's not being done for my benefit.'

'No. It's done for mine.'

He poured out the mineral water and said, 'Let's have a bottle of Brouilly.'

Two businessmen in suits that were almost identical edged on to the next table. They were talking about a property deal. At least Douglas wouldn't have to worry about them listening.

'I hope you didn't mind hearing from me,' Julia said.

'No. It just surprised me.'

'I thought Paris, Eurostar, you could just come over. It only takes a couple of hours.'

Douglas didn't want to tell her how long it had taken him from Glasgow; the effort he had made, the excuses he'd given.

'Well, here I am.'

'Did you think about not coming?'

'Not really. Did you?'

'I have to be here for my work. And there's an exhibition I need to visit. I thought I could combine it with seeing you. You're supposed to be the highlight of my trip.'

'Then I'll try and live up to your expectations.'

'Oh I didn't have any. I just thought we'd have lunch and see what happened.'

'I'm not sure I believe you.'

'Why, don't tell me you were hoping for something more?'

Douglas offered Julia the bread. He knew he had to be careful what he said before the corridor of uncertainty closed. It was ridiculous to think of a phrase from cricket at a time like this: *the corridor of uncertainty*. He was still not sure if Julia thought there was as much at stake as he did.

'When I got your message,' Douglas began, 'I remembered the last time we saw each other. Then I couldn't stop thinking about it.'

'I'm glad I made such an impression.'

'You did, believe me.'

Douglas worried that he was saying too much too soon. The kiss had been in the American Bar, just before Julia had left for the airport.

'Too bad you didn't make your move earlier,' she had said at the time.

The beetroot salad arrived.

'Oh,' she said. 'I can't eat that. They've put eggs in it. Why didn't they say?'

'Order something else.'

'No, I'll just have some of your pâté.' She reached over.

'Let me help you,' Douglas said.

'It's good to see you,' Julia said.

'It's good to see you too. I'd almost forgotten how much I liked you.'

'You just said you keep thinking about me.'

'Thinking isn't the same as feeling. You're much better in the flesh.'

'Steady . . .'

He should give it up right now, he thought. He should leave the restaurant while it was still safe, before anything happened.

'Sorry. I'm only saying what I feel.'

'You're very kind. I'm flattered.'

'I'm telling the truth.'

Douglas wondered how many other people were having assignations at this very moment; or if they

98

were waiting for the two-hour window after work and before their return home. In Paris he assumed it was commonplace, the *cinq à sept*. He tried to think what such a life might be like. Did people book regular hotel rooms or borrow apartments from their friends? What were the logistics of doing this regularly and how much money did you need?

Julia's steak arrived. It was too tough.

'Perhaps it's horse,' she said.

A waiter brought her a serrated knife and apologised but it made little difference.

'This place seems to be resting on its laurels.'

'I don't know,' said Douglas. 'People seem to come here all the time.'

'But the world has moved on since it became famous.'

'I suppose they don't come here for the food any more,' Douglas said.

'Why do you think people come here then?' Julia asked.

'It must be the romance of it all.'

The couple at the next table rose and squeezed past them. A waiter brought over a 'just in case' summer raincoat for the elderly lady. The man shook his hand and gave him a tip in cash.

'*À demain.*'

Douglas tried to picture the routine. Did the man have a different guest every day of the week or did he just meet his wife? Would they just order the *plat du jour* or study the menu every time they came? How long would it take before they were bored? What kind of marriage did they have? And surely the restaurant would have given them a corner table by now?

'Have you got somewhere to stay?' Julia asked.

'Yes.'

'And have they let you check in?'

'I've done all that . . .' said Douglas.

'Is it close?'

'It's just round the corner. I can't think why you're asking.'

'Neither can I.' Julia took a sip of water. 'So, you've made your arrangements.'

'Have you?'

'Yes,' she said, without elaborating further.

Douglas could not think what to say next.

'What would you like to talk about? Entertain me,' she said.

Douglas didn't feel like *talking* at all, he wanted her there and then, even in the toilets, but if they were going to stay in the restaurant then he might as well ask Julia a few questions about her life.

'Are you happy?' he asked.

The waiter refilled their glasses.

'Well,' she said. 'I'm not unhappy.'

This appeared to be all he was going to get.

Douglas realised, yet again, that he hardly knew this woman. What was he doing? He tried to think of other things to lessen the anticipation but he could not think of anything safe that was not dull.

'What about you?' Julia asked. 'Doing anything interesting?'

'Apart from talking to you?'

'Well, that is obviously a highlight.'

Douglas was almost irritated that the conversation had fallen back on him. He started to tell her about the television series he was making, the history of the relationship between art and anatomy.

100

'I'm surprised you haven't taken up life classes,' said Julia.

'I may well do.'

'Although I can't see you drawing men very well. I think you'd lose interest pretty fast.'

'Well, I do prefer women, Julia.'

'I'm glad to hear it. Shall we have something else?' She looked at the menu. 'You can have the pancakes, or the chocolate mousse, or, of course'—she looked up—'you can have me.'

'When?'

'That was a joke, Douglas. Shall we just have coffee?'

'Why bother with the coffee?'

People were beginning to leave, readying themselves for an afternoon in the office. He could see the tension returning to their faces as they rose from their tables.

'I'll get the bill,' Douglas said. 'I can't wait any longer.'

Julia smiled.

'I'll freshen up.'

Douglas wanted to follow her into the Ladies. He didn't think he had ever felt like this, wanting someone so urgently that he could think of nothing else. He signed the bill and waited for Julia. When she emerged he could smell her freshly applied perfume.

'Let's go,' she said.

'I didn't expect this, you know.'

'Expect what? I don't know what you're talking about.'

'I mean I didn't plan on it.'

'No, of course you didn't.'

They walked through the market and along the

101

rue du Bac until they found themselves in the midst of a group of demonstrators protesting about housing developments in the Languedoc.

'Honestly,' Julia said, 'only in France. A demonstration by archaeologists.'

The protesters handed out leaflets, chanted, blew whistles and let off flares and firecrackers as policemen on Rollerblades circled around them.

They neared the hotel.

'I suppose you do this all the time,' said Julia.

'No,' Douglas replied. 'I don't.' They walked into the foyer and he picked up his key. 'Could we have a bottle of champagne?' he asked. He didn't bother to speak French.

He let Julia enter the lift first.

'I bet the hotel hasn't seen this before,' she said. 'A couple going up to a room in the afternoon with a bottle of champagne.'

'Do you think we are a cliché?'

Douglas opened the door and waited as Julia looked round, assessing the size and the space, avoiding the bed. Douglas had booked the largest available double room. He waited until Julia turned and smiled and then he let the door close. He took a step towards her and they started kissing, eyes half closing, her body falling into him.

Douglas felt the heat and force of the kiss. He tried not to think of his wife and resented the fact that he had ordered champagne. They would have to wait until the concierge brought it up.

Douglas wished he didn't have to think about these things, that he could lose all sense of himself; kissing Julia so hard he could forget about everything else. He kissed her forehead, her closed eyes, her cheeks, her neck and her lips. He tried to

102

tell himself that he had neither anticipated nor planned what he was doing; that this was a conclusion, both natural and inevitable, and he could do nothing to avoid it.

Julia took a step back.

'Careful, my jewellery, my earrings.'

'Never mind about that.'

'I do mind.'

There was a knock on the door. The waiter looked unsurprised. He opened the bottle of champagne and poured out the glasses. As he did so, Julia took off her shoes. Douglas was surprised by her drop in height; how much smaller she became. He handed her a glass. Julia took a sip and watched the waiter leave. As soon as he had closed the door she looked back at Douglas.

'I want you,' she said.

'What about . . .'

'You don't need to worry about that . . .'

They moved over to the bed, kissing all the time. They started to take off their clothes, helping each other until they were naked and desperate.

'Come into me now,' she said.

It was all Douglas wanted: this moment, with this woman in this life. He wished he was younger and stronger and that he could make it last for the rest of his life; that he could go on like this, that he could die like this, that nothing mattered except what he was doing now, with her, in this room.

After they had finished they looked up at the ceiling and listened to each other breathing. Douglas fell asleep.

He awoke when the bedside light was switched on. Julia was sitting next to him. For a moment he did not know where he was.

What time is it? It's after seven. Why are you dressed? I'm sorry, I have to go, I have to get back to my hotel. Why? My husband will worry where I am ... He's in Paris? No, of course not, but I have to call him and I can't do that when I'm with you. Stay. I can't. You mean you don't want to? Don't make it hard. When will I see you? Soon, sooner than you think, I promise. I love you. Don't say such things too soon. I mean it. Don't you love me? Of course I do, just don't make me say it out loud, I have to go. Don't go. I have to go, if I don't go now I'll never go, I'll be lost. Then don't go.

In the doorway Julia tilted her head to one side to whisper that she was sorry.

Douglas finished the champagne and ordered room service. Then he sat up on the bed and watched French television. He wanted to see how long it would be until there was no longer any sense of Julia in the room; her footprints in the talc on the carpet, the smell of perfume and lipstick and newly washed hair, the champagne left in the glass, her weight on the bed and the fallen sheets as she had thrown them off. The next morning the chambermaid would come and erase it all.

He knew that he should go out, think of something else, and be active in the world, anything other than this lassitude.

He lay down and took in the remains of Julia's scent as if she was still there. He didn't normally sleep on the left side and he spread himself across the bed. As he did so he thought, involuntarily, of home, and of Emma.

He tried to shut out the memories of his wife; of the holidays they had shared, the hotel rooms they had slept in, her delight to be away from Scotland in places where she could feel the warmth on her face.

He wished he could stop thinking about her but he could not.

His head began to hurt with the speed of his guilt. Was it for desire alone that he had lost all sense of his life? Could lust, or whatever it was that had overcome him, so unravel every sense that he had of himself that he no longer knew who he was?

The next morning he visited the Musée d'Orsay. Outside there was a queue of tourists, penned into lines. He remembered that Julia had an Art World pass that allowed her to walk straight into almost any gallery in the world. She would enter as if she ran the building already, moving with an assurance Douglas knew he could never possess.

He had to queue for half an hour. He took the escalators up to the impressionist galleries on the top floor, past the determination of Caillebotte's woodstrippers, the exhaustion of *Les Repasseuses*, the unhappiness of *L'Absinthe*. A group of children sat on the floor with their lunch boxes as their teacher told them to close their eyes and imagine what it would be like if the whole of their lives were a dream.

He stopped at the Monet series of Rouen Cathedral and at Renoir's path through the high grasses: a daughter leading the way through the sunlit fields, her left arm outstretched, reaching for a butterfly. The mother's parasol matched the red of the poppies in the light of summer. It reminded him of his childhood: of home.

He thought back to the time when he had wanted to be an art historian rather than a television producer, studying early Italian

Renaissance painting in Glasgow, happy in galleries and libraries, drinking tea, yes, tea, for God's sake, sitting in cafés in the afternoons with his friends.

He turned into a darkened room of pastels by Toulouse-Lautrec. He remembered how Emma had given him a card on one of his birthdays. It was of two people lying in bed under the sheets, and turned towards each other. *Le Lit.* The woman on the left had hair that had sprung up in a tuft; the figure on the right had the same lips as Douglas's.

'Don't you see?' she had said. 'It's us—except they're lying on different sides. They're the wrong way round.'

He could sense the warmth and yield of the marital bed and the give of the pillows. He had once bought a new mattress for them both on Valentine's Day. It was pocket-sprung so that they could turn in the night without disturbing each other. 'It's got so much more give to it,' Emma had told him. 'We'll be in heaven.'

In the art gallery he shuddered at the familiar ease of the two figures in the painting. It was a portrait of them both: he could see that now.

He wanted to sit down but there were no seats. He didn't know whether he was going to cry or be sick. He thought of Emma and what he had done.

Her optimism. His bleakness.

Her affirmation. His drift.

He took a taxi to the Gare du Nord and crossed the river past La Samaritaine. They had once shared a meal together in the rooftop restaurant. It had been an anniversary weekend just after they had given up on having children. They had discussed how they were going to tell their parents.

106

It was raining when the taxi arrived at the Gare du Nord and Douglas had neither a raincoat nor an umbrella. He had not thought about the weather. Everyday life seemed to have nothing to do with him any more: people, escalators, walkways, security, passport control.

He boarded the train and edged his way towards his compartment. A man flirting on his mobile blocked the gangway: 'Smooth like the groove, baby!'

Douglas found his seat opposite an alert elderly woman who looked up from her crossword with a nervous smile. He hoped that she wasn't expecting a conversation.

As he sat down, Douglas imagined what it might be like to tell her his whole story, this stranger on a train, a woman that he knew he would never see again. She would be as good a choice as any, he thought, and perhaps he was lucky to have found her. Her face, even in repose, was a mixture of curiosity and joy. Already he envied her ease with the world. Was it faith, family, the love of one person on whom she could rely, or had she been born with such confidence?

The woman took out her knitting from a polythene bag. She was making baby clothes for a grandchild, a girl.

Douglas decided to order drinks and look out of the window. A bottle of red wine. He knew it looked bad but he didn't care. He overheard a man talking about his mother-in-law: 'The only reason she isn't dead is because she's more toxic than her cancer.'

He opened the bottle and the old joke came to him: *Is life worth living? It depends on the liver.* He

107

thought of the colleague who had failed to eat and who had deliberately drunk himself to death on two bottles of vodka a day (it had only taken a year). There was his Uncle Gordon, living in a house divided into two flats, his wife below, visited every Wednesday by a financial adviser who was also her lover. And he thought of Ansei, the Japanese poet he'd once met in Tokyo, a man who married a woman he hated because he thought the suffering might make him write better poetry:

Now that you are going to a far-off land,
Only your scent remains,
Lavishly infused with late-autumn rain.

On arrival in London he could still pass himself off as being in control. He did not need to resort to mints or aftershave to disguise his drinking. He would take the tube and then catch one of the last trains back to Glasgow.

Two girls opposite were talking about the previous night's party. One of them had been standing in a conservatory full of plants and a woman asked her if they were inside or outside. It was so hard to tell, she said, and the girl had said that she had often felt like that when she was blind drunk and the woman had replied, 'I'm not drunk. But I am blind.'

Douglas knew that he had often been that drunk.

He looked out of the window to see the flooding in the fields, a dull reflection of the bleak skies above, church steeples against low dark clouds. There were people throwing fireworks from bridges on to passing trains and traffic. They came as a series of sharp white explosions and distant smoke against brick and timber yards.

This was a countryside of car parks and abandonment, disused pumping stations and recycling centres, of land being cleared for out-of-town superstores, of desolate rugby posts that reminded him of his brother Angus, the sky darkening above them all.

Back in Glasgow an open-air concert was ending in George Square. Douglas watched people leaving, couples free from anxiety, the young and the newly in love, heading on for pubs and clubs all over the city, dancing at Corinthians, or Cottiers, or the Garage, anywhere, it didn't matter, getting wasted, slaughtered, trashed, bombed and wankered.

Douglas could not ever remember being as young as them.

He took a taxi to Hyndland. Most of the lamps in the tenement were out but an overhead light shone over the entrance. He unlocked the door to his flat and heard Emma call, 'Is that you, darling?'

He saw her walking towards him, barefoot, wearing his favourite pale-blue blouse over her jeans. She was young and alive and her whole face was smiling.

'I've missed you,' she said. 'Have you had a good time?'

CHAPTER FIVE

'If you're going to go far out you should wear a bright hat,' Jack said, 'so that passing boats notice

109

and steer clear.'

'Oh, I think they will notice me,' Krystyna replied. 'Don't you think?'

It was a Saturday and she had come out of town for a day. Jack had met her at the bus stop and she was already wearing a black halter-neck swimsuit under her cotton dress. She could not risk a bikini and knew that she had only a few weeks left before her pregnancy would start to show.

Jack watched Krystyna swim out to sea with the Bass Rock ahead of her. Her head was low against the surface, closer than he had expected, her body streamlined in the glide. She turned on to her back, circling her arms, churning the water with her feet.

Jack had been coming to the beach at Seacliff all his life; with his parents and his brothers when he was a boy, and then, in the early days of his marriage, with Maggie and the girls. He remembered the picnics and the ice cream and the shivery bites after all their swims. Every time he had come he had returned to his childhood. Now here he was again, beginning another chapter, resitting the exam of his life once more.

Guillemots and kittiwakes swept over the rocky outcrop by the smallest of harbours. Jack remembered calling his daughters in from the water and their inevitable disappointment, cold and impatient for immediate supplies of towels and chocolate biscuits.

Krystyna turned and swam butterfly back towards the shore. It was a continual, rhythmic movement and she appeared to be unaware of her surroundings, losing herself in the water. For a moment, Jack thought he was watching a different

Krystyna, a Krystyna that was confident and unafraid. Perhaps this was who she really was, before Sandy, before she had come to Scotland, before anything terrible had happened.

Once she was back in her depth she stooped to regain her balance and climb out. Jack handed her a towel and she began to dry herself.

'I will change at the house. It is easier.' She turned her towel into an improvised skirt and threw her dress over her shoulder. 'I hope you are proud of me, swimming in the North Sea. You should have come too.'

'It's too cold. My days of swimming in the sea are over.'

'I do not believe you. Next time I will insist.'

They walked back over the dunes to the bus stop, passing a row of holiday cottages. There were young pheasant in the roads, cabbage white butterflies quick and low over the fields, and then a burst of midges, flickering briskly in the air.

Krystyna smiled.

'Better with a car.'

'You know I'm not ready to drive.'

'I do not mind.'

'I can hardly remember what it's like.'

A man was shadow-boxing underneath a sprinkler in his garden, attacking the water as it fell through his fingers. A ten-year-old boy walked past accompanied by a mother wearing a T-shirt that read, *I am still a virgin*.

Jack wondered if his appearance with Krystyna was equally absurd. He was already trying to look younger so that it wouldn't seem odd when he was with her. He wore black jeans with deck shoes and pale linen shirts, clothes that had seen better days

111

but had some remaining class in the buttoning and the details. He still had his hair, and it was still dark-brown, but he knew that he had only a few years left in which he could try and pass himself off as being in his early forties.

Perhaps he was enjoying the uncertainty of it all. Krystyna was not a student that he could teach and occasionally tease and cajole; she was not a daughter, like Annie or Kirsty, whose emotions he could easily read; and she was not yet a friend, known over the years, who understood him well enough to forgive his faults.

After she had showered and changed they prepared supper in the kitchen. Krystyna had brought supplies from a Polish delicatessen and began to make home-made pierogi, combining flour, eggs, sour cream and buttermilk. After a few minutes Jack was dismissed for getting in the way. *Gdzie kucharek sześć, tam nie ma co jeść*. Where there are six cooks there is nothing to eat.

He began to see the house through Krystyna's eyes and was embarrassed by its state of disrepair. There were gaps on the walls where Maggie had taken her favourite paintings, their outlines in dust, the colour of the wall unfaded, the torn wallpaper around the nails like a swathe of fear across his life. He should have tidied it up, redecorated even.

As Krystyna began to knead the dough Jack could see her looking at the collage on the wall. It had been made by the children when they had rented a cottage at Tighnabruaich. He had taken them mackerel fishing. It had been one of his proudest achievements—*thirty-five fish, Dad*—and they had sold them door-to-door.

'It is funny,' Krystyna said, as she set the dough to rest. 'No one really knows I am here.'

'No one?'

'It is the greatest freedom. You remove yourself from the world and nobody notices. It is like having a holiday from my own life.'

'What about your friends; or your father?'

'I do not worry about them. I know they don't worry about me. Do you know where your daughters are now?'

'Roughly.'

'I do not believe you.'

'I know how to get hold of them, put it that way. I think you are far more elusive.'

'Elusive?'

'Hard to reach.'

'People can always call me.'

'Not when you keep your phone switched off.'

She began to work on the filling for the pierogi, chopping the onions and potatoes, preparing the cheese.

'Well, perhaps I do not want to be disturbed.'

Jack could not tell if she was flirting or if she always spoke in this way. What did she want from him and was he wrong to try to define it?

They sat out in the garden as they waited for the dough to prove. A flight of swallows swept across the lee of the woodland. Jack thought of Christopher Wren. *Nothing can add beauty to light*. He had once made a list of words to describe the fall into evening: *gloamin—'tide, daylight's gate, crow-time, owl-leet*.

He had always been precise about language. When he met people whose names formed sentences he would always stop them. *Philip*

113

Wood—would what? *Angus May*—but then again he might not. He'd even met a Dutchman called *Jan Smoulders*.

As they sat reading in the garden Jack tried not to stare at Krystyna's dark bare arms and her exposed midriff. He wanted to avoid looking at the rise and fall of her stomach, the gap at the top of her jeans, the whaleback thong visible when she bent over to pick up her clothes. He noticed that her movements were all about adjustment. Her hair was pushed back, swept round, or twisted in her fingers. Her flip-flops were slipped on and off. She toyed with one of them, letting it half fall from her raised bare foot. Her presence had sent him back to the world of attraction and desire, a world he thought he had left long ago.

'What are you reading?' Jack asked.

'Just a story. About love and a lie.'

She held it up so that Jack could see. It was Ian McEwan's *Atonement*.

'I thought it might be something Polish.'

'I can read English as well as speak it.'

'I know. I didn't mean to offend you.'

'You did not. Next year, of course, I will be reading Latin.'

'You are joking.'

'Who knows? It depends how good my teacher is.'

'You'd like to learn?'

'Why not?' Krystyna asked. 'But it is getting cold and I must finish the pierogi. Shall we go inside?'

'If you like.'

Jack normally sat in the garden until it was almost dark. He liked to watch the pace of the light.

Back inside the house Krystyna finished her preparations and then turned on the television, flicking between channels on the remote. The only programme that was not about middle-aged women having a makeover was a flower show. Presenters unused to wearing suits pronounced on nostalgic gardens filled with cottage flowers and low-tech junk—a mangle, a cider press and a rusting tin bath.

'Does your wife do this work?' Krystyna asked.

'How do you know?'

'Your mother told me.'

'She seems to have told you everything.'

'It's quite important, don't you think?'

Jack thought back to the disappointment of his parents when Maggie had left; his mother's weakened optimism and his own pedantic response.

'Is it fatal?' she had asked.

'Well, I don't think I'm going to die, Mother, but it's definitely over.'

'Such a pity,' his mother had said. 'She's a good woman. And the girls . . .' Her voice had faded away. In the silence Jack assumed that his parents were already thinking that it was his fault.

On the television exhibitors spoke about the importance of foliage and their dream leaf, mahogany and deep-veined. They extolled the virtues of architectural gardens with basalt and limestone, because, Jack heard a man saying, 'there's no beauty in concrete'.

'Is it true?' Krystyna asked.

'Yes. She makes gardens.'

'We should change channels.'

'No, it's all right. Let's stay with this.'

115

'Why did she go?'

Jack really didn't want to have to explain it all.

'You do not have to say.'

'She fell in love, I suppose.'

'She was not in love with you?'

'Well, I thought she was . . .'

'I'm sorry.'

Jack remembered when Maggie had left him.

'I tried, Jack. But I just couldn't. We weren't going anywhere, were we?'

Why this need to travel? he had thought. He didn't think they needed to go anywhere.

'I'm sorry.'

He had considered it enough. They were friends, like Angus and Tessa, he thought. They were comfortable and they never got in each other's way. Wasn't that what happened with most marriages after the lust had gone? When you were too tired to resuscitate passion, the energy drained away.

But Maggie had felt frustrated, living out of town (even though she was the one who had asked for a more rural lifestyle), commuting back into Edinburgh and all over the Borders. She had asked Jack what they were going to do to make their lives more tranquil. She kept using the word 'tranquil', and Jack had told her that he thought their lives were already quite content.

Maggie kept on. She asked for a sense of purpose and a vision of the future when all the time Jack felt it was hard enough for them to keep what they had. Didn't she understand that he was working as hard as he could just so they could stay where they were?

He thought he had done his best, but Maggie

116

told him that marriage was never constant even when you thought it was. You could sleepwalk for years and then wake up in a place you no longer recognised.

She had met someone, she said. She hadn't meant to fall in love. But it had happened. Guy and she were soulmates. She had never felt anything like it before.

'What about your children?' Krystyna was asking.

'Sorry?'

'Are you listening to me?'

'Of course. My children.'

It was so long since Jack had explained this. Perhaps he never had.

'They were angry with her at first and took my side but it's settled down a bit now. Annie's involved in corporate hospitality. Kirsty's training to be a lawyer, the usual kind of thing . . .' He waved his hand, as if swatting away a bee. He really didn't have the energy.

'Were you angry yourself?'

'I find anger rather tiring. Is that very lazy of me?'

'And you're not lonely?'

'You get used to it.'

Krystyna smiled.

'Well, now I can see why I came. It is not for me; it is for you.'

'Perhaps it is.'

'Do you see her?' Krystyna asked.

'Who?'

'Your wife.'

'Sometimes. Of course she's not my wife any more.'

117

'Will I meet her?'

'I don't think so. She lives in Bristol. Why?'

'I don't understand why she left you. It seems a bit random—is that the word?'

'I don't really know,' Jack said. Perhaps the whole of his life had been 'random'. It was one of his daughter Kirsty's favourite words.

He could still picture the first 'Dear John' letter he had ever received. His girlfriend had been called Noelle. *I'm sorry but I love Steve. And only him.* Even at the time he had thought the underlining unnecessary.

'You should have more confidence,' Krystyna said, 'and go out more instead of working all the time.'

Jack thought of the hundred and fifty exam papers he had just finished marking.

'I like what I do. I need to do it. And I don't have much time to do anything else.'

'You should make time.'

'That's probably easier for you to say.'

'You must not sound as if you have given up.'

'Perhaps there comes a time when you think you've had enough adventure for one life.'

'No,' said Krystyna. 'You must live dangerously. It is the only way.'

Jack was not convinced. The translation on which he was employed continually made clear the argument that intellectual pleasures (which were long-lasting and never cloying) were of far more value than physical satisfaction.

Sed fugitare decet simulacra et pabula amoris
Absterrere sibi atque alio convertere mentem
Et iacere umorem conlectum in corpora quaeque,

118

Nec retinere, semel conversum unius amore
Et servare sibi curam certumque dolorem . . .

Better to run away,
Escape from such illusions, frighten off
Such things as nourish love, and turn the mind
Anywhere else, disseminate the rank
    accumulation . . .

He thought of Krystyna. This was what he wanted to avoid, although their relationship, if that was what it was, didn't feel as bad as *rank accumulation.*

He knew that if he wanted to retain the calmness of his former life then he should avoid the distraction of her company. Already he could feel himself slipping, losing concentration. He had to finish his translation over the summer; before next term began.

They returned to the kitchen and ate the pierogi with salad. They tasted better than he had been expecting and he remembered the pancakes he had eaten as a child. He had worried that he was going to have to be polite but when Krystyna asked he told her they were the best pierogi he had ever had.

'But you have never had them before.'

'That is also true.'

'What are you like?' Krystyna asked.

'That's a Scottish phrase.'

'I know. Sandy used to say it. I'm sorry.'

'No, it's fine.' Jack did not really want to talk about Sandy. But he wondered how much Krystyna was keeping back; the good times, rather than the bad. 'Would you like some wine?' he asked.

'No thank you.'

'I thought you liked wine?'

'I do but I have stopped. I don't drink any more.'

'Oh.'

'I thought it best.'

'I suppose so. But it's the smoking you should stop.'

'That is impossible,' Krystyna said, almost too quickly. She was worried that Jack was referring to her pregnancy. Perhaps he had been waiting for her to tell him. 'Did you ever smoke?' she asked.

'No.'

'Did you ever take drugs?'

'Not really.'

'What do you mean "not really"?'

Jack remembered the one joint he had had at university. It hardly counted. Krystyna was almost amused, waiting for him to tell his story.

He was about to ask her the same question when his father phoned.

'Jack. Your mother has only just informed me.'

'About what?'

'About what happened: Krystyna and the boy who killed himself. Are you all right?'

'Yes, Father. What did Mother tell you?'

'Everything. Well, I assume it's everything. Why didn't you say?'

'It's complicated.'

'It doesn't seem complicated at all. It must have been awful. You should have told me about it when you were last here. We went for a walk, remember?'

'Yes, Father.'

'You should have stopped me banging on about my own burial and talked about your troubles.'

'It didn't seem right.'

'What are you doing about it? Are you talking to someone?'

'I'm talking to Krystyna.'

'I mean a professional. These things can affect people for a long time. Talking to that girl may not be enough. She will have her own problems. You might not be good for each other.'

'I know. But it's all I can cope with at the moment.'

'You sound very guarded. Is she with you now?'

'Yes.'

'Is she staying with you?'

'Not exactly.'

'Is she in the room with you?'

'Yes.'

'I see. So you can't talk.'

'Not easily.'

'Well, let me know when you can. Your mother's worried about you. We all are. You should have said something.' Jack's father was trying to be kind but was adding another layer of guilt.

'I'm fine, Father. Really.'

'You don't sound very fine.'

'I am.'

'It must be hard on your own. Bring her over if you want. We rather like her. You could come and see us together . . .'

Jack was not ready for family therapy.

'I can manage.'

'Come for lunch whenever you like. Don't be shy.'

'I won't. I just need some time . . .'

The conversation was ending but it was clear that Ian wanted more.

121

'Nothing else I can do?'

'No, it's all right.'

'Well, cheerio then.'

Jack put down the phone. He felt guilty that he had not asked his father a single question in return; how he was feeling or if there was anything he could do.

He finished his pierogi and poured another glass of wine. He knew he should talk more about Sandy and how much Krystyna thought about him.

'How is your father?' she asked.

'I don't really know.'

'You should see him.'

'I will,' said Jack, already imagining what it would be like if he took her with him.

'He is a generous man. A good father, I think.'

'Yes. He likes to think that he is.'

'Do you think we ever stop being children?'

The question surprised him.

'Only when we become parents ourselves.'

Krystyna nodded.

'I see.'

Jack was not sure that she believed him.

'You never stop being a parent,' he said.

'Even when you are old?'

'No, I don't think so.'

'I see.' Krystyna stood up to clear the plates.

'No, it's all right,' said Jack. 'I'll do it.'

'Let me, I'd like to. You make me think too much.'

'I don't mean to.'

'It doesn't matter,' she said.

'What doesn't matter?'

'It's OK. I need to do something simple.'

'Let me help . . .'

122

'No. You stay there. Or do some of your work. It's OK. I can do this.'

She appeared to be shutting him out. Jack did not know what he could have said to upset her. All he wanted was for her to like him.

'What is it?'

'It's nothing.'

'It must be something.'

'I can't explain.'

'Is it . . .' He did not reach the word 'Sandy' but Krystyna seemed to guess that this was what he meant.

'No, it's not that . . .'

She rested her wet hands on the sink. Jack knew he should probably touch her, hold her, comfort her, but her body was closed and turned away from him.

'I think it was hearing you speaking to your father . . .' she said.

'Because you can't speak to your own?'

'No. It's just that you have a father. Only that. And I was thinking what it was like not to have a father. I can't explain. I'm sorry. I have to go.'

'Don't go.'

'I must. I'm sorry. I should not cry.'

'Of course you can cry. You can do whatever you want.'

Krystyna turned at last. She smiled.

'Not really.'

'No, I suppose not. But then often we don't know what we want. If you see what I mean.'

'You do not have to talk,' said Krystyna. 'You do not have to have an answer for everything.'

'I feel I should.'

'Don't worry.'

123

'I do worry. I worry about you all the time.'

She put a wet hand on his shoulder.

'Then worry less. And fetch me a towel.'

Krystyna sat down at the table. She dried her hands and then her face.

'Sorry, I must blow my nose. I will go to the bathroom.'

When she returned she had her shoulder bag ready.

'You know I must go. I have to work tomorrow.'

'You could take the day off,' said Jack. 'We could go for a walk.'

'I need to earn money.'

'I can lend you some money, if you like.'

'That will not be necessary. It would not be appropriate.'

'Appropriate?'

'Yes. Appropriate.'

Jack smiled.

'Your English is very good.'

'Thank you.'

'I like its precision.'

'You must have to be precise in your work.'

Now she was humouring him.

'I like to be accurate.'

'I can tell. You can be, what is your word, "pedantic"?'

Once, when Jack had phoned his computer helpline and IT support had asked whether he had 'migrated his files' he had shouted down the line, 'migrate is not a transitive verb.'

'I think it's important to say what you mean.'

'And mean what you say. Although they are not the same thing.'

'I'm impressed.'

124

'I hope you enjoyed your pierogi.'

'Of course.'

Krystyna looked at the clock on the oven.

'I must get the bus. I do not want to miss it. There is one at nine, I think . . .'

Jack tried once more.

'You know, you can always stay.'

'We have to take our time. Then I will stay.' She smiled, trying to be kind but without wanting to lead him on. 'In my own room, of course.'

'Of course. I didn't want you to think . . .'

'I didn't . . .' said Krystyna. 'Perhaps next time . . .'

'Is that a promise?'

'Promises always lead to trouble.'

Jack did not take the conversation further. He heard the words he wanted to say in his head and tried to dismiss them. *Perhaps we want trouble.*

He walked with Krystyna to the bus stop. It was not yet dark. Jack remembered one of the first poems he had translated. *Qui nunc it per iter tenebricosum.* Now he travels the darksome road. *Illuc, unde negant redire quemquam.* Thither whence they say no one returns. Catullus. Perhaps it was wrong to feel so sad when the light was so beautiful.

The bus pulled up and Krystyna leaned towards him and let him kiss her on both cheeks. Anyone looking at them would have assumed that this was a daughter saying goodbye to her father. Jack didn't think it was like that at all.

CHAPTER SIX

Angus was sure he had the best marriage out of the three brothers but, given the competition, he didn't think it counted for much. He and Tessa were considered the most stable couple by default: conscientious, dutiful, and ever so slightly dull. But, for most of the time, Angus did not mind. Decency, discretion and stability might have become old-fashioned but they were still virtues worth preserving. He had provided for his family consistently and without complaint. What was the alternative?

He and Tessa had lived in the same house on the south side of Edinburgh for years. They drove a car that never broke down. The mortgage was almost paid off, and they were sure of their friends. It had been a life of few surprises. Then Angus lost his job.

He had no warning. He was told by a man who was twenty-four years younger in a room without windows. The firm was redirecting its focus towards new initiatives in China and India. Angus was 'one of the casualties of the shake-out'.

The man from human resources was called Tim. He had the largest nose Angus had ever seen and sweat stains under his shirt. He was clearly frightened of making a mistake. Perhaps he was worried the same thing might happen to him in a few years' time. He spoke as if he had learned some kind of script and argued that the company was doing Angus a favour. They would provide for a lawyer, make sure Angus's pension was unaffected, and offer him a severance payment.

Angus listened and said little. He could not believe the nerve. The company had simply spat him out. Even as the man spoke Angus knew that he was unlikely to find equivalent employment. He did not have the transferable skills necessary for what Tim was referring to as 'a portfolio of career opportunities'. But he felt far from retired, redundant, finished or whatever the word was for the outspat.

One of the senior partners who had been party to the decision even said that he was envious. Now Angus was free from all the hurly-burly of the rat race. He could do anything he wanted.

As the man spoke, Angus almost suggested that they swap places. Perhaps the senior partner might like to see what it was actually like to have his financial and social status removed without warning. Angus only just remembered to retain his dignity. Edinburgh was a small city. It wouldn't help to fall out with people.

He did not want to see his colleagues ever again. He had drifted into financial services as his rugby playing days ended and had stayed there ever since. He didn't think he'd ever actually *enjoyed* it. Every time he had taken Tessa to one of the firm's social functions they had felt excluded by the rapacious nature of the conversation: how to pension commercial property investment; the need to raise commission rates; how inheritance-tax planning could extract more money from elderly relatives.

The only person he would miss, he decided, was Janice, his personal assistant.

'She's paid so little we're keeping her on,' his

127

boss told him. 'It doesn't make much difference.'

Janice looked appropriately guilty (Angus was sure she must have known in advance) and told him that her working life wouldn't be the same without him. She said she thought they had let him go because he had been 'too nice'.

Although he wouldn't miss the work Angus recognised that he would have to find another way of describing himself. He had been defined by his employment. How would he introduce himself now?

At first he thought he might behave as if he still had his job. He would put on his suit and leave home, pretending that nothing had happened. Then he would read the financial pages in the library before doing something adventurous with all the other men who had been discarded in their mid-fifties. He would go to a gym, work on his golf, spend more time at the Rotary. He would need to work out the details, of course, but he reckoned he could keep up the pretence for a couple of years until the redundancy money ran out. Perhaps he would shave off his beard and buy a new wardrobe in an attempt to look younger.

He tried to contain his resentment. His life had been dominated by the pressure of work and he had given the firm over half of his life. He had spent years on his computer and on the phone, tracking stocks, and making what he considered to be shrewd investments. He was proud to have set up one of the first ethical funds in Britain, visiting smaller companies all over the country, avoiding arms, tobacco, gambling and nuclear stocks. He was a well-regarded manager but a cautious investor and his moral stance meant that he sometimes missed out on easier profits. His funds began to lag. They were described in the papers as 'solid' but 'lacking sparkle'. It seemed to sum up his life.

Tessa would have to be the first to know; then his children and, finally, his parents. It had been so different for them, he thought. His mother had inherited a house and his father had secured a job for life. As far as he knew they had never had to worry about money or redundancy or their marriage breaking down. At least Angus had managed to avoid that. It was about the only area in which he felt superior to his brothers. He was convinced he had the best wife.

Perhaps they could go away and live somewhere else, Italy perhaps, and forget all about Scotland and the struggle to keep up a cheerful face and a decent home. They would probably have enough money.

If they moved abroad Angus would not have to bother being polite to those friends and acquaintances who had no difficulty in hanging on to their jobs until their proper retirement age.

He was fifty-four. It was hardly old.

He began to practise how to tell people what had happened.

'I've lost my job. I've been made redundant. I've taken early retirement. I am now retired.'

The sentences were too defeatist. He had to learn how to take the initiative.

'I'm setting up a new venture. I'm going to do something different. We're leaving Scotland.'

Angus knew that he had to preserve his self-esteem. It was the emotional quality that mattered most, he decided; but it was also the one most

129

vulnerable to attack. He had seen it disappear from the faces of friends whom the NHS, the National Trust, local government and the BBC had all 'let go'. Employers that liked to see themselves as providing a nurturing, training environment soon lost interest when members of their workforce hit fifty.

There was his friend Roger who was made redundant while he was on sick leave; there was Anne who was removed because her employers told her they were sure she would not mind; and there was Tom who was dispatched between his mother's death and funeral. The man doing the sacking had begun with the words, 'I know this isn't a good time . . .'

No one had said thank you or good luck or given them any indication that the work they had done had been worthwhile. As a result they had lost their confidence. Angus was determined not to feel the same. He would not let his former employers destroy him.

He began to watch property programmes on television and conducted secret relocation searches on the Internet. He wanted to approach Tessa with a series of possibilities, he decided. They could carry on as they were, downsize, or move abroad. He preferred the last option but thought that he had better not sell it too hard. He would have to keep his nerve.

The thought of living abroad began to take hold. He started to think of a future life in Italy. He began to hope that Tessa might be glad to get away from Edinburgh, to go somewhere warmer and escape the demands of his family in East Fortune. He had noticed how she had already begun to mother his parents.

He would do something mad: buy a vineyard. *Viticulture*. He even liked the word. That would finish off his former colleagues. And if he managed to achieve this he decided that he would show no signs of stress or failure. He would take his revenge by being happier than the people he had left behind.

He confessed in the middle of a picnic in the Botanic Gardens. It was such a warm day, Tessa had said, and they so rarely did anything impromptu. Why couldn't they just pack a hamper and a cool bag and enjoy the day? She had bought bread from the Italian delicatessen together with Parma ham, melon, panforte and home-made lemonade.

The gardens were already crowded with keep-fit enthusiasts who had decided to ignore the *No jogging* signs and toddlers escaping their mothers. Angus was reminded of their children, Imogen, Sarah and Gavin. How innocent they had seemed, all those years ago, with their tricycles and scooters, their little crash helmets and their games of rounders with friends. Every time he saw a grassy bank Angus was reminded of their childhood roly-polies down the hill. He wanted to take off his glasses and do one just for Tessa—to show that he could still be young.

They found a spot by a large eucalyptus tree and unpacked the picnic together.

'Isn't this lovely?' said Tessa.

'It was such a good idea to come. I love this place.'

'It's extraordinary we ever find time for each other,' Tessa was saying. 'There's always a child to

131

worry about or a relation to visit. But I suppose that's what retirement is for.'

'Yes,' said Angus. He poured out the lemonade. 'Are you all right?'

'Of course I'm all right. Why do you ask?'

'You just seem a bit different.'

'How am I different?'

'I don't know. Perhaps you are keeping something from me.'

She appeared to know already.

'Why would I do that?'

'I've no idea. But you're up to something. I can tell.' Tessa began to lay the Parma ham and the slices of melon on a plate. 'Would you like some black pepper?'

'You've even brought that?'

'Of course.'

She was not going to say anything more.

'Well?'

Angus took a bite of the melon and the ham. If he closed his eyes he could be in Italy. He finished his mouthful. Tessa was waiting for a reply. He took a sip of lemonade.

'I'm leaving my job.'

'Oh.' Tessa broke off another piece of bread and began to butter it.

Angus waited for her to say something more but nothing came.

'I've quit.'

'I see. Would you like some more ham?'

'Thank you.'

'Don't you think we should have discussed this?'

Angus tried to retain the authority he thought he needed.

'I thought we could discuss it now. I wasn't ready

before.'

'When did this happen?'

'A few weeks ago.'

'A few weeks?'

'I'm sorry. I should have said.'

Angus could see that Tessa was being careful not to judge him too soon.

'Won't it be hard to find another job at your age?'

'I don't need another job.' The response was firmer than he had intended. It sounded like pique.

Tessa was still calm.

'But the kids? Gavin's still at university.'

Angus tried to soften his tone.

'There's a good pay-out. We'll have enough if we're careful.'

'A pay-out? I thought you'd resigned?'

He should have taken her into his confidence.

'Are you telling me everything?' she asked.

'Not exactly.'

'Was it your decision?'

'It was a mutual decision.'

'Oh Angus, why didn't you say? Why didn't you tell me?'

'I didn't want to worry you. I thought I should do it on my own.'

She leaned forward and hugged him.

'Oh Angus, I'm sorry.'

'No, it's all right. I'm fine about it.'

He waited as they held each other. He had to sustain his confidence amidst her kindness.

'It was a bit humiliating at first,' he said. 'I had to listen to a load of nonsense about corporate outsourcing and three-hundred-and-sixty-degree roll-outs, but apart from that I'm fine.'

Tessa smiled sadly.

'I could have helped you.'

'You didn't need to help me. I didn't need your help. I only need it now. That's why I'm telling you.'

He poured out more lemonade, and unwrapped the panforte. Icing sugar drifted on to his trousers. He tried to show his wife that it did not matter.

'That stuff gets everywhere,' he said.

'What are you going to do?' Tessa asked.

'I don't know. I've had some thoughts . . .'

'And?'

'What do you think about living abroad?'

'Oh Angus . . .'

'I thought France, or even Italy. We remortgage the house, use the redundancy money, and buy a little smallholding—a little vineyard even. What do you think?'

'Italy? You know I've never been back.'

'I know. But perhaps we should go back. Live again. Have an adventure.'

'Is that what you call it?'

It was the brightest of days. The trees contained a myriad of greens against the blue: olive, lime and emerald. Tessa remembered the Italy of her youth, the accident when she had burned her arm. She thought what it might mean to go back. It didn't seem possible.

'And what am I supposed to do about my job?' she asked. 'I can't just give it up.'

'I know. I haven't thought that bit through.'

'We can't really afford it.'

'We can if we live somewhere else, somewhere cheaper.'

'But Italy . . .'

Angus put his hand over hers.

'I know, I know . . .'

'Are you sure you've thought about this properly?'

Angus smiled.

'Of course I haven't. I'm just trying to be brave.'

'And what about the family, your parents?'

'They can come and stay. It'll be an adventure.'

Tessa started to clear away the picnic.

'I'll have to think about it, Angus. It's quite a lot to take in. When will you tell people?'

'When we know what we're going to do and where we might go. I don't want to worry anyone.'

'Or change your mind . . .'

'I won't do that . . .'

'I don't know.'

'Trust me. I want to start again. I want to leave everything behind; everything except you.'

'And the children.'

'Of course, the children . . .'

Tessa stood up, put the wicker basket to one side, and began to shake out the rug.

'I'm glad I've survived then.'

'I can't do anything without you. You know that.'

'It's just as well. I don't think your parents could cope with another of their sons' marriages collapsing . . .'

'There is that . . .'

Tessa folded the rug and handed it to her husband. Her tone was still jovial but it contained mild steel.

'You mean you're only staying with me to please your parents?'

'Of course not. I love you.'

'Good. I'm glad we've got that sorted out.' She

handed Angus the cool box.

'Aren't you supposed to say you love me too?' Angus asked.

'Of course I do. I just need to keep you on your toes. I can't have you taking anything for granted.'

'Believe me,' Angus replied, 'I don't take anything for granted any more.'

They walked back through the Botanics. Angus began to breathe more deeply. He had told Tessa and now, whatever happened, it was going to be all right.

He could do almost anything as long as she stayed with him. His job was nothing, he said to himself, and his wife was everything. It was his last chance to reinvent his life.

CHAPTER SEVEN

Krystyna knew that she would either have to tell Jack about the baby or stop seeing him altogether. They could not go on as they were.

Travelling on the bus to see him once more, she thought back to when she was little: mushroom picking with her father in the woods and forests outside Kraków. It was one of the few things they had done together, seeking out special places that the family had passed on for years, gathering supplies of *czubajki kanie*, bringing them home and frying them up for breakfast.

She tried to think how different her life would have been if she had had no father; if her mother had had to do it all on her own.

When she arrived at the house she could see

that Jack had not been out for days. There were piles of washing up in the sink, dirty coffee cups on his desk, overflowing waste-paper baskets.

'I've been very busy,' he explained.

'Perhaps I should not have come.'

'You're always welcome, Krystyna, you know that.'

'I'd like to take you out. We should go for a walk.'

'Yes, of course.'

'I thought we could find some mushrooms.'

'I don't know if there are any round here.'

'I have seen the woods close to your house. There must be some there.'

Jack stopped his work.

'The girls used to gather them but I was always scared they might be poisonous. Maggie was the one that knew. After she left, of course . . .'

Krystyna was not going to let him talk about his wife.

'Did you never go out with the children yourself?'

'Of course. But I was always busy. I suppose the word is preoccupied.'

'You didn't like spending time with them?'

'Of course I did. But I never realised how quickly their childhood would disappear.'

'And what about when you were young? Did your parents take you out?'

'Yes, but I always preferred reading.' He gestured to the desk. 'I'm always with my books and papers.'

Krystyna did not believe him. Jack couldn't have been reading Latin from the age of five.

'Are there mushrooms in your work?' she asked.

137

'Does your poet talk about them?'

'I don't think so, although Lucretius likes the bark and roots of trees, the woodland floor, nature dispersing itself . . .'

Krystyna wondered how long Jack could speak before realising that he was sounding ridiculous.

'Really?'

'And I think the Emperor Claudius was killed by mushroom poisoning. It's in Tacitus.'

'What kind?'

'A death cap, I think . . .'

'*Amanita phalloides*. Don't worry. It's too early in the year for them. I think you will live.'

'Are you teasing me?' Jack asked. He had never seen her so—what was the word—*larky*?

'Of course. Didn't you notice?'

'I'm not sure I notice anything these days.'

Krystyna pulled open the kitchen drawer and picked out two knives.

'I think we should take the pastry brush, too. What do you think?'

'I don't make pastry.' Jack tried to sound helpful. 'I'm sorry. I know I should . . .'

'We can use it to take off the soil. Don't look so anxious.'

'I'm not anxious.'

Krystyna picked up a basket.

'There's nothing to worry about. I think you might be more worried if you could see yourself sitting at your desk all day.'

'But I like my books. I'm happy doing what I do.'

'Are you really?' Krystyna asked. 'You don't think you could be happier? You can't see your life differently?'

'Believe me. I like solitude.'

138

'I don't think people are supposed to live on their own.'

'I used to think it was the only way I could get any work done. And after everyone had left I was used to it. Then, of course, when all this happened . . .'

'What?'

'I realised . . .'

'What?' Krystyna smiled.

'That I'm even happier when I am with you.'

'Then I am pleased.'

'I'm sorry if that's too much.'

'Of course it's not. But perhaps you overestimate me. I can be quite boring . . .'

'I mean it.'

Krystyna was almost amused by his intensity.

'No, you don't.'

'I do. I promise . . .'

She stretched out her arm and pulled Jack out of his chair.

'Come on. Let's go out. We can't stay inside on a day like today.'

They left the house, crossed the main road, and headed past a disused airfield into the hills. Jack was sure they were not going to find many mushrooms. It wasn't the season but Krystyna kept encouraging him to crouch down at the base of birch trees to look for chanterelles lodged under leaves or clustered amongst moss. She taught him to recognise the safe from the dangerous, talking of blushers and grisettes, *pieprznik jadalny* and *podgrzybek brunatny*.

'You're making these names up, knowing that I can't possibly understand you,' said Jack.

'I'm not, I promise.'

139

They spent an hour stooping down amidst the damp resinous smell of the woodland ('Is this poisonous?' 'No, it's a brown birch.' 'How am I supposed to know?')

Working low, at the base of the trees, Jack was a small boy again, searching amidst worms and earwigs, surprised by the minutiae of ants and spiders, delighting in the unseen activity of natural life: beetles in rivulets of bark, a woodlouse in the crevice of a broken branch.

The earth was alternately hard and spongy underfoot, broken up by roots and fallen branches. The rotting stumps of dying trees gave life to fungus and lichen, grub and fern. Looking at the woodland floor, Jack was forced to slow his life down. When he stood up, he even saw the sky differently. He had a dizzying, vertiginous sense of his own place in the world, caught between the overarching blue above him and a woodland floor whose roots travelled as deep into the earth as their growth climbed into the air.

'How are you managing?' Krystyna asked.

'Better than I thought.'

'You see. It is good for you. I am sure you will work better after you have done this.'

'I'll certainly be keen to get on with it,' said Jack.

At the edge of the wood he could see a white fog approaching, the haar off the sea, shrouding the distant fields and heading towards them. He had known this mist since childhood and yet it always surprised him, filling the valleys and the woodlands with its speed and thickness.

'We should get back,' he said.

'I am not ready,' said Krystyna. 'We haven't enough.'

140

Jack pointed to the advancing haar.

'Soon we'll hardly be able to see our hands, never mind the mushrooms.'

'What is it?'

'It's the east coast of the North Sea, the fastest fog you'll ever have known.'

'Do you know the way home?'

'You may have to hold my hand.'

'Let me finish with this tree.'

Krystyna stooped down, brushed aside some leaves and made a firm incision in the base of a young cep.

The sky had already darkened; the light in the clearings had faded.

'We must get to the main path before we can't see.'

'It's so bad?'

'Trust me.'

The air filled with storm. Jack was becoming impatient. He held out his hand.

Krystyna swung her basket over her shoulder and looked down her muddied arm.

'I should not have worn a white blouse.' She took his hand.

They reached the path just as the fog closed around the trees. Jack insisted they walk slowly, looking down at the uneven track and then ahead to check the way forward. There were steep ditches on either side.

'You are very tense,' said Krystyna. 'I can feel it in your hand.'

'I don't want you to stumble or fall.'

'I will be all right. I am quite strong,' she said.

'It always takes people by surprise,' said Jack, 'this haar.'

The ash and birch by the roadside disappeared into a mist which was thick and bright, more luminous than the day had been, with dusk behind it. It was like the ground of a painting. Darkness would fall as soon as the layer of light had been stripped away. A wood pigeon flew out of the hedgerow directly in front of them.

'It's like being in a horror film,' Krystyna said. 'I never know what is going to happen next.'

'Stay with me,' said Jack.

They kept to the margins between road and ditch, following the lines of hedge and fence through the enveloping whiteness. They could hear traffic but could not tell how close or far it was. Then they saw the lights of a Land-Rover, crossing their path, distant in the fog.

'Perhaps we can get a ride,' Krystyna said.

'They won't see us. Keep to the edge of the track . . .'

'Are you frightened?' Krystyna asked.

'Of course not.'

'I think you are.'

'I'm only worried about you.'

'I'm used to the countryside.'

Krystyna thought back to the dark mornings when she had risen with her father, putting on as many clothes as possible and setting off in the Fiat 126, going into the woods with torches so that they could be sure of being the first to find the best of the mushrooms as dawn broke. It was so cold and her father was always determined, involved in a personal battle with nature itself; angry and cheated when they failed, victorious and loving when they were successful.

Now she worried about twisting her ankle and

142

did not know how she would be able to help Jack if he fell himself. The wind in the mist was colder than anything she had anticipated. It brought with it a relentless dampness. Krystyna could feel her hair matted against her head, the cold and the wet in her face, and swore that she would never go for a walk in Scotland again. It was July and here she was, lost and freezing with a middle-aged man in the middle of nowhere.

'Nearly there,' said Jack.

The white light was passing beyond them, leaving a clouded darkness that was almost transparent. Krystyna sensed that the haar was easing; but in the distance, she could see a further band of whiteness unfurling towards them.

They waited until there was no sound of traffic and crossed the road. Two sheep skittered away in front of them.

'They are so stupid,' Jack said.

'Almost as stupid as us,' said Krystyna.

It had been so long since Jack had walked out into the woods that he had become confused on their return, taking the long way round through the whiteness. Only when he saw the farm buildings with the grain store beyond did he know that they were almost home.

'It must be this way,' Krystyna said as they neared the house. 'We were lost. Why didn't you tell me?'

'I knew we'd find our way in the end,' said Jack.

Krystyna sat down on the bench in the porch and took off her shoes. She was relieved to be back in the warmth.

'I'll fetch you a towel,' Jack said. 'I hope you weren't too afraid.'

143

'You were the one that was afraid.'

'Never.'

'Not of the mist. Of me.'

'Nonsense.'

Krystyna turned on the shower. She felt the water soak into her skin and washed her hair free of its cloying dampness.

Jack set out warm towels and waited for her while pretending that he was working.

Half an hour later Krystyna walked into the kitchen and turned the hob on low. She began to melt butter and crush some garlic ready for the mushrooms.

'We can have mushrooms and toast,' she said. 'And you can have wine . . .'

'I thought you had to be careful with alcohol and mushrooms.'

'I won't be having any . . .'

'Nothing?'

'Just the mushrooms. If your brother Douglas was here . . .'

'There's no need to bring him into it.'

'I like him.'

'Don't tell me you prefer him to me?'

'It's not a competition, I think?'

Krystyna dropped the mushrooms into the saucepan and began to coat them with the butter and garlic.

Jack poured Krystyna a glass of water. Then he opened the red wine.

'How much garlic are you using?'

'A lot. You like garlic?'

'I only worry about bad breath.'

Krystyna picked up her water and teased the glass below her lower lip.

'We are not going to be kissing.'

'No. I don't think so.'

'You don't think? You mean it's possible?'

'I didn't say that, Krystyna.'

'I am joking. There is no need to be scared. I'm just going to make the mushrooms.'

'Good.'

Krystyna gave them a final stir.

'Don't sound relieved.'

'I'm not.'

Krystyna poured the mushrooms on to the toast.

'I think you are supposed to be disappointed. It would be polite.'

Jack pulled out his chair and sat down.

'I don't know what I sound like.'

Jack added black pepper to his mushrooms and drank the red wine. Before Krystyna arrived he had always eaten his meals too quickly. Now he took his time, enjoying the silences between them.

When Krystyna had finished she looked up and smiled. Jack wondered if she had been waiting to say something but had then thought better.

'What?' he asked.

'Nothing . . .'

'No. Go on . . .'

'You are good-looking. In your own way. If you tried harder.'

'I don't believe you.'

'I am sure that if you wanted you could find a very nice woman.'

'It's all right.'

'Don't you ever want to? You are free, aren't you?'

'Yes, I suppose I am.'

'Then what would be the harm?'

145

'I can't,' Jack said. 'I just can't.'

'Then that's a shame.'

Jack couldn't imagine what it would be like to be in love again; the desperation and the need: how much he would have to risk and how it would unsettle his life.

He thought of their return from the walk, and seeing Krystyna's cold red hands taking off her shoes, the dark hair falling in front of the pale face, and then her looking up at him:

You were the one that was afraid.

Never.

Not of the mist. Of me.

CHAPTER EIGHT

Douglas missed the excitement of being with Julia. He knew it was wrong but he did not care. He no longer had the morals for resistance.

They had arranged to meet in Amsterdam and were staying in a hotel by the Vondelpark. The stairwell was decorated with portrait busts of Descartes and Spinoza. Douglas and Julia were told that there were philosophical discussions in Dutch every Thursday night.

A long quotation about absolute beauty from Plato's *Symposium* had been painted on the wall of their room. The white gauze curtains were embroidered with a poem telling them that life should be taken 'little by little'.

'This could become annoying,' Julia said, as she locked the door and started to take off her clothes.

'Yes,' said Douglas, 'there's even a mirror over

the bed, for God's sake, *Heb lief en doe wat je wilt.* Have love and do what you will. We could give it a go, I suppose.'

'You suppose? Is that all?'

Julia tilted her head to one side and took off her earrings. Then she pushed back her hair and waited for him to speak.

Come here. Have patience. I can have patience later, I want you now, is there anything wrong with that? No, nothing's wrong with that.

She started to unbutton her blouse.

'Come on then.'

Here he was again, Douglas thought. He could do nothing but this; and it was for this, he thought, that people wrecked marriages, ruined careers, and destroyed lives: and it was this that, when denied or abandoned, made people despair and drink and die.

'What now,' she said, 'what next?'

*　　*　　*

The next morning a whole new set of messages had been posted in the Hotel Filosoof. *Beginning to think is beginning to be undermined. Fear cannot be without hope nor hope without fear.* Douglas was amused that even the toaster had a message stuck to it. *Silence is a friend who will never betray—Confucius.*

'I wonder if Confucius had any friends.'

'Only very silent ones,' Julia said.

They walked to the Rijksmuseum. An opportunistic busker was singing 'Waterloo' outside the Hotel Abba. One of a group of English stag-weekenders was enjoying his first pint of the day, telling his mates how he had been punched for trying to take a photograph of a prostitute in the red-light district.

Inside they began to walk freely through the galleries, aware of each other's presence but never coming too close. They spoke so little that at one point Julia came up behind Douglas and whispered, 'Hello, Confucius.'

They stopped in front of a painting, a Brueghel featuring a series of miniature dramas set in a small town square. It was a folk painting, earthy and unsentimental. There was country dancing and drinking, there were children playing with spinning tops and men with dice. In the foreground, the figure of Carnival sat astride a beer barrel. He was preparing to joust with Lent, an elderly woman with a bee-skelp on her head.

'What do the bees mean?' Douglas asked. He thought of his father tending the hives in East Lothian, smoking them out while wearing his large hat and veil.

'Diligence. Temperance. Something you might need to work on.'

'I'm very diligent.'

'Just not so good on the temperance.'

The painting was a minute depiction of the daily process of living. It was a world without individualism, a song to the unsung. A woman had climbed a ladder to clean her windows, another sold fish, while a beggar with a bedridden child received money from strangers.

'Let's see if we can find ourselves,' Julia said. 'Who is most like us?'

'I'm not some sixteenth-century peasant . . .' Douglas began.

148

'Look. There you are,' she said. 'In the top window of the pub, observing the action.'

Douglas tried to think what it would be like to film the scene from a high angle. He tried to find someone who looked like Julia, but the women all wore headscarves or danced with their backs to the picture frame.

'I can't see you anywhere.'

'Of course not. I'm far too glamorous.'

Douglas looked at her and then at the dead in the painting, unnoticed amidst the revellers, the crippled and the blind.

'Haven't you got any work to do?' she asked.

'I've done most of the filming; I've just got a little more setting-up to do. I've called this a recce.'

'I hope I'm not compromising your work.'

'Does that mean I'm compromising yours?'

'Well, we certainly can't do this at home.'

They looked at simple paintings of Dutch interiors: a woman taking off her stockings, a mother delousing her child's hair, a roistering man proposing a toast.

They stopped in front of Rembrandt's painting of the *Jewish Bride*. Julia pointed out the sweep and volume of the groom's golden arm, his right hand on her breast, her left hand on his; pearls and jewellery, cream and gold, ochre into darkness.

The husband was trying to give his wife comfort. Her eyes were past and beyond him, saying, 'I don't know . . . I don't know.' She was wearing bracelets of pearls, four twists on her right hand, and one on her left. Douglas could imagine her distracted with her jewellery, playing with the weight of the gold.

149

'What if that was us?' he asked.

'Look at their hands.'

'I can understand being him,' Douglas said, 'reaching out . . .'

'They seem so gentle with each other. So full of care.'

Douglas began to think that perhaps this was a painting not about themselves but about their partners. He and Julia were already corrupted, fallen. And here it came again, without warning, the same feeling that he had had in Paris after Julia had left; the thoughts of Emma, the inevitable guilt. Was this going to happen every time or would he get used to it? He wanted to ask if Julia felt the same, if she was thinking of her husband.

They walked back through the streets and along the canals, avoiding the movement of trams and bicycles. It was warm on the bridges and in the sunnier streets but Julia insisted that they walk through the shadier parts of the city. The sun was too bright and unforgiving. It showed her age, she told him. Douglas should know this. She didn't allow overhead lighting at home, she said. She liked the darkness.

They visited a shop full of mirrors on the Herengracht and saw themselves reflected back and forward, their images repeating in infinite regressions: Julia with her blonde hair and her red coat, Douglas with his black jacket, jeans and Converse trainers. Despite the distortion they looked like an ordinary couple. Douglas felt a fraud.

He bought blue flowers for their room, irises and cornflowers, and they browsed in bookstores and antique shops in the Jordaan. Douglas wondered how soon he could suggest they went back to their hotel.

Julia took his arm.

'Isn't this fun?'

'Yes,' said Douglas, unable to imagine how it was ever going to last.

Back in the hotel Julia said she was tired. She didn't want sex. She just wanted a rest. It was the first time she had said no to him.

Douglas raided the minibar and watched her sleeping. Her head was turned away from him, her blonde hair falling over her shoulders. Her sleep seemed so careless and he was almost angry with her for not being as tensely, vibrantly, anxiously elated; for sleeping through the storm of this uncertainty and desperation; for being so calm and detached when he was so engaged and complete.

He wanted to make love to her again. It would be the only way he could stop thinking, by losing himself in her, by embracing the darkness, by exhausting himself to the point of collapse and oblivion, finding that sated sense of self where nothing could reach him.

He pulled back the sheets and looked at her naked body. He remembered asking if she had a birthmark and she had said no, she had no marks anywhere, not even a freckle. He listened to her breathing and adopted its rhythm himself, rising and falling, trying to calm himself down, but it was useless.

Julia stirred.

What is it? I can't sleep, I want you. Again? Yes, again. Come on then.

She was still half-asleep, letting him do what he

151

wanted. He tried to raise her energy, to stimulate her into some kind of response, but she lay back, more passively than she had ever done before. The excitement had gone.

It was like being married, Douglas thought. It was their first experience of bad sex.

Are you all right? I'm fine, I'm sorry it wasn't very good. That's all right, don't worry.

Her agreement came all too readily.

'It doesn't matter,' Julia said.

But it did. Douglas knew that he had pushed it too far and felt ashamed. He felt worse than when he had begun. Now he would not be able to rest at all. He would have to wait until they were both ready and try again. He could not afford to mess it up. He wanted to make it right.

Julia was sleeping again. Douglas knew that he would never be able to make any sense of what he was doing. He could see no present and no future; only the past and everything that had led to this moment in which he was trapped, fearing the loss of this love, the end of his marriage, and all sense of himself. He had no idea how he was ever going to get out of it.

CHAPTER NINE

Sometimes Krystyna worried that she was spending too much time with Jack. He had begun to look anxious when she spoke. She wondered once more if he was scared of her. She did not think she had ever frightened a man before.

He had taught her a new word.

Discombobulated. It had come out by mistake and she had stopped him as soon as she had heard it.

'I'm sorry. I'm a bit discombobulated.'

'What do you mean?'

'In a flap, uncertain, thrown off balance.'

'And why would that be?'

'I don't know. It happens every time you visit.'

'I'm sorry.'

'I don't mind. In fact I quite like it. I just need a bit of time to get used to it, that's all.'

Krystyna asked him to repeat the word so that she could learn how to pronounce it.

'Discombobulated.'

He had already taught her some of his favourite Scottish words: 'fankle', a mess or entanglement; 'stramash', an uproar or disturbance; 'croozumit', a person living alone. She liked the sound of his voice; the softness of his accent.

She made Jack go through the variants.

'I am discombobulated. You are discombobulating. This is a discombobulatory conversation.'

She had learned to tease Jack when he became too serious. It was good for him, she decided. Even though he was used to lecturing in front of hundreds of students, there were times when he appeared to be incapable of normal conversation.

'Don't you ever see your friends?' she asked.

'I like being at home. And I like you being with me. I don't need anyone else.'

'But we don't say very much.'

'We can still enjoy each other's company,' Jack said. 'I think they're called "sofa moments".'

'And what are they?'

'It's when we just sit and read the papers, or

153

listen to music. The idea is that we're so at ease with each other that we don't need to say anything.'

Krystyna stopped to think it through.

' "Sofa moments". Because they are plural does that mean you have to have more than one?'

Jack smiled.

'No, I think you can have one sofa moment at a time.'

'I think I prefer conversation.'

'I suppose it's what the Americans call "hanging out". The Scots word is "niffle-naffle". You just trifle away some time together.'

'I thought trifle was a kind of pudding.'

'It is. But most English words have more than one meaning.'

'It's so confusing.'

'It's not meant to be. It just shows how versatile language can be. "Trifle" can be a pudding, or a small insignificant object. We could look it up, if you like. I think the pudding probably came first . . .'

Krystyna laughed. She was still amused by Jack's enthusiasm for language. He could get so excited about so little.

He walked over to the bookshelf and pulled out a dictionary.

'Here we are. Golly, it's not what I thought . . .'

Krystyna had never heard anyone say the word 'golly' before.

'*A false or idle story told to deceive or amuse; a matter of little value; a literary work that is light or trivial in style; a small sum of money; a dish composed of cream boiled with various ingredients. Now, a dessert of sponge cake (especially flavoured with sherry or spirit)*—I see, the sponge comes in

154

later. Perhaps it started life as a kind of syllabub. The pudding seems to be seventeenth century; the nonsensical story is from the Middle English *traif*. Fascinating, don't you think? There's even a bit of Henry James. *I stayed. I dawdled. I trifled.*'

'Do you do this with every word when you are translating?' Krystyna asked.

'Yes. Well, a lot of the time. It's my job.'

'So that is why it takes so long?'

'I enjoy it, Krystyna.'

'I can see. You could be lost for hours.'

'By the way,' Jack continued, 'talking of puddings, it's my mother's birthday next weekend. I was hoping you might like to come. There's a dinner party.'

'I am sure I am not invited.'

'You are. They told me to ask you. My parents would love to see you again.'

'I will be shy.'

'You're not shy. And everyone loves you. Besides, you wouldn't have to talk to me all the time.'

'I like talking to you,' said Krystyna.

'Do you?'

'Of course. Why do you think I am here? You are the one who looks worried during our conversations: not me.'

'I am sure you understand why,' said Jack.

'No, I don't understand why.'

'I just worry.'

'And what are you worried about?'

He might as well say it, he thought.

'I'm worried about liking you too much.'

Krystyna laughed. It was the first time he had seen her do so.

'How can you like someone too much?'
'You know what I mean.'
She put her right hand to her mouth.
'You are so funny.'
'I don't mean to be.'
'That's what makes it funnier.'

*   *   *

Jack's mother thought back to the birthdays of her childhood. She remembered being taken into Edinburgh for her first party dress. It was black velvet with a white lace collar and she wore it with white socks and black ballet pumps. She could still recall the children from the village walking up the lane or arriving on farmers' carts carrying the presents for her party. Then there was the excitement of organised games: pin the tail on the donkey, blind man's buff, sardines, and singing games:

> *There was a farmer and a dog*
> *His name was Bobbie Bingo*
> *B-I-N-G-O, B-I-N-G-O,*
> *His name was Bobbie BINGO.*

After pass the parcel her father would come into the room with the cake and candles. The year before he died there had been eleven.

Now she was going to be eighty.

Angus, Tessa and their children were staying the night. Elizabeth had asked them to make a weekend of it. She saw so little of her grandchildren and she knew their presence would cheer up her husband. They could pretend that he

156

was not as ill as he was.

The family arrived with flowers, champagne and presents. Jack and Krystyna brought an antique music box.

'Lovely to see you, Krystyna. You look stunning.'

She was wearing a tailored white blouse and a mother-of-pearl scallop-shell necklace.

'I hope it is not too much.'

'Of course not. Did you choose the music box?'

'No, I did,' said Jack. Maggie had always picked the presents in the past.

'Such a pity Annie and Kirsty couldn't be here,' said Elizabeth.

'I'm sorry,' said Jack. 'They're both away.'

'I understand. I don't mind. And it's lovely to see Krystyna.'

'Our children are here,' said Angus. It irritated him that his mother missed the relations who were absent rather than appreciate those who had made the effort to come.

Gavin had taken the train up from London but surprised his grandmother by sporting a hairstyle that involved a shaved stripe across the right side of his head.

'What on earth have you done to your hair?'

'The razor slipped, Granny.'

'You're not expecting me to believe that, are you?' Elizabeth also noticed that he was wearing a *Proud to be Pakistani* T-shirt. 'And you're not from Pakistan, as far as I know . . .'

'My mother was born there,' said Tessa, defending her son's choice of outfit. It had been hard enough to persuade him to come without policing his dress code.

'Which makes me a quarter Pakistani,' said

157

Gavin. 'So I'll be safe, come the revolution.'

'What revolution?'

'When Britain becomes a Muslim state. Just think, Granny, a teetotal Britain . . .'

Elizabeth couldn't imagine the Taliban thriving in East Fortune. At least her nieces were well presented. No tattoos or piercings *yet*, as far as she could see.

She opened her presents: three bottles of bath oil, a cushioned dining tray, a friendship book, and a bottle of gin. The family began to look embarrassed.

'Sometimes I feel about a thousand years old. I'm giving Methuselah a run for his money, I can tell you.'

Gavin gave his grandmother *The Worst Case Scenario Handbook*. Now she would know how to escape from quicksand, perform a tracheotomy and fend off a shark.

'Sorry, I couldn't think what to get you.'

'At least it's better than hand cream and bath essence,' Elizabeth replied. 'That's all I seem to get these days.'

'Well, I'm sorry,' said Sarah, who had given her exactly that, 'but it is high quality.'

'I'm not complaining.'

Ian gave a low chuckle.

'Oh I rather think you are.'

There was a ring at the doorbell and a barking of dogs as Douglas and Emma arrived. They were late. It was obvious that they had argued in the car and that Douglas had been drinking.

'Happy birthday, Mother.' He had brought some flowers that had clearly come from a petrol station. Emma had wrapped up a cookery book.

158

Douglas gave Angus a hug and inspected him for his dress sense.

'You look like a schoolteacher who's been sacked for a bit of indiscretion.'

'We can't all afford Armani.'

'Sorry, I suppose that's a bit tactless.'

'I haven't been sacked.'

'Oh, sorry, I thought . . .'

'Not in front of Mother.'

They were eleven at the table: Ian and Elizabeth; Angus, Tessa and the three children; Jack and Krystyna; Douglas and Emma.

Douglas insisted that he sat in the middle between what he called his 'favourite nieces'.

'We're the only nieces here,' said Imogen.

'You don't like Jack's children?' Krystyna asked.

'I was joking, Krystyna.'

'Still. It is rude.'

Douglas was surprised to be taken to task.

'Well, I'm very sorry.'

'It's all right,' said Jack. 'It doesn't matter.'

Elizabeth tried to give Douglas something to do.

'Will you open the red wine?'

'I think Angus has already done it. He's just a bit slow on the delivery.'

'I suppose not everyone can keep up with the speed of your drinking,' said Emma.

'There's no need to draw attention to it.'

'I'm not. You're perfectly capable of doing that yourself.'

'Now, now,' said Ian. 'That's quite enough. It's Elizabeth's birthday. We are here to enjoy ourselves. And I'm going to start with this rather marvellous chicken.'

He began to carve. Jack tried to anticipate what

159

it would be like when his father was no longer with them; how the family dynamic would change.

'Did you get the chicken from the farm?' he asked his mother.

'I think it was about the most expensive organic bird I've ever seen.'

'None for me,' said Sarah.

Ian stayed his knife.

'Aren't you having any?'

'I'm a vegetarian.'

'Since when?' Angus asked his daughter. 'You don't even like vegetables!'

'I do.'

'I'm not sure you've ever eaten a vegetable in your life. It's been nothing but pizza and chips.'

'That was when I was fifteen.'

'It's all right,' said Tessa. 'Let her have the roast potatoes.'

'You could have warned us.'

'I thought you knew.'

'I did tell him,' said Tessa, 'but your father has had a lot on his mind.'

'Hitler was a vegetarian,' said Douglas.

Angus turned to his brother.

'What's that got to do with it?'

'I've always thought it explains a lot. That and the watercolour painting.'

He wondered how far he could push it. Didn't Saddam Hussein become a vegetarian in prison? And wasn't Pol Pot a vegan? Perhaps there was enough for a documentary: *The Vegetarianism of the Great Dictators*? He began to think that if he drank enough he might even enjoy himself. He could bait his brothers and even, perhaps, get back at Krystyna.

160

Sarah gave him a nudge as he cut into the meat. 'Murderer.'

'It's just a chicken.'

'Do you know how they are kept?'

'Perfectly well. So you don't need to tell me now. And are you wearing leather shoes?'

'Don't start . . .' said Jack.

Angus had chosen a light Burgundy, which, he said out loud, was crisp on the palate and long on the finish.

'You don't really mean that, do you?' asked Jack.

'It's refreshingly unpredictable,' said Douglas, 'the hint of bubblegum enhanced by the sharpness of barbed wire.'

'All right, *all right*,' said Angus. 'I don't know why we always have to argue.'

'We're not arguing,' said Jack.

'Yes, we are,' said Douglas.

He remembered a Christmas long ago, when his parents had still seemed young. The girls had given their grandparents bath salts.

Steep the bug in the bath, Ian had read from the packet.

'That'll be you, my darling. Now what do I do with the salts?'

His wife had left the table and refused to eat her pudding. Now the tension was just as palpable.

Douglas sneezed.

'*Na zdrowie!*' said Krystyna.

'I'm sorry?'

'It's what we say when someone sneezes.'

Douglas sneezed again.

'It also means "Have a drink soon"—like "Cheers".'

'Have a drink soon,' said Emma. 'That shouldn't be too much of a problem. You're not having any wine, Krystyna?'

'No, I don't drink.'

'Oh well,' said Emma, 'perhaps you could pass on a few tips. How you've done it, that sort of thing . . .'

'I do not think your husband will listen to me.'

'He doesn't listen to anyone.'

'That's enough,' said Douglas. 'I only sneezed, for Christ's sake.'

'And how is your film coming along, Douglas?' his father asked. 'Got a good researcher?'

'I'm doing most of it on my own.'

'Don't you normally have an attractive girl in tow?'

Emma poured herself some mineral water.

'They're getting a bit young for him these days, aren't they, darling?'

'I don't know about that . . .' Douglas looked at Krystyna. 'Age doesn't always matter, does it?'

'Anyway, it's not the researchers I'm worried about,' Emma said. 'It's all those other women.'

'What other women?' Ian asked.

'The ones he meets on his travels. He thinks I don't know about them but I do.'

Douglas let out a theatrical sigh. Why on earth was his wife starting on this? Was she deliberately trying to provoke him in front of his family?

'It's all very boring,' he said quickly. 'I spend most of my time waiting around. There are long periods when nothing much happens and then when it does it's all over very quickly. It's a bit like sumo wrestling: a lot of build-up and then, bang, it's over.'

162

'It's nothing like sumo at all,' said Emma.

'You must meet many famous people,' said Krystyna.

'They're not famous. I make documentaries.'

'Have you met Michael Palin?' she asked.

'No. Everyone asks me that.'

Emma tried to explain.

'Douglas prefers working with women.'

'No, I don't. I work with everyone. It doesn't make any difference what sex they are.'

Elizabeth tried to calm her son down.

'It's all right, darling. There's no need to be cross. We all love you.'

Krystyna caught her eye. She was not sure she loved Douglas at all.

Imogen tried to cheer up her uncle.

'Tell us one of your funny stories. What have you been doing?'

He could only think about Julia.

'Oh, you know, the usual. Poncing about.'

'Then tell us about your poncing about.'

Douglas could hardly tell them all *that*. Instead, he started on his list of anecdotes about television presenters behaving badly in restaurants:

Never mind the fucking cutlery. Bring me my Pinot Grigio.

His mother interrupted, 'Try not to swear so much, darling,' but Douglas went into full anecdote mode, telling stories of the celebrities he had met, their eccentricities and their demands:

I cannot sleep in this hotel. That's the problem with Rome. The Vespas go on all night.

I know. Those Gregorian monks never know when to stop.

I mean the scooters . . .

163

He told a story about Windsor Castle and seeing Charles and his new wife leaving.

'Camilla Parker Bowles is, of course, a sentence,' said Jack. He stood up to clear the plates but then stopped. 'I keep thinking of her in her whites on the village green.' He performed an underarm gesture. 'Camilla Parker bowls . . .'

Douglas looked at his brother. It was extraordinary to think that they were related.

'Your work sounds very glamorous,' Krystyna said to Douglas. 'You must travel all over the world.'

'I don't know. I'm sick of airports.'

'You should be so lucky,' said his father.

'I used to love to travel . . .' his mother began.

Soon, Douglas realised, she would be talking about Switzerland after the war and dancing through the night with people who 'knew how to behave'. Then it would be a short skip to *The Sound of Music* and everyone's plans for Christmas.

Douglas drifted off to think of Julia. He wondered what she might be doing and the type of family she had. Did they have intimate dinners at home, sit in front of the television, or go out to restaurants? He found it hard to imagine her as a wife and mother and impossible to think of her meeting his parents.

'You're not listening at all,' said Emma. She appeared to be expecting a response.

'Sorry?'

'I was just saying how you find going away a lot more interesting than staying in boring old Glasgow with me.'

'No, that's not true . . .' Douglas replied but he

was too late.

Ian was determined to keep the mood good.

'We all need to bring things back from the world into the home. Marriages can become very introverted, I find.'

Elizabeth cut in.

'Speak for yourself.'

'I'm not talking about *our* marriage, of course.'

'I should hope not.'

'Every marriage is different, isn't it, Douglas?' said Emma.

'It is. And that's what makes it so interesting.'

How much longer was he going to have to keep up this pretence, and how was he going to avoid giving himself away? He couldn't stop thinking about Julia at all.

He helped stack the dishwasher in the kitchen while Elizabeth made the coffee. He knew that people were already beginning to notice that he was tense as well as drunk.

His mother suggested that he should see a doctor.

'You know how I can always tell when something's the matter.'

'There's nothing wrong.'

'Do you have someone to talk to?'

'I don't need to talk to anyone.'

'Jack's always been a good listener.'

'My brother is the last person I'm likely to talk to. What's he still doing with that girl?'

'She's not a girl.'

'She's young enough to be his daughter.'

'No, she isn't. Would you like some coffee?'

'No. I think I'll just have brandy.'

'I presume Emma is driving.'

'You shouldn't be doing this, Mother.'

'I like doing it . . .'

Douglas knew he should apologise.

'I'm sorry about everything. Sometimes I just can't do it all. I don't think anyone realises the stress I'm under.'

'It's all right. You're home now.'

It was absurd how much he was giving away. In his drunkenness Douglas asked himself if it was because he wanted to be discovered. Then this whole charade would be over.

He had to stop. He could hardly bring Julia to East Fortune and introduce her to his family. It would be absurd.

This is Julia.

He couldn't imagine it at all.

*   *   *

'It's not good, is it?' said Tessa as she began to undress.

Angus was already in bed.

'I know. But at least we got through it. The children were great.'

'Honestly, though, your brothers.'

'What about them?'

'Where do you want me to start?'

'I don't know. It was the same old story with Douglas and Emma.'

'They seem to get worse every time they come. And I don't see why he always has to get so pissed.'

'It's become a bit of a routine.'

'You should say something.'

Angus cupped his hand under his beard as if he was checking that it was still there.

'I don't know. Every time I try he just flies off the handle.'

Tessa climbed into bed.

'You don't think he's having an affair, do you?'

'Why do you say that?'

'He just seems so grumpy all the time.'

'That doesn't mean he's having an affair.'

'No, but . . .'

Angus turned away, preparing for sleep.

'Jack's the one having the affair . . .'

Tessa gave her husband's shoulder a little shake.

'Actually, darling, that's just where you're wrong.'

'Of course he is. I don't know why my parents are so accommodating and I can't believe Jack has the nerve. Even the children are embarrassed.'

'I think they're more amused than embarrassed. But there's no hanky-panky. It's separate rooms, you know.'

Angus turned back.

'Are you sure?'

'That's what she told me.'

'How did you get that out of her?'

'People tell me things,' said Tessa. 'You know how frightened Jack is of women.'

'He's not frightened. He's just distant.'

'And he's terrified of sex.'

'No, he's not. Don't be ridiculous. And even if he is, how would you know?'

'Maggie told me.'

'God,' said Angus. 'Why can't people be more discreet? There is such a thing as too much information. I hope you didn't start telling her about *our* sex life.'

'Of course I didn't. Anyway, what would I have

167

to complain about?'

'Yes, I see your point.' Angus put his arm round his wife. 'She might think that you were showing off.'

'Careful. It's not that good.'

'Oh really?'

'Only teasing.'

Tessa began to stroke her husband's face.

'Let's not worry about anyone else.'

'I can't really believe it about Jack and Krystyna.'

'I hope you're not jealous,' said Tessa.

'Of course I'm not. What would I have to be jealous about?'

'Are you sure?'

'Honestly.' Angus turned away once more. 'You don't think I fancy her, do you?'

'Just checking,' said Tessa.

*   *   *

Krystyna was given the same room in which she had stayed on the night of the play. Elizabeth had told her that the three Henderson boys had all been born in the house.

She thought of the child growing inside her. It was fourteen weeks old. She had always been thin but surely it was obvious now? She tried to think who else might have suspected. Tessa? Emma?

She could not keep up the pretence for much longer. It was not fair on this family and it was not honest to Jack.

She felt the yield of the bed and tried not to think of the future. She wished that she could sink further; that she could leave everything behind.

168

She was frightened of everything.

Perhaps that was what it had been like for Sandy.

She dreamed of his dead body: how white he was, how the stubble still grew.

She tried to understand the fear he must have felt on his last day of life; fear of the night streets and of the future without her; fear of pain, or loss, and of being alone; fear of hope, fear of love, fear of trust, the very fear of being alive.

What would it mean to have his child?

CHAPTER TEN

Tessa was still not convinced that it was a good idea to start a new life abroad but had agreed, despite her reservations, to a holiday in Rome. Angus wanted to use the time to talk about the future without distraction.

They stayed in a boutique hotel near the Orange Garden. The small, feminine bedroom contained painted rococo furniture that looked as if it had come straight out of an interior-design magazine. Angus was amused by the fact that as soon as they put their suitcases on the bed the look was ruined.

'Perhaps we're not supposed to live in it at all. We're just expected to admire it.'

'I think it's charming.'

'It would be all right if you were a dwarf.'

He laughed as he tried to move round the bed. Tessa noticed that Angus was amused by most things these days; the fact that they were away and alone, that the future was so uncertain, and that they could do whatever they liked. He was like a student who had left university and decided to do something ridiculous rather than earn a living.

On the first evening they wandered through quiet squares and the deserted fish market, the shut blue stalls looking like old English police boxes, the pavements still waiting to be swept free of cigarette ends.

Tessa knew that no one would mistake her for a local even if she could translate the graffiti—*Lazio Merda. Napoli Colera*—but she didn't care. She wanted to feel she belonged.

She had decided to paint in the Orange Garden. She remembered the last time she had been in Rome. She had been so young. Now she worried about ageing and the fact that she had let herself go. What would it be like to be young like her daughters or Krystyna, to wear jeans and a white blouse with layered knitwear and silver necklaces? How would it be to go back to that time when men always turned to admire her and she could carry their looks, leaving them with nothing more than a waft of Camel Lights and the scent of Rive Gauche?

It had been in the late-1970s. Tessa had spent a year in Rome, learning Italian and taking an art history course. Within weeks she had met Edoardo and found herself on the back of his silver Vespa, riding round the Piazza del Popolo, buying *calzone* from hole-in-the-wall pizza ovens late at night, and making love in dangerously public places.

It was 1978, the year Aldo Moro was kidnapped and then assassinated. Fear ran through the city. Police were stationed on every corner but Edoardo told her to ignore them. Instead he took her to

170

parties where they met other students, musicians, and girls who seemed to have come straight out of *La Dolce Vita*. He loved the fact that Tessa didn't look Italian. He told her that when her hair fell across her back it was like ribbons in the snow. It reminded him of the end of a party, *finita la commedia*.

Edoardo was spoilt and he drank too much. At one of the parties he threw a can of petrol on the fire for a laugh. He had wanted to see how big the flames could be. He gave no warning.

Tessa was standing too close when the fire burst out. There had been no time to escape. First the curtains, then her dress and hair. People were screaming, ripping blankets off the bed, and turning on all the taps, filling the bath and buckets of water. There was no fire extinguisher. Tessa had fallen on to the marble floor. Crawling away from the fire, she put her hands over her face but could feel the flames in her hair. My eyes, she thought, I must protect my eyes. She could hear her friend Kate from London shouting, 'Oh my God, put her *out*,' and people running. Then she could feel blankets and water as she rolled across the floor to rid herself of the flames.

She was in hospital for two weeks, the left-hand side of her body burnt, her hair singed, her ear and her face bandaged. At least I can see, she thought. At least I am still alive. She did not know why Edoardo was not by her side, or if he had told her parents.

The nurses were all nuns. They moved slowly; halfway between this life and the next. Perhaps this is a dream, Tessa thought. Perhaps I am already dead.

171

She had been given a breathing tube and could not speak for three days. Her mouth was dry and she was frightened that she might choke. She tried to think of all the Italian words that she might need and the first things that she might say:

Ho sete. I am thirsty.

Ho troppo freddo. I am too cold.

Quando posso andarmene? When can I leave?

C'è qualcuno in quest'ospedale che non sia una suora? Is there anyone in this hospital who is not a nun?

She was taken to a hydrotherapy room where the side of her head was shaved and the wounds were cleansed. Tessa could not understand how Edoardo had been so stupid, or why he hadn't visited her. Perhaps he was with the police. Perhaps he had been arrested.

Tessa wanted to ask if she would ever get better, if the scarring would be permanent. The nurse told her not to worry. She would be beautiful again.

She wanted to reply that she was not so sure she had been beautiful in the first place but knew that such a conversation would take too much effort.

'When?' she asked.

'In a few months. With God's help.'

She was bathed twice a day. The burning was worst on her arm. It began to itch and she found it hard to move. She was given Percocet to relieve some of the pain and the nurse covered the wounds with antibiotic cream, gauze and bandages. In the ward she could hear people crying out, praying to the Virgin Mary, asking for mercy, unable to sleep. This is hell, she thought, this is like being in bloody Dante, in the second circle amidst all those whose lives love had rent asunder.

172

She knew that her arm would never be the same again. People would look at it and she would have to decide whether to tell her story or not. She could not imagine ever taking her clothes off in front of a man again.

At last Edoardo came to the hospital. He was carrying an enormous toy rabbit with a ridiculous smile.

'*Questo ti piacerá.*'

He placed it at the end of the bed so she could see it. The bunny was called Valentino. Tessa hated it as soon as she saw it.

Edoardo said he was sorry he had taken a few days to come and see her. He had felt terrible. He had been in shock.

He told her that he would buy her a new dress. One that wasn't so flammable.

Ah, Tessa thought, so it is all the fault of the dress now.

Edoardo said it had all been a terrible accident. He had no idea that it would happen. He wasn't even sure that it was petrol.

Tessa wondered when he was going to apologise, but he was already saying that hospitals made him nervous and that he hated seeing her like this.

She asked what he had been doing. He told her that he had been trying to behave as normally as possible in order not to think about what had happened. He had just been getting on with his life. Whatever tragedy befell a person life had to go on, he said.

The nurse asked him what was going to be done to help with Tessa's recuperation. People would need to look after her. She would not be able to cope on her own.

'I have a sister,' Edoardo said.

'Let me talk to you,' said the nurse. 'Privately.'

Tessa heard her arguing in the corridor outside. She had never heard a nun shout before.

A few days later Edoardo returned to say that his father had spoken to the landlady and paid off Tessa's rent. The family had a flat in Trastevere in which she could recover as their guest. Normally it was rented out to students but she could have it all to herself for three months and they would pay for everything. It was only right. Then it would be spring, and she would be better and she could be happy again.

Tessa recognised the deal. Three months' free accommodation for a lifetime of scarring.

'And my course?' Tessa had asked.

'They will send you books, if you like. And when you are better my sister will take you to the galleries.'

'Why not you?' she wanted to ask.

When she asked Edoardo to help with the dressing on her arm he told her that it was something his sister Maria would do. It wasn't something he felt able to manage himself.

'So you find it distasteful.'

At first he didn't understand what she meant. *Schifoso.*

'No, no,' he said in English. 'It's not that.'

'You know it is.'

'I am not a nurse. I would be frightened of making a mistake. Of infection.'

He was flustered, he spoke too quickly, but she was too tired to push it further.

'It's all right,' she said.

'Do you still love me?' he asked.

That's not the question, Tessa thought. It should be the other way round.

'If you love me you will forgive me,' he said.

His sister Maria came to the flat with simple food from her parents: yoghurt, bread and mortadella, the last of the autumn apples. One evening she made a soup, *tortellini in brodo*, but Tessa could not bear anything hot. She only wanted food that was cold and easy to swallow. The nights were frosty now but the fridge in the apartment was filled with ice cream and mineral water. For weeks it was all Tessa ate.

'Soon you will be well,' Maria said.

Edoardo brought her a selection of exotic birds to keep her company. They came in wicker baskets and elaborate wrought-iron cages that dated back to the eighteenth century. Each day he brought a different bird and lined the cages with copies of *La Stampa*.

'The man said I ordered so many he thought I was going to ask for a case of flamingos.' He thought this was funny: *una cassa di fenicotteri*.

She learned the names for all of them: ring-necked parakeets, umbrella cockatoos, cheery-headed conures.

The man from the pet shop came to see how she was managing. He told her about the subtle variations in colour, how they changed as the birds aged. He taught her what to feed them and how to weigh and wash them, controlling dust and dander. She had to monitor the doors and windows to prevent accidental escape when they were out of their cages.

At first Tessa found them beautiful; black-

175

cheeked, peach-faced Nyasa lovebirds. Her flat filled with peeps, chirps and squeaks and, because she couldn't bear to close the cages, the birds kept flying around the room. They gave her comfort: the illusion of freedom.

On Christmas Day she stood at the back of the Church of Santa Maria in Trastevere, watching Edoardo's family make confession, receive communion, and light candles that she was still too afraid to go near. Perhaps she should have recuperated at home but she had chosen to separate herself from her family. She thought of them all singing carols in the darkness of St Mary's Cathedral in Palmerston Place, followed by the turkey lunch in a Georgian town house that reaffirmed the worldly success of her father. He would be complaining about the bluntness of the carving knife already.

Tessa looked at the devotion of the old women crossing themselves in front of a life-sized icon, La Madonna della Clemenza, at the servers processing with their silver candlesticks and at children clutching their unwrapped presents: dolls and drums, twists of sweets, a new leather football.

I am not part of this, she thought. I am not part of anything at all. What would it mean to let go and have faith? Would I no longer be afraid?

It would have been so much easier to believe.

In the new year the winter set in. The flat had a gas heater which Tessa was too frightened to light and so she was permanently cold. If she put on extra layers of clothing they felt too heavy on the burns.

Maria made visits, as did old friends from her course, but Tessa did not feel that she was getting

176

any better. The pain continued and she slept badly. Every morning she made an effort, dressed herself, and sat in cafés on her own in order to keep warm. She brought out her books on Italian literature and art history but found that she could not concentrate on anything other than Agatha Christie and P.G. Wodehouse. Then in the afternoons she was so tired that she had to go back to bed for a siesta.

It meant that she was unable to sleep at night.

She thought back to the summer, hoping that she might be able to imagine herself warm. She dreamed of the old Roman restaurants with their heavy pieces of wild boar grilled over open flames. How well they had eaten and how much Chianti they had drunk! She could still see the door swinging open with people selling roses, watches, lottery tickets and cigarette lighters. She remembered the laughter, late nights, and a heat that would never recede.

But the cold continued and the birds stopped eating and talking. They slept on both feet during the day. They no longer preened their feathers, or opened their eyes fully, but sneezed and became colder and quieter as the winter progressed. They lost weight and had difficulty breathing. Some sat on the floor of their cages, too weak to sit on a perch.

'You are not looking after them properly,' Edoardo said. He worried more about the birds than he did about her.

Tessa stopped listening. He was going to have to do his National Service and he would be away before long.

The birds began to die, shuddering away from

the window, freezing to death in the corners of the room. There was nothing Tessa could do to stop it apart from light the fire that she was too scared to go near.

She needed to go somewhere warm, where it was as light as possible, where there was no need for fire or naked flames. She wanted to go to a place where birds were free and didn't drop down dead on to a cold terrazzo floor.

In the early spring people in the square outside were carrying bunches of mimosa for the Festa della Donna. The yellow of the flowers reminded her of the healing around the burns on her arms, of iodine and wounds about to be dressed. Maria took her to a park on the outside of the city in the Colli Albani. They followed paths flanked by old ilexes and maples, lindens and oaks. In the pools of light between the trees Tessa thought that she could see fallow deer. For the first time the temperature felt even, neither the cold of winter nor the fierce heat of summer.

They passed sequoias and magnolias, and then an aviary and a small zoo. By the pond were a dozen flamingos bowing and bending their necks, running back and forth as a group, and then suddenly taking flight to wheel around the edges of the lake.

Tessa stopped to look at the deep-pink plumage, their carmine-red bills with black tips, their orange eyes.

'They are the only animals that don't fight others for food,' Maria said. 'They flock together. Their only enemy is man. You know the Romans ate their tongues as a delicacy?'

Tessa watched the flamingos rise and fly over

the lake, their necks and feet stretching far from their dark-pink bodies, their wings black along the trailing edges.

It was as beautiful a night as any before the accident. Tessa had been in Trastevere for three months. She would leave before the embarrassment of asking if she could stay longer.

She would not say goodbye to Edoardo. In all probability she would never see him again. The next morning she would go to the train station and start the journey home without telling anyone other than Maria.

Once she had returned Tessa gave up any thought of reading art history and studied law instead. She shared a flat in Edinburgh with two other girls. There were no naked flames: no fires, no matches, no cigarette lighters and no candles; not even on birthday cakes.

At times she was afraid that she would never mend. Perhaps, she told her friends, we never fully recover from the defining moments in our lives. We only learn to accommodate them: the death of a parent or a lover, the break-up of a marriage.

But she found love quickly and more easily than she had ever thought possible; with Angus, who was passionate about rugby and loved her from the start. He had thick eyebrows, and slightly crooked teeth that seemed too small for his mouth, and he was so tall that when she spoke to him he had to lean down towards her.

'Show me,' he said.

He cupped his hand under her arm. It was one of the largest hands she had ever seen but he supported her so gently that Tessa thought she was going to cry.

179

'I'm sure we can live with this.'

'We?' she asked.

'If you'd like.'

'You're not put off?'

'Why would I be put off?'

He took her to meet his parents and they greeted her as the daughter they had never had.

'You have such beautiful hair,' Elizabeth announced.

Tessa felt at home in East Fortune. The Hendersons were relieved that their son had found someone to love; and the fact that their future daughter-in-law was training to be a lawyer meant that she hardly had to say anything to win Ian's approval.

'So there is a God,' he announced after her first visit.

Angus told Tessa that if she wanted someone to love her unconditionally then she did not have to worry. As soon as he had met her he had known. There was never going to be anyone else as far as he was concerned. If she said no to him then he would be single for the rest of his life.

'You say that now . . .'

'You don't understand,' said Angus. 'I know. I will only ever love you.'

She was almost put off by his certainty. But he had been true throughout their marriage. Even at the beginning Tessa recognised that she had found what her mother would have called 'a right man'. He wasn't going to be making love to her in the bathrooms of the Villa Borghese or in the car park of the Quirinale but he wasn't going to set fire to her either.

She went to watch Angus play rugby at

Myreside. He had once had a game for Scotland 'B', and Tessa was surprised how quick and authoritative he was, turning out for Watsonians in a maroon-and-white-hooped shirt and muddy white shorts, directing the three-quarter line, taking the kicks and shouting instructions during the scrums and line-outs. The other players kept calling him Hendo, and Tessa imagined it was a nickname he must have been given at school. If so, he had escaped lightly since other players were called Psycho, Fatboy and Captain Scum.

Angus had talked her through the first game in advance, telling her patiently about offside and what was expected of a stand-off, and one freezing Saturday she had even seen him score a try, cutting inside from just outside the twenty-five, shimmying past the opposition full-back and placing the ball right underneath the posts. He had been so pleased with himself that he had fluffed the conversion: instant hubris.

In the pub afterwards he told her that it was one of the best trics he had ever scored.

'And if you had to choose between scoring that try and meeting me, which would it be?' she asked.

'Meeting you, of course.'

'And you expect me to believe that?'

'Love me,' he said.

In the beginning it was friendship more than passion, but Tessa had faith in it lasting and, over the years, their relationship had grown into something she had never imagined. They had been wrong to assume that everyone else had what they had or enjoyed stronger, more passionate relationships. She only had to look at her friends, or at her brothers-in-law, to recognise that they had done more than survive. They had found a place of safety, a refuge beyond passion, and she was determined to let nothing threaten it.

Now, twenty-seven years later, Tessa raised her head to see her husband coming towards her. The look was instinctive, a moment of minor telepathy, as she sensed his arrival. He had bought a new panama hat that shaded his face but she could see that he was smiling.

People were leaving the Orange Garden now; their early-evening walks were at an end. Church bells rang out across the city, summoning the faithful to the last Mass of the day. Tessa thought of his words all those years before.

Love me.

Angus sat down on the bench beside her.

'What have you been thinking?' he asked.

'So many things . . .'

He looked at her watercolour and then out at the view of St Peter's.

'I'm sorry I haven't been more for you. You know, that I haven't done better.'

'I don't think that at all . . .'

'It's been a pretty ordinary life.'

'That's what most people want,' said Tessa.

'Do they?'

'And now we're going to do something different.'

'If you're happy . . .'

'I was frightened of coming here . . .' Tessa began.

'I know that.'

'But it was so long ago and now I'm here it all seems to belong to someone else's life rather than mine. I can let go of it all now . . .'

182

'And you're happy to leave home?' he asked.

'I never quite know what people mean by home. Of course I know really; it's a building, a place, a marriage, a family; but sometimes it's both more and less than that. You're my home.'

She looked at Angus and knew that they would grow old together. She thought of her marriage: such an odd word, 'husband'. Such a far-off country, the past.

CHAPTER ELEVEN

The next time Douglas saw Julia they had no privacy. It was at the opening of an exhibition in London and it was the earliest time Douglas could see her without having to make a complicated arrangement or find another excuse. He organised a few spurious meetings and flew down from Glasgow.

The exhibition was so crowded that it took a long time to find her. Julia looked up, saw him, and separated herself from the people she was speaking to.

Douglas leaned forward to kiss her on the cheek, as if they were acquaintances.

Julia held on to his arm.

'We can't be seen talking to each other. The slightest thing could give us away.'

'I've hardly touched you.'

'Don't even joke about it. My husband is here. He'll guess.'

'You never told me he was coming.'

'How could I? Is your wife with you?'

'No. We live in Glasgow.'

'Well, we live in London.'

Douglas did not want to see her with her husband. He could not stand the thought of pretending that he didn't know her.

'I have something for you,' she said, reaching into her bag. 'It's a letter. It explains everything; or as much as I can. Read it when you are alone. Then destroy it.'

It was a tightly folded piece of orange paper with *Bundestagswahl . . . und was das Grundgesetz dazu sagt* written on it, a flyer for an open-air dance event in a small German town. The dance steps were drawn in diagrammatic form.

'It looks very odd.'

'I had to wait for a flight back,' Julia said. 'Don't let anyone see it. It says too much already.'

Douglas could see other guests coming towards them: Steven, the owner of an art gallery, a dandyish painter in a lemon-yellow suit, a woman whose name he could not remember.

'I didn't know you two knew each other,' Steven said.

'We don't,' Julia replied.

'I'd have thought you'd get on rather well . . .'

'Another time, perhaps,' said Douglas, obeying Julia's instructions. 'I have to be going.'

'Of course.' Julia smiled. 'Another time.'

Douglas found the nearest pub. He ordered a pint of Guinness and looked for a place where he could read her note. He found a light by the slot machine.

He had not seen Julia's handwriting before. It was rounded and scarcely joined; almost printed. He wondered how long it had taken her to write it (had there been a previous draft?) and what a graphologist might make of it:

Dear Douglas,

Don't ask me what's on the other side of this paper. I think it's dance steps meets nuclear physics. I am killing time before the flight, soaking up the um-pa-pa atmosphere. The brass band has left the stage and now I am confronted with an aerobics performance. Yesterday I went to a small medieval village near by. We took a boat upriver, past the vineyards and a charming industrial area complete with its very own nuclear power plant. But I know you don't want to hear all this. You want to talk about us. What a difficult thing to do. Every day I think about us. I know it is impossible and can only lead to disaster. We must stop. I think the longer it goes on the harder it will be. I can feel myself slipping and before I know it I will not be able to break away. This is why I keep my distance. I have made a life with John. Now the aerobics team has left the stage and been replaced by a chorus singing 'Zip-A-Dee-Doo-Dah' in German. What a weird country. Nothing matters to me more than my children. You know there really isn't such a thing as a free lunch. So when can I see you again? Hopefully I can deliver this letter to you in person Thursday night.

Love,
Lonely, obsessed, confused, intoxicated, sensual, paranoid
Julia

185

Douglas read the letter again. It was a form of thinking aloud. He thought of writing a reply. But he realised he still didn't want to *say* anything. If anything he wanted to silence Julia, be with her physically, their mouths together and bound so fast that no speech was necessary. He wanted to call her, be with her, never leave her again. He didn't want a letter. A letter wasn't enough.

He said little on his return from London.

Emma was in rehearsals for a musical play and was tense because only half the songs had been written.

'Honestly,' she said, 'this happens *every time*. And there's a whole song about consumer goods that's supposed to represent the decadence of Western culture but it's impossible to learn. You know, every soap, every breakfast cereal, every bread and every biscuit. They want to do it as a kind of rap but none of us can get our heads round it—are you listening?'

'Of course I'm listening.'

'Then what did I say?'

'Something about breakfast.'

'And?'

'In your show.'

'You will come, won't you?'

'Of course I'll come.'

Douglas couldn't understand how he was getting away with it; why his wife didn't suspect anything.

'God, they're impossible. The men who run that place . . .'

'I like them.'

'I like them too. That's why I am there. But they can be so infuriating.'

186

'They mean well.'

'What do you know, Douglas? You're hardly ever there.'

'Have I ever missed a show that you've been in?'

'No.'

'There you go then.'

'There's no need to be smug about it.'

'I'm not being smug.'

'Oh, for God's sake.'

'Don't be angry.'

'I'm not angry.'

'I'll leave you then,' said Douglas. He thought what it might mean to use the phrase for real. He couldn't imagine it. A different life. What was he doing?

'Don't leave, you're supposed to comfort me.'

'Sorry.' He opened his arms and gave his wife a hug. He did not know how much longer he could keep up the pretence.

'I just need you to look after me.'

Ten days later he was sitting in an aisle seat at the back of the theatre watching the first performance of his wife's play. Although the show wasn't as slick as it could have been Emma had a presence, vivacity and a drive that forced people to look at her. Douglas was both proud and afraid. He didn't know how he could ever tell her, or explain himself, or keep what he had done from her.

'Wasn't Emma great?' the director asked afterwards.

'You got there in the end.'

'We couldn't have done it without her.'

Emma came out to the bar with the other actors and kissed her husband.

'Was I OK?'

'You were great. You always are.'

'You're just saying that.'

'No, really you were.'

Nothing made any sense any more. Here Douglas was, surrounded by writers and actors, people he knew and liked, good, generous people who occasionally ranted about their lack of money and recognition but who had always been welcoming and accepting.

What was wrong with him? This was a perfectly decent world. He had been lucky with his work, his marriage and his friends. He had nothing to complain about.

But he kept thinking of Julia.

He remembered going to a production of *Les Liaisons Dangereuses* in London. Madame de Tourvel: *I was innocent, at peace with the world: it was meeting you that destroyed me.* And there was Lancelot and Guinevere, even though what he was doing with Julia was never as noble. *Thorow thys same man and me hath all thys warre be wrought, and the dethe of the most noblest knyghtes of the worlde; for thorow oure love that we have loved togydir ys my most noble lord slayne . . .*

There was no way out or back. He could see that now. There was nothing he could do to right his life.

CHAPTER TWELVE

After four days of rain Krystyna had begun to feel restless.

'This is mad,' she said. 'It's August. And it's still cold.'

Jack had persuaded her to come and stay for a week.

'We can light the fire.'

'You do know how crazy this is?'

'It's global warming,' said Jack.

'No, it isn't,' Krystyna replied. 'It's Scotland.'

There was a log-and-coal store at the back of the house. As Krystyna collected supplies she remembered what it had been like at home in the past with so little food in the shops and the family gathering as much as they could from the land. Had she left her country only to repeat what had happened? What would it have been like if she had stayed there; never come to Scotland, never been with Sandy, and never met Jack?

She carried the logs in from the store and started to lay the fire. She could not see how their relationship, if that was what it was, could have a future with a child. Every time she walked through Jack's house she tried to picture what it might be like. There would have to be a buggy by the door, toys in the front room, stair gates and changing mats. They would get in Jack's way. He would be irritated and distracted. It didn't seem possible.

Jack could tell that Krystyna was restless. He had tried to ignore it, hoping that her mood would pass with a new day, a walk, or a change in the weather. But the tension persisted.

'What is it?' he asked.

'You know I must go tomorrow?'

He tried not to sound relieved.

'Yes, but you can always return. You can come back whenever you want.'

189

'I know that.'

'Then is it something else?'

'It is nothing.'

'Then let's eat.'

They were having a simple supper: omelettes, salad, bread and cheese. On some evenings they listened to music, or even read to each other, but Krystyna didn't want to do any of these things.

'I worry I'm not good for you,' she said. 'I am too distracting.'

'No, you're wrong. You give me great comfort.'

'You think so?'

'I know so. It was odd at first but now I think we're used to it. Don't you? It's almost a routine.'

'Yes. I see that. I am sorry.'

'Why are you sorry?'

'I'm sorry because I have to go.'

Krystyna could talk about Sandy, she could tell Jack about her past and even what she wanted to do with her life, but she could not speak about the only thing that mattered.

'I am not sure it's good for me to be here,' she said.

'Perhaps we should not think about it too much. Introspection can be dangerous,' said Jack. 'I know. I do it all the time.' He was trying to cheer her up but could see that it was not working. 'What is it?' he asked again.

'It's nothing. I don't know. I am sorry. I do not mean to be like this. Perhaps it's the end of summer. It is not you, I promise. Tomorrow I will leave and then you can work without interruption.'

'You'll go back to Edinburgh?'

'At first. And then perhaps somewhere else.'

'Where?'

'I don't know.'

'Back home?'

'I have no home. But it does not matter. I will make a home. I am used to it.'

'There's always here . . .'

'I know. You are very kind.'

Jack realised that there was nothing he could do. He took the dishes to the sink.

'You do know that I remember everything about you,' he said.

Krystyna did not answer. Sandy had once said the same thing. The memory was as involuntary as a dream. If only he could retain the hours they had together, he had told her, then they could become an eternal moment, a virtual piece of time that would run in parallel with real life, so that whenever they were troubled or apart they could return to those flashes of happiness and live within them until the separation or the trouble passed.

She didn't want to have to think or explain anything any more. She came over and put her hand on Jack's shoulder.

'I'm going to read in bed,' she said. 'Don't work too late.'

'What else am I going to do?' he asked.

*   *   *

The next morning Annie let herself in with her own key.

'Hello?' she called. 'Are you there? Dad?'

Jack came downstairs in his dressing gown and found his daughter looking at his work.

Be on guard,

191

As I have taught you, don't be taken in.
It's easier to avoid the snares of love
Than to escape once you are in that net
Whose cords and knots are strong . . .

'Not like you to lie in bed,' she said.

'I didn't know you were coming.'

'Well, I thought I'd just look in.'

Jack had kept Annie's bedroom as it was before she left for university. All the remnants of her adolescence remained: star cushions, belts and school photographs; a Wallace and Gromit alarm clock, an article ripped out of a magazine: *I Don't Need a Man to Be Happy*.

'How have you been?' he asked.

Annie leaned against the sideboard and began to describe the corporate hotel she had just assessed in Italy: Americans ordering egg-white omelettes, worrying their muscles had shrunk from a lack of working-out.

Jack was surprised by her confidence. For a moment he couldn't remember how she had ever come to be his daughter.

'Were they all very rich?'

'Put it this way, Dad, not many of them were wearing *Make poverty history* bracelets.'

'They probably want to keep 'em poor.'

Annie told her father about the hotel's state-of-the-art spa and handed him its posh brochure with the Latin tag, *Salus per aquam*. The cosmos in a water drop.

'That's not a proper translation, of course.'

'I thought you'd say that . . .'

Looking through the expensively produced pages, Jack sat down and read about balneotherapy, and algae reducing-compresses, of passive exercise machines and thalassotherapy for mental and physical fatigue.

'What's wrong with a swim?' he asked.

Annie began to laugh but stopped when Krystyna walked into the kitchen. She was barefoot. She picked up the kettle to fill it with water.

Then she looked up.

'Sorry.'

Jack stood.

'No, it's all right.'

'I'll go upstairs. I didn't know you had company.'

Jack had neglected to tell his children that Krystyna was staying.

'This is my daughter, Annie.'

Krystyna turned back upstairs.

'I'm sorry, I don't want to interrupt.'

Jack said, 'No, stay.'

'I must go.'

Annie waited until the sound of her footsteps had faded.

'Jesus, Dad . . .'

'It's not what you think . . .'

'It is what I think. How long has she been staying?'

Jack began to defend himself.

'Only a few days.'

'And what is she doing here?'

'She needed help.'

'You're the one that needs the help, Dad. It was bad enough you listening to my music. Now you're dating people my age.'

Jack hoped Annie was not going to lose her temper. When she was two years old she would

193

deliberately stop breathing, her face scrunched up against the world. People would tell her to stop but she couldn't, and there would inevitably follow the fall to the ground and the rush to the hospital.

He looked at his daughter.

'She's not your age and we're not "dating".'

'Can't be for want of trying. How long has she been here?'

'Krystyna needs company.'

'And you think you're the person to give it?'

Jack reached up for the pot in the cupboard. He assumed that his daughter wanted the coffee he was making.

Krystyna appeared, dressed and in the doorway.

'I must go,' she said.

'No. Stay. We haven't talked.'

'We have. Now I must go.'

'Don't.'

'Oh,' said Annie. 'I'm sorry. Am I in the way?'

'Yes.'

'Jesus, Dad. Are you telling me to leave my own house?'

It occurred to Jack that Krystyna was far easier to live with than his daughter; and that if people had a choice of who to share their home with then they wouldn't necessarily choose their own children.

'It's not a good time, Annie.'

'I can see that. Perhaps you'd like to tell me when it *is* a good time; when you can fit me in.'

'Don't be angry with me.'

'You don't give me much choice.'

She turned away and slammed the door of the kitchen, the front door of the house, and the door of her car.

194

Jack walked to the porch to check that his daughter had left. He wished he had been able to avoid such a confrontation, but it was too late now.

He remembered the way Annie held his hand as a little girl, crossing the road on the way to a party, red ribbons in her long black hair.

He could still see her as a small child, holding on to the end of a brass bed, jumping up and down and laughing. He remembered how she used to time everything with her first watch; how long it took to eat a boiled egg, to clear away the plate, to climb the stairs, to clean her teeth, to organise her model farm and say goodnight to all the animals. How quickly her childhood had disappeared.

He walked back into the kitchen. Krystyna had packed her shoulder bag.

'You know that now I must go too,' she said.

'I wish you wouldn't.'

'I can't stay for ever,' Krystyna said. 'It is not right.'

'I'm sorry.'

'About your daughter? Don't worry.'

'No, it's not that. I was just trying . . . I don't know . . . I wish you wouldn't go.'

'Please don't make it so hard.'

'I just wanted to help you,' Jack was saying.

'You did. You have done.'

'You sound as if it has finished. Whatever "it" is.'

Krystyna looked down at her bare feet, inspecting her right sole.

'I'm sorry. You must think I am ungrateful.'

'Stay a bit longer.'

'I can't.'

'Why not?'

Krystyna lit a cigarette. Jack wondered why, when she said that she was going, she was prolonging her departure. Was this to give him time for one last appeal? He wished she wouldn't smoke in the house. *Smoking can cause a slow and painful death.* They could hardly make it more obvious.

He tried to think how he could explain the difference she had made to his life. He looked down, trying to think what else he could say, and noticed his work.

Surely delight comes in a purer form
To sensible men than to your love-struck
  wretches
Who, on the very verge of consummation,
Can't make their minds up, thrash about,
  uncertain
Which they should pleasure first?

'You don't have to decide everything now,' he said.

'I don't think I'm well enough to make decisions. I can't think any more.'

'Then stay.'

Krystyna looked down at the translation in front of him. She could see that Jack had crossed out the word 'delight'.

'I am stopping you working.'

'It's all right.'

She finished her cigarette.

'I'm sorry. It's my fault. Perhaps you wish you had not invited me.'

'No,' Jack said. 'I don't think that at all.'

She put on her shoes and her linen jacket and

196

lifted her bag on to her shoulder.

After so much rain the bright light of a still summer day was unfamiliar and oppressive. Scarps of white cloud were stationary in the sky.

Jack offered to walk Krystyna to the bus stop but she told him it would only make it worse.

'You know I could not stay for ever.'

'You could.'

'Don't be crazy.'

'Are you sure this is what you want to do?' Jack asked.

'I am not sure.' Krystyna put on her sunglasses. 'But if I do not go now perhaps I never will.'

'Isn't that a good thing?'

'I don't think so. But I am sorry. I will miss you. Thank you for everything.'

Jack walked over and held her. His left arm was round her waist, his right arm covered her shoulders. He tried not to hold her too tightly. He listened to the rain die away in the distance. The church bell struck the half-hour.

He felt her hand against his hair and decided to wait until she broke the moment. They stood without moving. At last Krystyna stepped back. She did not meet his eye and pushed a strand of hair away from her face.

When she was further away she looked at him once more.

'Thank you,' she said. 'It's best if I go. Please don't make it difficult. I'm sorry.'

Jack stood by the front door and watched her leave.

'Goodbye then.'

It was as if she was going for a walk, up into the hills or out into the woods. Jack realised that his life now consisted of people walking away from him rather than towards him.

He thought of the times when it had all been so different; of his daughters, running out of school or across the beach, pleased, even delighted, to see him.

He remembered Maggie smiling at him with her head tilted to one side and the light in her hair. At the time he had not been able to believe his luck in finding her. *My wife.*

Then there was his mother turning from the bottom of the garden, putting down her weeding basket and taking off her gardening gloves, signalling that his very presence meant that she could stop and that all was right with the world.

There was even his father, coming out of the study and into the hall, still uncertain whether to kiss him or shake his hand or give him that half-embarrassed hug on which they had finally settled.

He could hear their voices: *Daddy . . . Darling . . . Good to see you, Jack . . . Son . . .*

Now they were all going away.

They flee from me that sometime did me seek.

Jack tipped the cigarettes out of Krystyna's coffee cup. Was this what it had been like when Maggie had left, a feeling of inevitability, that there was nothing he could do?

He walked through the rooms until Krystyna's presence faded. He wondered why he could not hold on to people and when he would have to tell his parents.

Later, at night, he listened to the wind gusting over the roof slates, against the windows and inside the chimney, seeking out the frailties of the house. Rain spattered into the gutters in sudden flurries,

198

like the sound of fledglings slipping, pecking at the tiles, attempting to fly and falling back. A summer storm. He had no idea where Krystyna was. He hoped that she was safe.

The glass shuddered in the windows. Jack worried about the trees in the garden; branches snapping, trunks unearthed. The storm was growing in momentum: bright lightning, distant thunder, a sudden artillery of hail.

He thought of his daughters, Annie and Kirsty, and how full the house had seemed when they were with him. He remembered Kirsty as a child holding up her right hand. She had drawn a spider inside in black felt-tip pen. She clenched her fist. She had written *THIS* on her fingers.

'This—is—a—spider,' she spelled out, opening and closing her fingers.

'This spider is'—and she clapped her hands together—'*squished.*'

Annie called to apologise. It had been a shock, she was saying. No one had warned her. She knew she had overreacted but if her father had only told her the full story then she would have been more sympathetic.

'It's a complicated story to tell.'

'I had to get it out of Grandma. I started ranting about it and she stopped me and explained everything. No one tells me anything in this family. But I suppose I shouldn't be surprised. Jesus, Dad, you lot know how to complicate your lives . . .'

'It is complicated. I can't explain it. I was only trying to be kind; to do what was right. That was all that I was trying to do.'

'She must be in such a state.'

'She is. But perhaps it doesn't really matter any

199

more.'

'Why? Has she gone?'

'Don't sound so relieved.'

'Where is she?'

'I don't know.' Did he have to go into all of this now?

'Did you end it or did she?'

'It's not an ending. At least, I don't know if it's an ending or not. I don't really want to discuss it.'

'That means she did.'

'It wasn't like that.'

'What was it like then?'

'I'm not sure you're the best person to talk to about it, Annie.'

'Well, don't see her again, that's all the advice I'm going to give you. Make a clean break and be grateful you've escaped so lightly.'

Jack put down the phone and tried to think what to do next. He knew he would not be able to work.

He remembered how he used to bounce Annie up and down on his lap in the garden when she was a baby. She smiled and laughed in her pink dungarees. She was clutching a little wooden rattle, the one with the bell inside.

Then it fell to the ground.

Her face changed, and Jack stopped the bouncing. Annie looked down on to the grass but could not see the rattle at all.

'Gone!' she said.

It was the first word she had uttered aloud. She had seen something disappear and could not understand how it had happened; suddenly and unexpectedly. It was her first experience of loss.

'Gone!'

Jack stood in the kitchen and listened to the

sounds of night. He thought how hard it was to love people in the way they wanted to be loved.

CHAPTER THIRTEEN

Angus was determined to sustain his momentum. He discovered a smallholding on the Internet, a two-hundred-year-old hilltop farmhouse between Asti and Alba in Piedmont. The place was falling apart but it had three acres of land.

He handed Tessa his laptop.

'A lot of work,' she said as she clicked through the images.

'We have time.'

'Are you going to do it all then?'

'What else am I going to do?'

'We don't know anyone there.'

'We don't have to live there all year. And people can come and stay.'

He showed her the outhouses, the hayloft, the slope for the vines. There was even a flattened area where they could have a swimming pool.

'You're sure we're not too old for all this?'

'I'm sure we're too young to do nothing.'

Angus printed out the pages and took them to his parents. It was Tuscany without the tourists, he said. He showed them pictures of the property from a distance, pointing out the seclusion and the proximity to the Alps. He talked about the local farmer who tended the vines, showed them the plot with its south-facing courtyard, and drew their attention to the kitchen with its own pizza oven and the outhouses where they could stay.

201

'You mean we're not invited into the house itself?' Elizabeth asked.

'No, I don't mean that. Of course you can come into the house. But this would give you privacy.'

'How much time are you going to spend there?'

'As much as we can.'

'What about your work?'

'I won't be working for ever.'

'Well, I think it's wonderful,' said Ian. 'I only wish I was well enough to muck in. Have you actually bought it?'

'Not yet. I wanted to talk to you about it first.'

'And can you afford it?'

Angus had not told them about the redundancy.

'The firm has given me some money. We're all right.'

'And why have they done that?' Elizabeth asked.

'It's a kind of bonus. You know; in time for Christmas.'

'I don't remember them being so generous in the past.'

Angus shied away from the truth.

'Well, Mother, times change. We've been very busy.'

After lunch Ian asked his son if he wanted to go for a walk. They wouldn't go far. It would just be a breath of air with the dogs.

It was early September. Ian put on his coat, his scarf and his peaked hat. In the afternoon sunlight Angus noticed that the flesh around his father's cheeks had sagged. His eyes were pink-rimmed. He walked with a stick.

Angus worried that his father was going to try to dissuade him from Italy.

'So. This is news,' he said.

'I hope you approve, Father.'

'I wanted to say that I could help out with some inheritance money if you need it: if I don't die in time.'

'There's no need to joke about it.'

'I'm not joking. There is an inevitability to all this. We are all cut flowers.'

'How have you been feeling?'

'Not too bad. People keep phoning me up and asking how I am. I have to stop myself from telling them I'm still dying.'

'I suppose they prefer a bit of optimism . . .'

'How is Tessa about the move? Are you sure she's all right? Will she give up her job as well?'

'Not at first. She'll take a leave of absence. It's a bit like maternity leave. They're being a lot more accommodating than my firm.'

'I take it the decision to leave wasn't entirely yours.'

'No, not entirely.'

'Don't worry. I won't tell your mother.'

'I'm sure she will have guessed.'

'She likes to think the best of you all. Your brothers have provided her with enough to worry about. I don't think we need to tell her a little thing like this.'

'Is that why you asked me for a walk?'

'That, the money, and the pleasure of your company . . .'

The sky was beginning to darken and Angus could smell the first woodsmoke of autumn. It made him think of childhood: the return to school and the first few games of rugby when the ground was still soft. The low sun behind the goalposts would sometimes shine right into his eyes making the kicks far harder.

They walked down the lane to the stream by the kirk. His father knew the curve of every path and the slope of each hill. In the distance they could hear the sound of a shooting party; beaters and flankers with whistles in the woods; a flurry of pheasant; shouts of 'Mine' before the firing.

Ian was almost amused by his son.

'I rather like this new side of you.'

'What new side?'

'The unrealistic part of your character. It suits you.'

'It's good of you to say that.'

'I only wish I'd had your courage. Your mother's lived in the same house all her life.'

'It doesn't appear to have done her any harm.'

'It might have been nice to try a few alternatives. You will look after her, won't you?'

'Of course.'

They had walked for less than a mile and Ian was already out of breath.

'I don't like to think of her on her own.'

'She won't be on her own.'

'Friends disappear rather fast, I've noticed. It's all right for the first year and then the invitations stop. You will make sure she survives?'

'Of course I'll make sure.'

'Your brothers seem rather distracted so it'll be up to you, I'm afraid.'

'She can come and live with us, if she likes.'

'I don't think that will be necessary. I can't see her leaving here. But it would be good to make the offer. I'd like her to have everything she needs.'

'Of course.'

Ian was more agitated than Angus had ever

seen.

'I've never quite told her what a good wife she's been.'

'I'm sure you have.'

'No, I'm not so sure . . .'

'And there's still time.'

'Sometimes I wish I'd loved her more.'

Angus had never thought that his father could talk like this.

'You did love her.'

'I know. But did I love her enough? That's what worries me.'

They stopped to see where the dogs had gone. They were running towards a field of sheep.

Ian whistled and then shouted out, 'Cadbury, Hoover, come on.' The drugs had made his voice higher and frailer.

They rounded the corner of the lane. Elizabeth had already turned on the outside light and drawn the curtains. Angus was sure she would have lit the fire.

Ian stopped and leant on his stick.

'It's a handsome house, isn't it? You'll stay to tea?'

Elizabeth had laid out a tray and made a Victoria sponge.

'After all that lunch?' Angus asked.

'I want to make sure you miss me,' his mother said.

'I'm not going anywhere yet.'

'But I can't be too careful, can I?'

'Nothing's certain.'

Before he left Angus asked his father if he could have a look in the library. He knew his father's appetite for history and travel. There had to be some books about Italy in there somewhere.

'Take whatever you like,' said Ian. 'I'm hardly going to be reading any of them again.'

'Now, now . . .'

'I don't mean to be bleak.'

'You are being bleak,' said Elizabeth.

She had been brought up to believe that illness was a sign of weakness, a failure even of character. Her mother had once boasted of how there had been no cancer in the family but that was before Ian's diagnosis; before the realisation that the Henderson family were no more immortal than their peers.

'I'm not afraid of what's going to happen, you know,' her husband was saying. 'The great adventure . . .'

Angus walked into the library. The wall by the desk was filled with legal textbooks and court reports. Boxes of old papers stacked above the top shelves. All of this would have to be cleared, he thought. All this work and all this life.

He found Berenson's *Northern Painters of the Italian Renaissance*, a biography of Garibaldi, and a guide to the Italian lakes. He wondered how long it would take him to acquire a similar library, and if the house in Italy would accommodate such a thing.

When he returned he found his father alone in the sitting room. He had taken off his jacket and had his arms folded against his stomach. He was rocking himself back and forth, shuddering as he did so, trying to hold back the pain.

He saw Angus watching him.

'I'm all right.'

'No, you're not.'

'It doesn't matter.'

'Have you been taking your pills?' Angus asked.

'I don't want to sleep all the time. I don't want to lose control. I want to beat this bloody thing.'

'Father . . .'

'I suppose it's good for you to see pain.'

'I don't know what I can do.'

'Leave me. It will pass . . .'

Angus went to find his mother.

'How long has he been like this?'

'It happens every night,' said Elizabeth. 'I don't think I can stand it any more.'

Angus opened his arms and his mother started to cry. It had come to this, he thought. He tried to avoid thinking of how much worse it could get or how he was ever going to be able to leave.

A few days later he phoned the local surgery to talk about palliative care.

'You must be well,' Dr Hunter said. 'I haven't seen you for years. Firm keeping you busy?'

'I'm managing to survive.'

'I'm sorry about your father. How is he?'

'The pain's worse.'

'I'll pop in and see him. Your mother is determined to keep him at home.'

'You mean he should be in hospital?'

'Or a hospice. Then we could monitor him more consistently. But he's more cheerful at home, and it lets your mother feel that it's not as serious as it is . . .'

'And it is serious . . .'

'I'm afraid you reach a stage when there's not much more you can do.'

'And we've reached that stage?'

Dr Hunter was not going to commit to any kind

of resignation.

'Hope is always important . . .'

'I see.'

Angus remembered him jogging through the country lanes with his wife. Thirty years ago they had been so full of vitality. Now he was treating the children of the patients he had seen as babies.

'Try to keep him comfortable, and I'll see what I can do about the pain,' Dr Hunter said. 'There may be more time than we think. There's no point giving up just yet.'

Angus remembered his father singing Harry Lauder songs on long car journeys.

Keep right on to the end of the road.

CHAPTER FOURTEEN

Douglas wished he could find a way of seeing Julia more regularly. He tried to find an excuse to meet her in London and sent her coded text messages that received guarded replies. She did not want him to come. London was impossible. The risk of being seen together was too great. They would have to wait until she was going to some other European city.

He knew that he should forget all about her; that if he left it for long enough the memory would fade and he could return to whatever normality he had left. But in the gaps between work and home, in the moments when he did not have to concentrate, every empty thought filled with her. He stopped when he saw people in the street who looked like her or who wore similar clothes. He read the books she had mentioned and looked up the exhibitions she had organised on the Internet. He found her perfume in a department store, opened the bottle and drank in the smell of her: Joséphine by François Rancé.

He thought he was going mad. His only consolation was to drink enough red wine to sleep his way through the anxiety.

Even then he dreamed of Julia. They were together in foreign cities and hotel rooms, walking through streets, sitting in outdoor cafés, waking in soft beds with nothing else to do but be with each other. He could see her leaving at airports and then coming forward to greet him. He tried to recall every part of her body, the softness of her upper thigh, the magnified pores of her skin, the fall of her hair as she slept.

One morning, as he tried to sleep off his hangover, he was half woken by Emma moving in and out of the room. He was used to the sound of her getting up before him, holding her tights to the light to see if they were navy or black, dressing quietly so as not to disturb him but then coming back into the room ten minutes later and changing into something different because the first outfit she had chosen was 'hopeless'.

On most days she dressed quietly and let him sleep but now she was emptying the laundry basket. It had become something of a Saturday-morning routine. She created separate piles on the floor, dividing whites from colours, putting other clothes aside for dry-cleaning. Douglas remembered that they were due at a party in Edinburgh that night and so she was probably thinking about what she was going to wear. After fourteen years of marriage Douglas could predict her movements in and out of the room and had learned not to ask any questions or say anything about the noise. He was lucky she took charge of all the laundry, he thought. In fact, he was lucky about most things in his marriage. He really had nothing to complain about and no excuse for indiscretion. He would just let his wife get on with the laundry, doze a little longer and then work his way through a couple of cafetières of coffee.

He listened to the lid of the laundry basket opening and closing. He could hear the shirts being unbuttoned and shaken out, and the fall of jackets and trousers as they were thrown on to the chair by the window. Emma was unusually aggressive, working at speed, getting the job done as quickly as possible. Douglas did not know what the hurry was for. He could hear her going through pockets, pulling out handkerchiefs, bus tickets, receipts and loose change and then *Christ* . . .

'What is this?'

Even then, he knew. He should have thrown it away as Julia had told him but he had wanted to hold on to it.

'Douglas . . .'

'What?'

'Look at me.'

His wife was holding Julia's letter. Douglas almost knew it by heart. He certainly remembered the end:

Lonely, obsessed, confused, intoxicated, sensual, paranoid

Julia

210

'What's this?'

'It's nothing. Bits of a script.' He turned away.

'It's not your handwriting.'

He could picture the weird dance steps and the German text.

'No, it's just some research.'

'Research? It doesn't read like research. Look at me, Douglas.'

It was the last thing he wanted to do.

'Who is Julia?'

'A researcher,' he said.

'I hope you're not going to deny it.'

'Deny what?'

'Oh for God's sake. Just answer my question properly. Who is Julia?'

'It doesn't matter.'

'I think it does. I think it matters more than anything has ever mattered—certainly in our marriage if you have any desire to hold on to it.'

'Of course I do.'

'How long has this been going on?'

'Nothing's been going on.'

'Oh really? When did you first meet her?'

'I don't know.'

'I'm sorry, Douglas. You seem to be under the impression that I am very stupid.'

'I have never thought that.'

'More stupid than her, obviously.'

'You're not. You're much cleverer than her . . .'

'Who is she?'

'She works for the British Council.'

'I don't think her profession has got much to do with it.'

'She organises lectures and conferences.'

'And why is she lonely, obsessed, confused, intoxicated, sensual, and, it appears, paranoid?'

'I don't know.'

'Is she your lover?'

'I don't want to talk about this.'

'That means she is.'

'It doesn't mean anything.'

'Oh for God's sake.'

Emma threw the letter on to the bed.

'Who is this fucking bitch?'

'She's not a bitch.'

'What is she then?'

'Someone I met.'

'You did more than meet her, you bastard. What did you think you were doing?'

'I don't know.'

'Is she married?'

'I think so.'

'God, you don't even know that.'

'Yes, I do, she is.'

'And does she have children?'

'Two.'

'Oh well, that's all right then. I suppose she won't mind having some more then.'

'That's got nothing to do with it.'

'It's got everything to do with it.'

'I didn't want children. We discussed this. Everything was all right.'

He wished he could have been more discreet, or kept silent, denied everything.

'I'm sorry.'

'Sorry? Is that all?'

'I don't know what else to say.'

'You're pathetic. Absolutely pathetic.'

It wasn't so much the infidelity, Emma said, as

the fact that he had done so little to avert it. Douglas had surely seen it coming. He could have talked to her and even if he had made one drunken 'error of judgement' (such a ridiculous phrase, but Emma couldn't think of anything else) then they could have spoken and done something about it. But this appeared to be a sustained and secret operation that had been carried out behind her back for months.

'Part of me wants to know everything,' said Emma. 'Whether I've met her, what she looks like, what she wears, what attracted you to her—everything. Did you know that you were going to do this from the start? Did you do anything at all to stop it—although obviously you can't have done because you wanted to and you were just too fucking selfish to stop, I can see that—but I'd like to know whether *at any stage* you thought of me and what you were doing and whether it might, it just might, you know, be *the wrong thing to do* . . .'

'Of course I did . . .'

'*Don't interrupt.*'

'I'm not interrupting.'

'*You are.*'

'I didn't want to hurt you.'

'You suppose that makes it all right?'

'I'm not saying that.'

'What are you saying?'

'I don't know, I was lonely, I didn't mean to do it; I thought I could avoid hurting you or you finding out.'

'Every word in that sentence is rubbish and you know it.'

'I don't know. I don't know anything any more. Perhaps I did it because I thought you'd be better

213

off without me.'

'I think I'm the one that decides that.'

'I'm sorry.'

'I don't understand you at all. You've kept this letter when you could have destroyed it. Perhaps you wanted me to find out all along and didn't have the courage to tell me face to face. The next thing you'll be telling me is that you only did it as a favour to make our marriage stronger or that I should be grateful to you for giving me the excuse to leave.'

'I don't think that.'

'It never occurred to me to be unfaithful, do you know that? Even though I work in the theatre and people somehow expect it of me. They assume, because I am an *actress*, that this is what happens, that I must have so many opportunities and I'm always at it but I'm not. It's not in my DNA. But you—one whiff of an opportunity and your trousers are down and in you go.'

'It wasn't like that.'

'No? Well, what was it like? Actually, no, don't tell me. I really don't want to know about your sordid four-minute sessions in hotel rooms round the world or wherever you *fucking* did it. In fact, come to think of it, I'd rather know nothing. I've heard enough of your so-called confession—the one that's supposed to make our marriage stronger.'

'I didn't say that.'

'*I'm the one doing the talking.* So in fact what I'd like to happen, what I'd like you to do now is just leave, get out, don't talk to me, keep your dirty little secrets to yourself.'

'I don't know where to go.'

214

'There's a hotel round the corner, you can stay there—or why don't you just move in with her?'

'It's complicated.'

'What? It's *complicated*? Of course it's fucking complicated. If it was easy everyone would be doing it. But now, of course, it seems that everyone *is* doing it. I suppose you could always just fuck off and live with her.'

'I can't do that.'

'Why? Because she's married?'

'She won't leave her kids.'

'Do you really think I need to know this? Is that supposed to make me understand that she has some kind of conscience? Can you not see that every sentence you utter is full of the most *complete crap anyone has ever heard*?'

'Don't be so vile.'

'Well, I'm sorry. Perhaps you should have thought this might happen. Perhaps, when you were taking your trousers down, you should have stopped and thought—do you know what—maybe I shouldn't be doing this, maybe I should stop—put it away, pull my trousers back up, leave the room, or wherever you were, maybe it was some crap toilet in an airport, I don't know—and never see her again. But then it was too late, I suppose. Then you were "committed", as you are supposed to be to me—well, you were supposed to be to me—but that's all gone now. I could just about forgive the drinking and the absences and the selfishness and the sheer lack of awareness of anything to do with me. I know you didn't really want children but I did. I wanted two or three, in fact, but now of course off you go and fuck someone else and soon there'll probably be a whole nursery of little

215

Douglas Hendersons popping out all over the place and how do you think I'll feel? How do you think I'll live with that?'

'It won't be like that.'

'No? What will it be like then? Do you think we can just carry on after this and pretend nothing has happened—or that you could go on seeing her? Perhaps we could have her round to dinner and you could compare the two of us face to face. Tell you what: let's invite the whole family round. You could turn it into a reality show on television. *Wife or Mistress—the Family Decides*. Then the public could vote. You'll probably need the money by the time I've finished.'

'Don't be ridiculous.'

'I'm not being ridiculous.'

'I wish I hadn't told you.'

'Well, it's a bit late for that.'

'Couldn't you tell that something was wrong?'

'*Of course I could tell*. I just didn't expect you to be such a walking cliché. I thought you had a bit more muscle than that. A bit more moral fibre. But clearly you haven't.'

Emma sat down on the chair by the window.

Douglas hoped that it had all come out and there would be no more.

'At least we've talked about it.'

'And that's all we're going to talk. I can't face speaking to you any more. You'll have to do it through lawyers from now on.'

'Already?'

'Yes, already, Douglas. You don't expect me to forgive you, do you?'

'No. But isn't it a bit soon for lawyers?'

'No. It's a bit late. I should have seen it coming,

216

found out sooner, acted more quickly, and then I would have been spared all this *crap*.'

'It's not crap.'

'It is crap.'

'Emma . . .'

'Don't you "Emma" me.'

She stood up and started pacing the room.

'Don't you dare use that wheedling tone with me. Don't even *think* you can get out of this. This is it. Just forget that we were ever married or that you ever had a chance or that you ever thought you could ever talk your way out of this.'

'Don't be like this. Please . . .'

'Like what?'

'So fierce.'

'Well, I am fierce. If you don't like it you should just carry on and get out.'

'You really mean it?'

'Of course I mean it. I've never meant anything more in my life.'

*   *   *

Douglas checked into a Travelodge. He visited a series of pubs, read the newspapers without concentrating, and drank throughout the day.

Perhaps, he thought, he could get a taxi to the airport, catch a flight down to London and see Julia? He could even turn up at her work, surprise her, and tell her that all he wanted to do was to start a new life with her.

Perhaps not.

In an alley behind a restaurant he could see a woman pouring discarded mussel shells from plastic boxes into black bin liners.

'I'm taking them back to the sea,' she said.

She looked like a younger version of his wife.

Douglas thought back to when they were first married and how contented they had been. Emma used to sing as she moved through the house, unaware that he was listening.

When I last rade down Ettrick
The winds were shifting, the storm was waking,
The snow was drifting, my heart was breaking,
For we never again were to ride thegither,
In sun or storm on the mountain heather,
When I last rade down Ettrick.

Douglas realised, as he walked past the dark-red sandstone tenements, uncertain where he was going or what he was doing, that he had ruined his life.

Emma had warned him that without children they had needed to find an even greater determination to love each other. There was no one else, nor was there going to be. They had to share absolute trust.

He remembered an evening years ago with his brothers, a kitchen supper with red wine and lasagne back in the family home. Angus and Tessa had been at the table with Jack and Maggie. There had been singing and Tessa had said how happy the evening had been, with the Henderson brothers together and at ease in each other's company, and Emma had said yes, she knew it had been a good and rare night. It was that special, she said, and they had to promise to remember it, because such times didn't happen very often.

They had laughed and they had been happy;

confident and free to say whatever they wanted. They were protected from the world by family and by companionship.

What a privilege it was, Emma had said, to be cocooned in this way.

But then she had stopped and begun to clear away the plates because even at the time, in the midst of all that happiness, she had known that it was only fleeting and she couldn't bear it.

You can never rely on these moments, she said. They don't come round very often and you can't anticipate them or expect them to last.

They were unexpected gifts, temporary moments of respite, and even then they weren't always enough to sustain you through the bad times; because, as she had said even then, you can never trust a man not to throw away his own happiness.

CHAPTER FIFTEEN

Jack tried to think what it would have been like if he had done things differently; if he had persuaded Krystyna to stay, or thrown everything in his life to one side and gone wherever she was going.

He called her mobile but it was switched to automatic answer. He tried to work out what he felt:

Fear. Krystyna had never got on the bus at all but had hitched a lift and been abducted. Perhaps he should report her missing. It seemed a bit melodramatic.

Anger. She was back in Poland, thinking of no

one other than herself. It was thoughtless, ungrateful and selfish.

Jealousy. There was another person with whom she had been in love all along; not Sandy, not Jack, but someone so secret that he could not be mentioned.

He did not know if he loved her, missed her, or hated her for disrupting his life. Krystyna could do anything and go anywhere, losing herself in the world, whereas Jack had withdrawn into solitude.

He knew that it would be so much easier if he forgot all about her and concentrated on his work. He returned to his desk:

Respice
Look Back

Item quam nil ad nos anteacta vetustas
Temporis aeterni fuerit quam nascimur ante
Hoc igitur speculum nobis natura futuri
Temporis exponit post mortem denique nostram.
The everlasting time before our birth
Has been to us as nothing; this, therefore, is
    the mirror
Which nature holds up to us, showing the
    time to come
When we at last must die.

Numquid ibi horribile apparet? Num triste
videtur quicquam?
Is there anything terrible in that? Is there
anything sad?

Non omni somno secures exstat
Is it not

220

The safest sleep?

He thought of Krystyna and then of Sandy lying in the road: *the safest sleep*. He turned back a few hundred lines.

Non potius vitae finem facis atque laboris?
Why not rather make an end of life and trouble?

He had avoided the word 'labour' but was 'trouble' sufficient? A 'troubled mind'. Could that really describe Sandy's emotional state? And what about Krystyna? He looked at another translation.

If life is only wretchedness, why try to add more
    to it?
Why not make a decent end?

He wanted to find words that expressed the fear, the anxiety, and the terror: not of dying but of living. He remembered that Creech, one of the commentators on Lucretius, had once noted on his manuscript, *NB. Must hang myself when I have finished*.
He did not know if he would ever see Krystyna again.

*   *   *

A few days later Maggie called to say that she was coming to Edinburgh. She wanted to see him and there were things they needed to talk about. Jack wondered how much he would have to tell her and how long it would take.
He chose a neutral venue, an Indian restaurant,

near the university.

Maggie was surprised at the choice.

'Are you sure? You don't even like Indian food.'

'I thought it would make a change.'

'You know how it doesn't agree with you.'

'It's the only place I know that's quiet.'

'I thought we might be going somewhere Polish.'

'Annie's spoken to you?'

'There's so much you haven't told me, Jack. I'm really shocked. To keep it all from me . . .'

'It's over now.'

'I'm not sure these things are ever over.'

The restaurant was dark and deserted, with red-and-gold-lacquered chairs, painted screens and a ceiling that looked like the dance floor of a 1970s discotheque.

Maggie had lost weight and wore a fitted grey dress with yellow stripes. Jack thought it looked as if it had been made out of curtain material. He noticed that it was cut lower than the clothes she had worn when they were married. He assumed she was going on to something more important later. Perhaps Guy was waiting for her.

She ordered confidently: dosa with dhal, Hyder Abadi, and a glass of lassi. Jack was less familiar with Indian food and plumped for an onion bhaji and marinated chicken tikka masala. He really didn't want to think about this. He was in the wrong restaurant with the wrong person at the wrong time. To make it worse, the waiters were behaving as if it was their wedding anniversary. Yes, he would have a bottle of Cobra.

Maggie spoke brightly. Jack remembered how her voice was always higher when she was trying to pretend not to be nervous.

'Annie told me what had happened,' she began. 'I couldn't understand what you were doing until she mentioned the accident. Why didn't you tell me?'

'It wouldn't have been appropriate. I didn't want to get you involved.'

'We used to be married to each other.'

'I didn't want to talk to anyone. And I didn't want to annoy Guy. You know, the ex-husband coming round with a spectacular tragedy just when you were settling down.'

'That's very considerate of you. But he wouldn't have needed to have known.'

'You mean you have secrets from each other?'

'No, that's not what I mean.'

'What do you mean then?'

'There's no need to be aggressive.'

'I'm not being aggressive. I'm being specific.'

'Well, it's good to see you haven't changed, Jack.'

The starters were served. Maggie was right. It was a mistake to have come to an Indian at lunchtime. Jack wondered if he could escape by two-thirty.

'How is Guy?' he asked.

'Do you really want to know?'

Guy was a sculptor in Bristol. He was older than Maggie with grown-up kids and he had inherited enough money to keep them both going. There was some kind of workshop attached to the house and so he spent most of his time at home. When he had first met him Jack had been surprised how similar he had been to himself and almost questioned Maggie about the wisdom of her departure. It was like trading in a Vauxhall Vectra

223

for a Ford Mondeo. There didn't seem to be much point.

'Actually,' Maggie was saying, 'this is what I wanted to talk to you about.'

'Not Krystyna?'

'Only if you want to. The fact is that Guy has asked me to marry him.'

'I see.'

'And I wanted you to know before anyone else. I didn't want anyone else to tell you first.'

'So you've said yes?'

'Not quite. I just wanted to make sure you were happy.'

'You don't need my permission.'

'I know that. But it would be nice to have your blessing.'

'Of course.'

'You don't mind?'

'How can I mind?' Jack said.

He did not know what he thought. If Maggie hadn't left then everything would have been different. He would not have been out on his own on election night; he would not have killed Sandy; he would not have met Krystyna.

As they ate Jack could hardly remember being married to Maggie at all. Perhaps he had made it all up? His marriage, his children, his life. Sometimes he thought that his past was a dream and his future was carrying on without him.

The waiters asked if everything was satisfactory, but Maggie was still talking about Guy.

'He keeps referring to "the Third Act",' she said, 'as if life is some kind of unfolding drama.'

'And it's not?'

'Of course it isn't.'

Jack tried to banter.

'I suppose I'm still in Act Two.'

'Well, I'm sure you could move on to Act Three.'

'I don't think so. I think everyone left at the interval.'

'Jack, don't be like that. Is it all over with your friend?'

Friend.

'I don't know. I'm not sure what it was all about anyway.'

Maggie's Hyder Abadi turned out to be lemon sole with almonds. Jack wished he had asked for something equally simple. He remembered how his life had been so much more ordered when his wife was with him. Now here she was, giving him advice about whatever love life he had left.

'Why don't you phone her?' she asked.

'She doesn't answer.'

'I suppose that is a bad sign. Where is she?'

'I don't know.'

'Then why don't you find out?'

'I'm not sure she wants me to.'

'Perhaps it's a test.'

'Maybe it is but I don't really want to be playing games . . .'

Jack knew that he had to make more of an effort but he was worried about looking desperate.

'You'll never know unless you try,' said Maggie.

'I know. It just feels a bit adolescent, that's all.'

'I wouldn't worry about that. No one's looking.'

'I don't know. My family certainly seem to have a few opinions.'

'Stop worrying about them, Jack. It's your life.'

'And the girls . . .'

'I know. The moral superiority can become a little tiring. But I think we have to ignore them. What have you got to lose?'

Jack recognised that he could, at least, look for Krystyna. He tried to recall the names of her friends: Eva, Myra and Magda; Josef, Tadeusz and Jan.

'You can't throw these things away,' Maggie continued. 'Especially when you get to our age . . .'

'Our age? We're not old. Anyway, you don't seem to have had much difficulty.'

'That's because I made an effort. Honestly, Jack, if you're keen you should try a bit harder.'

'I don't know if I am keen.'

'Elizabeth said you were . . .'

'You've spoken to my mother about it?'

'She phoned. She told me she was concerned about you.'

'That's all I need.'

'Honestly, Jack, it's only because we care.'

'Really?'

'*Yes, we do*. God, sometimes I despair of you.'

'I thought most of the time you despaired of me.'

'I'm sorry. I didn't mean to go into all this. I just wanted your blessing.'

'And you have it.'

'Isn't it extraordinary how we argue more when we are apart than we ever did when we were married?'

'It must be another one of life's little ironies,' said Jack.

Outside it had begun to rain. He remembered looking for Krystyna all those months ago, hoping to meet her by chance around Easter Road. It couldn't be that hard to find her again.

The streets were crowded with Hibs fans going to the first game of the season:

We are Hibernian FC
We hate jam tarts and we hate Dundee,
We will fight wherever we may be
Cause we are the mental HFC

A group of Polish men with rucksacks were smoking at the foot of Calton Hill, waiting for friends with beer so that they could all climb up together. He could hear their exchanges: *Ceść—Jak sie masz—dobrze—dziekuje*. Perhaps Krystyna knew them. He tried her phone once more. There was no reply.

*   *   *

Eventually Krystyna's friends realised that none of them knew where she was. She did not answer to anybody. She had forgotten her father's birthday. No one had seen her.

It had been a month. Hospitals were checked. The Edinburgh flat was searched. Krystyna's bank was asked when and where she had last withdrawn any money.

Friends and colleagues were asked when they had last seen Krystyna and why she might have gone missing. Then one of her friends mentioned Jack. He had been, she told the police, 'most attentive' after Sandy's death.

'"Most attentive",' the policeman was saying. He was sitting in Jack's kitchen, having refused a cup of tea.

227

'I wouldn't put it like that.'

'But that's how it was put. What do you think her friend meant by "most attentive"?'

Jack wondered how many times he was going to repeat the phrase.

'I did have a reason to see her.'

'Of course you did. It was an unfortunate incident. You were very unlucky.'

DI Morrison asked when was the last time Jack had seen Krystyna, what her state of mind was at the time, what clothes she was wearing, whether she was on any medication (antidepressants?), and if she had told him where she was going.

'She only stayed a few times.'

The policeman asked how long they had known each other, when exactly she had stayed with Jack, and if she had communicated with him since she had left. It could be that he was the last person to have seen her. Had she left anything behind, had he taken any photographs of her, and did either he or she keep a diary?

'Why do you need to know all this?' Jack asked.

'I'm trying to assess the level of risk.'

DI Morrison asked for a description and Jack realised how unobservant he had been. He could just about manage 'collar-length dark-brown hair, a lightly tanned complexion and green eyes' but he had to think about whether there was colouring in the hair or highlights, if she had any marks, scars, tattoos or distinguishing features. He hesitated over her height and weight, he did not know her shoe size, and it took him a long time to remember that she wore contact lenses. He was pleased that he could say what she had been wearing when she left: the jeans, the lime-green singlet and the

228

cream linen jacket, but he did not know any of the brands or labels and it was only afterwards, when the policeman had gone, that Jack realised that he had failed to mention the birthmark on her arm.

'Is that everything?' the policeman had asked.

'So many questions.'

'We need to do everything we can to ensure that your friend is safe.'

Your friend.

'Of course.'

'Was there anything in her state of mind that might lead you to believe she would put herself in danger?'

'I don't think so.'

'Had you had an argument?'

'Not an argument as such.'

'As such?'

'You know what I mean. She left.'

'No, Mr Henderson, I don't know what you mean. What was her state of mind when she left?'

Jack realised that he had yet to define what it had been like. Perhaps Krystyna had been relieved to go.

'I would say resolved.'

'Resolved?'

'Sad but resolved.'

DI Morrison was confused.

'They seem a bit different to me. You don't often see people who are sad and resolved at the same time, do you?'

'That's the only way I can describe it. She likes mystery; people not knowing where she is.'

'Do you know if she's gone missing before?'

'Perhaps.'

'Perhaps?'

'It seems possible. But I don't know her very well.'

'Oh come on, Mr Henderson. If you didn't know her very well then what was she doing in your house?'

'She needed space, time, a place where she could escape.'

'Do you have any male students to stay or is it just the girls?'

'She's not one of my students. She's too old. It's not like that.'

DI Morrison noticed the pictures of Maggie and the children on the kitchen dresser.

'Is that your wife?'

'We're divorced.'

'And your children have left home?'

'They have.'

'They must be about the same age as Miss Gorski.'

'No, they're younger.'

'Have they met her?'

'My whole family have met her. My parents, brothers. Not my wife.'

'Of course,' DI Morrison conceded. 'Well, I may have to have a little chat with them. I'll need their addresses.'

'Do they have to know about all this?'

'You don't seem to understand, Mr Henderson. If your friend is missing, and there are suspicious circumstances, then the whole world is going to know about this. Not just your family.'

'But there aren't any suspicious circumstances. I'm sure she's just gone away somewhere . . .'

'Well, if you're sure then there's no need to worry. The only problem is that I need to be sure too. It can't just be you that's sure, you see? That isn't quite enough for us.'

Jack could see that DI Morrison was irritated.

'If we get a response when we put out an appeal then there's no need for any alarm. But if there's no response, and we can't find her, then things may escalate quite a bit.'

'Escalate?'

'We have to do everything we can. You're not planning on going away anywhere, are you?'

'I don't have any plans.'

'Because it would be good to let us know if you were going anywhere far. Just in case . . .'

'I'll just be here,' said Jack. 'I'm always here.'

*   *   *

He was given a more senior officer.

'It's important that we look at all the possibilities,' Chief Inspector Murray informed him.

'You don't mind the tape recorder, do you? I know you've seen one of these before.'

'But not in these circumstances.'

'I'm sure you normally try to avoid them. But these things happen, don't they? How well did you know Sandy Crawford?'

'I thought this was about Krystyna?'

'It is.'

'I didn't know him at all.'

'The problem is that I'm not sure we really believe you, sir.'

Previously Jack had been called 'Mr Henderson'. Now he was 'sir'.

'But why would I have come across him? How

231

could I possibly know him?'

'And you never met Miss Gorski before the first incident?'

'Of course not.'

The Chief Inspector started to write in his notebook. It seemed odd, given the fact that he had the tape recorder. Perhaps he didn't trust it.

'When did you first sleep with her?'

'I didn't.'

'What day of the week was it?'

'I said I didn't.'

'In the daytime or at night?'

'Look . . .'

'Indoors or outdoors?'

'I have not slept with her.'

'I find that hard to believe.'

'It's the truth.'

Chief Inspector Murray leant forward.

'Perhaps you would like me to spell this out. This is what troubles me, Mr Henderson. A young man is hit by your car.'

'He threw himself in front of me.'

Chief Inspector Murray appeared to be changing facts that had already been accepted.

'A young man was hit by your car. It looks like suicide but perhaps we have been a bit hasty in thinking like that. Perhaps it wasn't suicide at all?'

'Hasty? This is ridiculous.'

'Let me go back to the beginning, Mr Henderson. A young man was hit by your car. His girlfriend is seen with you shortly afterwards.'

'At the funeral. It wasn't "shortly afterwards".'

'There may have been other times.'

'There were not.'

'I don't know that though, do I?' Chief Inspector

232

Murray continued. 'As I said, you were seen with her shortly afterwards. If you knew her before, perhaps the young man found out about it. Perhaps he was jealous. Perhaps they had a row. Whatever happens he finds himself under *your car*. Perhaps you and the girl needed him out of the way.'

'This is absurd.'

'The girl comes to live at your house.'

'She was just staying with me temporarily, that's all.'

'Staying or living? It doesn't make much difference, does it? Like many things in this case, it's all kept a bit of a secret, isn't it?'

'Not really. My family knew.'

'That's as may be. The fact is that her family did not. She doesn't tell anyone, as far as we can gather. Her father in Poland begins to worry because she doesn't return his phone calls. In fact he worries so much that he calls his daughter's friends and then they call us. Then, and what makes this even more strange, the girl really does go missing. No one knows where she is. And your story is a bit, well, shall we say, "hazy"? Would that be the right word?'

'I've told you everything I can.'

'Yes, but each time you remember a little bit more. And now I've begun to outline some of the possibilities, I hope you realise that we might need to keep having these little chats. Perhaps you can see why it doesn't look very good for you, Mr Henderson? Perhaps you can understand why your memory needs to improve and why, perhaps, you might need a lawyer?'

'I'm as worried about Krystyna as everyone,'

Jack said.

'We're all worried about her, Mr Henderson. That's why I'm here. That's why we're all here. And that's also why we are going to have to search your house. And, I'm afraid, your garden.'

*   *   *

Jack was surprised by the numbers. The search team began inside the house with an open-door investigation, inspecting cupboards and wardrobes, the loft and cellar. They looked under beds and behind furniture, pulling out clothes, crockery and Christmas decorations, looking for hiding places, signs of Krystyna, evidence of crime.

Outside, and within what the Police Search Adviser called 'the curtilage' of the home, men with dogs fanned out in a spiral, first in the garden and then outside its walls, looking down on to the ground, picking up objects and inspecting them in gloved hands before discarding, tagging and bagging.

They found a pair of flip-flops, a plastic water bottle and a lipstick-stained cigarette end.

Jack was asked to wait on the terrace. He remembered Krystyna bringing him a drink in the early evening after one of their swims. *Nothing can add beauty to light.*

Chief Inspector Murray came out to ask, 'Is this hairbrush Miss Gorski's or does it belong to one of your daughters?'

'Krystyna may have used it. I don't know.'

'And the toothbrush?'

'It's mine.'

'You use a pink toothbrush?'

'I didn't think about the colour.'

'Well, I suppose you've got more important things to think about than toothbrushes.'

Jack called Tessa for legal advice and asked her not to tell his father. The request was ignored.

Ian Henderson telephoned immediately.

'What the hell is going on, Jack? Why didn't you tell me about this?'

'There's nothing much to say.'

'Where is she?'

'If I knew then everything would be all right.'

Jack could hear his father's breathing become theatrical: the slow intake and the infuriated exhalation.

'I don't know. First your brother Douglas deliberately throws away his marriage . . .'

'He's told you then?'

'No, of course he didn't. Emma told us. We haven't seen him for weeks. But that's not the point. That's not why I'm ringing . . .'

'I know. I'm sorry.'

'What happened? Your mother was always worried Krystyna was too young . . .'

'It wasn't like that.'

'Did you have a row?'

'No. I don't think so.'

'You don't think so? It's so hard to get a straight answer from any of you.'

Jack tried to listen to his father.

'What am I supposed to say then?'

'Tell them the truth, of course. Provided you've got nothing to hide.'

'Of course I haven't.'

Ian sighed. Jack could tell that he did not want to get into an argument.

'You'll just have to keep ringing her until she answers.'

'I don't think there's much chance of that. She's probably thrown her phone away.'

'I thought young people were on the telephone all the time?'

'Not Krystyna. She's different.'

'She's certainly that. Sometimes I wish you'd all just stuck to the relationships you started with. Only Angus seems to have managed to do that.'

'We don't do it deliberately, Father.'

'I know you don't. But it's so upsetting.'

'Yes,' said Jack. 'That's what people keep telling me.'

Ian wanted to make his position clear, summing up his own phone call.

'You must inform the police about everything. Are you sure Krystyna hasn't done herself harm?'

'I don't think that's likely.'

'Anything's possible.'

'I know . . . but not Krystyna. She's too wilful . . .'

'You think you know her well enough to be sure?'

'Yes,' said Jack, 'I think I do.'

'Well, I hope you're right. Let me know if there's anything I can do. I don't want any more of your silences. Tessa can always sort out the legal side . . .'

Jack wished everyone would leave him alone. He should try to work, he decided, even if he could not concentrate: *Praeterea pro parte sua, quodcumque alit auget, redditur*. For every benefit requital must be given.

He kept stopping, unable to find his rhythm: *Ut*

236

noscas splendore novo res semper egere . . .

He thought of each word in turn: *You may see things need light ever new. Things for ever need renewal of shining.* The phrases did not fall as he wanted them. Perhaps he needed to be less literal.

He decided to stop, make a cup of tea and go to bed. He picked up his pen, crossed out the work he had done so far, and wrote in one quick sentence: *Things forever need renewal to shine.*

All he had wanted was to be kind; to do the right thing.

CHAPTER SIXTEEN

Douglas had never had to worry too much about money in the past (it was one of the few advantages of childlessness), but now that he was on his own he was going to have to make some adjustments. Emma had made it clear that, as far as she was concerned, he had no claim on anything other than the clothes he stood up in. Their flat was now on the market and she would only communicate with him by text or email. She did not want to have to hear his voice.

Can I see you?
No.
Can I ring you?
No.
Is there nothing I can do?
Nothing.

Douglas asked for forgiveness but Emma
237

insisted that it was too late. He was mad to think that she would ever trust him again. He had wasted their love and destroyed their companionship. The only thing he could give her was a divorce.

Douglas did not approach Tessa for legal advice because she was already dealing with Jack and, in any case, she liked Emma too much to be sympathetic.

He wanted to keep it separate. He could not stand any more disapproval from his family. They all made it clear that he had been a fool. His mother was the worst: trying, and failing, to find something positive to say.

'Perhaps if you're very penitent . . .'

'I've tried that . . .'

'I'm sure she might come round . . .'

'I don't think so, Mother. She hates me . . .'

'She doesn't hate you, Douglas. Nobody hates you . . .'

But Emma was relentless in her fury. Douglas suggested divorcing online as it was cheaper and less personal but Emma left him in no doubt what she thought of the idea.

Don't contact me any more with your stupid cheap thoughts.

Douglas found an expensive lawyer, a friend of a friend in London, who advised him to rethink the way in which he lived his life: no designer clothes, no taxis (unless he could claim them on expenses), no posh restaurants, no foreign travel, and preferably no alcohol.

Douglas was not sure that he could live without the alcohol but promised that he would always choose the cheapest wine on the menu.

'That implies you are still going to restaurants,'

his lawyer argued.

Douglas had picked her because he found her voice reassuring. Now he wished he had chosen a man.

'And your credit cards?' she continued. 'I assume you have more than one?'

Douglas had been kiting his accounts for years.

'We need to budget for everything and then put a plan in place. I don't want to see you destitute.'

'Does that happen often?'

'Not if you do everything I say.'

'It's as bad as that?'

Douglas tried to think of a television idea that would sell all over the world and make him proper money: a series on seven-star hotels, the secrets of the rich and famous, an exotic holiday show offering luxury on a budget. He was never going to survive directing documentaries about the relationship between art and anatomy.

His work was mainly in London and so he left Glasgow and rented a room in a friend's house. They had converted the storage cellars in their basement flat to provide ideal accommodation for a nanny, a granny, or now, it seemed, Douglas.

He left early for work each morning, had a coffee that he knew he couldn't afford, and headed on to his production company in Soho. Previously he had hardly been there at all, working from home, only attending vital meetings, but now he surprised everyone with his diligence. He only hoped that no one had guessed it was because he didn't have anywhere else to go.

He had begun to edit two out of the three films in the series but there was still more research to be done on the final programme. He visited Windsor

Castle once more to look at a selection of Leonardo's drawings. He turned over the pages, seeing Leonardo's location of the soul in a drawing of the skull. He looked at a representation of the female urinogenital system, and his observation of perforations in the pericardium for the transition of spirit.

As he leafed through the studies of the female form he thought of Julia. He began to think what it might be like when he saw her again, especially now that he was in London. But he remembered her obsession with secrecy. 'Never call me,' she had said. 'Store my number under a man's name. I will send you texts.' She would never have left a letter in a pair of trousers ready for dry-cleaning.

Douglas decided to call her office. He wanted to hear her voice.

It took several attempts; not because Julia avoided him but because he kept cancelling each call as soon as he had dialled her number. It was absurd, he thought. He hadn't even planned what he was going to say.

The most important thing, he decided, was to call her before he had anything to drink.

The first time he managed to dial her number and let the phone ring Julia was out. He did not leave a message on her voicemail and felt strangely relieved. He even had a glass of white wine to celebrate. After he had drunk the whole bottle and started another he called her again.

This time she was in.

'Well, hello,' she said. 'I didn't know you had this number.'

'It was easy enough to find.'

'You know you're breaking the rules?'

240

'I'm sorry, I couldn't resist it.' He tried to sound charming rather than drunk.

'It's bad behaviour.'

'Then forgive me.'

'What can I do for you?'

'You make me sound like a business meeting.'

'I'm *at work*, Douglas. People can come in at any minute. I have to look and sound professional.'

'I'm sorry. It's just I haven't seen you for such a long time.'

'I'm sorry. I've been busy. Haven't you?'

'Yes, of course, but I just thought . . .'

'It's not easy, Douglas.'

'I know.'

'We have to be patient.'

'I'm in London . . .'

'You know the rules, Douglas. Not London. I let you know when I'm going somewhere exciting and then you arrive. It seems to be working well so far.'

'Then when can I see you?'

'I don't know. Is something wrong?'

'No. It's all right.' He reminded himself not to say anything about Emma. He did not want to sound desperate.

'You don't sound good. Have you been drinking?'

'No.'

'I'm not sure I believe you.'

'Just a little.'

'You shouldn't drink so much.'

'I know.'

'I can't get away very easily. John's away next week and I have to look after the boys, take them to the Aquarium, stuff like that . . .'

'I still want to see you.' Douglas knew that he

241

was sounding too desperate.

'Something has happened, hasn't it?'

'No. It's all right.'

'I have to go now. I might be going away next month. I'll let you know. Around the 23rd. Is that any good?'

'I might be filming.'

'Keep it free—a few days either side of the 23rd. I'll call. Sorry, someone's coming into the room. Thank you for your call, Mr Henderson; I'll see what I can do. Of course. Goodbye.'

Douglas was determined to see her even if it was only to remind himself what Julia looked like (she had refused to allow him to take her photograph in case someone discovered it—*was he crazy?*).

The only clue she had given him was that she was going to the London Aquarium. He decided that the following week he would go there every day and wait for her.

He knew it was mad but he didn't care.

*   *   *

The Aquarium was hot and crowded, a world full of noise and hazards. The only animate objects at peace were the fish. Douglas learned that a hundred and nineteen different species were discovered in the Thames each year, and that, in 1984, in Upton Park, smelt and flounder had fallen on the streets of London from the sky.

'I don't think so,' a man was saying. 'I think it was West Ham fans having a laugh.'

All around him parents were becoming increasingly exasperated by their children.

'That's *enough*, Frank.'

'Do your shoes *up*, Katy.'

'For God's *sake*, Matt.'

Douglas watched couples kissing, holding hands and pushing buggies. He would probably never know what it was to be a father.

Children filled the corridors.

'Which one's Nemo, Mummy?'

'Where's Doreen?'

Douglas stepped back to let other families pass. This has nothing to do with me, he thought. I have nothing in common with anybody here. I only want to be with her.

It took him three days to meet Julia and he had begun to give up hoping, knowing that he was making himself ridiculous. In the end, she must have seen him first. He could see her walking briskly away.

'Julia,' he called.

She turned round and pretended she had not known he was there.

'Douglas? What are you doing here?'

'Looking at fish.'

'I didn't know you were interested in marine life.'

'You'd be surprised what I'm interested in.'

Douglas could see her two children looking at him.

'Hello,' he said. 'I'm Douglas.'

'This is Mr Henderson,' Julia interrupted. 'He's a colleague from work. This is Tom, and this is Sam. Say hello, boys.'

Her sons looked at their own feet.

Tom was a spiky-haired nine-year-old dressed in a Chelsea football shirt and a baseball cap. Douglas realised that he was the type of boy that parents describe as 'full of energy' but everyone else thinks a pain in the neck. He ran ahead, banged on glass walls that had signs specifically imploring visitors not to disturb marine life, and put his hands into every tank he could, roughing up the water and shouting, 'Die, fish, die!' His younger brother Sam was the opposite: a freckle-faced redhead who clung to his mother at all times.

Julia was looking for some kind of escape but recognised she was trapped.

'Go ahead and look at the fish, boys. Stay on this level. I'll join you in a minute. Go on!'

They waited until the boys were looking at the sharks, mirroring their movements through the glass, trying to provoke them.

Julia's formal tone changed.

'What the hell are you doing, Douglas? Are you crazy?'

'I'm just a colleague from work. We bumped into each other.'

'Don't you dare start following me around.'

'I'm not. I was here anyway.'

'I don't want you stalking me.'

'I'm not stalking you. I just happened to be here. I'm not desperate or anything.'

'I'll be the judge of that. Honestly, Douglas. I told you to wait.'

'It's just a coincidence.'

'Since when did you start visiting aquariums? Don't *ever* do this again.'

Tom interrupted.

'Mummy, can I have a shark?'

'In a minute. Mr Henderson is just leaving. Go and look at the piranhas.'

Douglas waited once more until the boys were

out of earshot. He knew that this was his last chance.

'Where are you going next?'

'God, you'll be lucky after this performance.'

'It's not a performance.'

'I don't believe you.'

'Trust me.'

'Never.'

'Where are you going? When can we meet? You can tell me.'

'Moscow.'

'Is that around the 23rd?'

'I'll send you a text. This is mad. You were insane to come here.'

'I've told you. I was here anyway.'

'That's such a lie.'

'Just let me come to Moscow. I promise I'll behave.'

'That's another lie.'

'It depends what you mean by "behave".'

'You'll need a visa.'

'Thank you.'

'I'm not promising anything.'

'I'm not asking you to make any promises. I'd just like to see you. But if it's difficult I can wait. You don't have to do this. I was only asking. If you can't see me then I'll understand . . .'

Douglas had managed to retract as much as he dared and could feel Julia relenting.

'I suppose we could just "bump into each other" there,' she said. 'It'll be freezing but it's a great city. The corruption is almost refreshing. You can get anything you want as long as you have money . . .'

'I'll get a visa.'

'I have to go. Remember what I said. Just

don't . . .'

'I won't.'

'I mean it . . .'

'I said I won't . . .'

'See you in Moscow then.'

She leaned forward. Douglas thought she was going to kiss him but she whispered in his ear.

'Bastard.'

Douglas left the building and decided to take a walk by the river. He would stop in a wine bar and think about what it might mean to keep seeing Julia.

He realised he had pushed it too far and damaged his cause. But he also knew that wherever Julia was he would seek her out. Every time she offered him the possibility of a meeting he would go.

CHAPTER SEVENTEEN

Before the Lent term began Jack took to his bed. He was determined to stop worrying about Krystyna and finish his work on the *De Rerum Natura*. He unplugged his phone and scattered papers, dictionaries and rival translations of Lucretius all around him, only leaving his room for further supplies of coffee in the morning and tea in the afternoons. He hardly washed. He did not shave. His life of disciplined withdrawal was complete.

He had reached the description of the plague of Athens. This had always been considered an abrupt ending to the poem and many scholars thought that Lucretius had died before he could complete it. Jack found a certain irony in the fact that the last word was *desererentur* from the verb *deserere*—to forsake, leave, abandon. Lucretius had left the reader with an apocalyptic description of piles of corpses on makeshift pyres and given up on any attempt at consolation. He could have been describing the end of the world.

Jack was enjoying the bleakness of the vision. The writing was so rich that part of him did not want to finish. He was trying to make his translation as perfect as possible, leaving something he could not improve, stretching himself to the limit of his ability, knowing that he could not have worked harder or better.

As he reached the end he realised that it was the only part of his life that he had successfully completed. Everything else was unfinished, or had fallen away without reaching a conclusion. He did not know when he would see his wife, his daughters, his family, or Krystyna again. They had either given up on him or assumed that he was too busy to see them. Perhaps, he told himself, when he finished the poem he would have more time to invest in the relationships he had neglected—although there were times when he recognised that he had retreated so far into his own world that it was going to be hard ever to get out of it.

He was just reaching the end, before his final revision—*Nec iam religio divom nec numina magni pendebantur enim*. Neither the worship of the gods nor their powers were much regarded—when the doorbell rang.

Jack assumed it was the police continuing their enquiries, even though he had told them all he knew. What could they possibly want with him now?

Looking through the window, he was relieved to see that the vehicle parked outside was not a police car but a black Nissan Micra. A wet figure in a hooded anorak was standing in the porch. He had curling hair and glasses.

He seemed familiar, yet distant, and when Jack opened the door he started with an apology.

'Sorry, I was supposed to get here sooner.'

Jack couldn't think who he was.

'I hope you remember me . . . you know . . . from the funeral.'

Then Jack realised. It was Allan, Sandy's brother.

'Of course.'

As soon as he spoke it was clear that Allan was not going to stay long.

'I hope you don't mind. I'm just a postman really. I've brought something for you. A letter.'

'Won't you come in?'

'I'm on my way south. Krystyna asked me to deliver it personally . . .'

'Krystyna?'

'She's in the Highlands.'

'I'm sorry?'

'She knows she should have told you.'

Jack couldn't think what to ask.

'Is she all right?'

'It's been a bit weird. But I'm not allowed to say anything . . .'

'Not allowed?'

'In case I get it wrong. Krystyna promised me the letter explains it all. I only agreed to do this if I didn't have to tell you anything myself. All I have to do is give you the letter. Here. Take it. Please . . .'

'Tell me what?'

'What's in the letter . . .'

Jack accepted the envelope. The handwriting was foreign and young. It reminded him of a French pen pal he had had at school, writing on lined paper in formal English. *Jack Henderson only.*

'Is it bad?'

'No, it's not bad. But I'm not allowed to say. She wants to tell you herself . . .'

'Then why didn't she come herself?'

'You'll see. It's been a bit of a time . . .'

'What do you mean?'

'After Sandy . . . you know . . . it's not for me to say . . . I can't tell you any more.'

'OK . . . I understand.'

'Krystyna didn't want anyone to know where she was or what had happened . . .'

'Yes . . . well . . . she certainly achieved that.'

'She changed her name,' said Allan. 'And we've got this cottage, opposite Mull. She phoned me and I gave her the keys. But she made me promise not to tell anyone. Not even you or my parents. No one . . . I shouldn't even be telling you this . . .'

'But the police . . .'

'I know. I heard. I'm sorry. That's why she's written.'

'She lives in the Highlands now?'

'Until the summer. Then we rent it out.'

'Are you sure you won't come in?'

'No. It's all right. I'm sorry. I think you've had a hard time but we didn't know. Krystyna thought she could disappear and no one would worry. When she found out she did phone the police to tell them she was safe. They should have told you.'

'I'm sure they will eventually. But it would have been good if she'd done it sooner. Are you sure you wouldn't like a drink?'

'I'd love one but I'm driving. And I have to get down south.'

Allan was embarrassed. Jack knew that he should let him leave.

'It was kind of you to come. Thank you.'

'That's all right. I made a promise. My brother would have wanted me to keep it. Life's strange without him. I keep hearing his voice; but I suppose that's mad.'

'I don't think it's mad at all.'

'No, well . . . we all have to deal with things . . . in different ways . . . I can't be very profound about it. We just have to get on with it, I suppose. I'm sorry it took so long to give you the letter. And I'm sorry about . . . you know . . . everything . . .'

'It's all right.'

'Krystyna promises she's explained everything.'

'I'm very grateful,' said Jack. 'It can't have been easy for you to come here.'

'No worries.'

Allan nodded, saying goodbye, his duty done. He went back to his car in the dark and the rain.

Jack watched Sandy's brother drive away. Then he looked at the envelope in his hand. The ink was beginning to run. On the back was the name of the sender: *K.E. Gorski*. He did not know what the 'E' stood for.

He returned to the kitchen table and remembered what it had been like when Krystyna had last sat opposite him. At the time he had almost forgotten that he could live in that way, at ease with another person, even in the silences.

Ardtornish
Morvern
Scotland
5 January 2006

Dear Jack,

I should start by saying that I'm sorry it has taken a long time to write. I have so many excuses but none of them are good.

My first excuse is that there is so much to say and I did not know where to begin. My second is language. It is hard to find the right words in English, especially because I am writing to a man who is always careful to put correct words in the right place. I am frightened of making a mistake, of saying the wrong thing, and I am frightened of irritating you, although I have not seen you be angry. Perhaps you were angry after I left? I do not know, of course.

I think then that I must start (although now this is no longer the beginning) by saying sorry. I am sorry for disappearing and for going away without contacting you again.

I must also say thank you for looking after me and for letting me meet your family. I hope they are all well, especially your father. I know you worry about him even if you do not say so. Please send him and your mother my best wishes. They made me welcome in a country I do not always understand. You did that too. I miss your welcome.

I have been thinking what it must have been like for you on that night when Sandy died and

251

*during everything that happened afterwards.
You did not need to see me. You did not have to
be so kind. I will always remember what you did
for me and how you helped me to recover.*

*It is hard to explain what it was like for me. I
think it is like when you wake in the night in the
darkness and turn on the light. It is very bright
at first and then you get used to it. That was
what it was like with Sandy. It was bright all the
time so that I could not see anything else.*

*Then, when the time came and the light went
off, I could still feel the remains of the light
behind my eyes, even when it was dark and my
eyes were closed. The light kept on going and I
could not darken it. I could not sleep.*

*I went to see Sandy's brother and told him
my news and what had happened. He has been
kind to me and now I am living in this cottage
in the Highlands. His parents say I can stay here
as long as I like, although I do not know how
long that will be. You will remember that I am
not good at deciding when to come and when to
go.*

*It is often very cold here and there is a big
wind but the sea is always near and I like the
sound of it. It makes me think that there is
something constant, whatever happens.*

*Why am I not telling you my news? It is
because I am scared what you will think. If I
write it down then you will know and perhaps
you will not think kindly of me. But I must write
it down. I will write it down now.*

I have a child.

Perhaps that was not so bad to write.

That is why I had to leave you. I could not

stay any longer because you would guess or know and I would have to tell you and I had waited too long. I should have told you at the beginning but I was not sure and then it became harder and harder until it was impossible. I have always been proud to be honest. I do not like to lie. But I know my silence was a kind of lie. Please forgive me. I hope you will forgive me.

He is called Adam. He was born in December. Sandy is the father. That is why his parents have been so kind to me. They helped me at the hospital and afterwards and they have made sure that their friends here come and see me and check that I am not making too many mistakes. You never stop when you are a mother. I did not know this before. I am busy all the time.

I think you may be angry with me but I hope you can understand why I had to leave you. I was trying to do the right thing. I know you like to do the right thing too. That is something you have taught me.

I knew that it would be impossible to visit you or be with you or stay in your house if I had a child. I had distracted (is that the right word?) you enough and I know that you were worried about your work even though you tried not to show it. Have you finished it yet? I cannot imagine how you must be feeling. I do not know what you will do next or how your life is. Perhaps you have a new girlfriend? (I am joking, although perhaps I am not.)

Adam is sleeping but soon he will wake. He has a lot of hair already. I like the smell of him.

253

I like to hold him close to me. I did not think I could feel so much love and so much fear at the same time. He has blue eyes but I have been told that many babies have blue eyes and they change colour as they grow older. His grandparents are proud of him. One day I will take him back to Poland and show him to my father and my brother. I do not know if they will be pleased. I do not have the same family as you. I think I would prefer to show him to your family rather than my own. Perhaps if you forgive me I will be able to do that one day.

You see, I am going on too long. What else is there to say? There is one thing perhaps. If you would like to see me again, if you can accept my apology for all my weaknesses, and for going away, and for not telling you the most important thing (so many failures!) then I am here. You can come. You must come. Perhaps it is your turn to visit me. I would be so happy to see you. Do not be scared!

I think I have forgotten to say thank you. Perhaps I did this earlier, but if I did not, let me say thank you again. Thank you for looking after me and for being my friend. Thank you for letting me meet your family. I think they gave me confidence to have this child. They showed me that it could be possible; that a happy family can exist in the world. (Although I know you will tell me that your family is not always happy. How is Douglas?)

Come and see me if you can. If you can forgive me.

I will not forget what you did for me.

Your Krystyna

As soon as Jack had finished he read the letter once more.

I have a child.

Jack could not believe that he had been so stupid not to think of this. He worried that the rest of his family had guessed and said nothing. And yet it had never occurred to him.

Perhaps, if Krystyna came back to East Fortune, they would think that the child was his. There would be so much to explain; not a grandchild but a new person, another beginning.

At first he couldn't imagine it. Then he started to think what it might mean.

He began to hear Krystyna's voice. He even knew what they could say to each other.

As he thought about these things Jack realised that the loss in his life had lifted. He was no longer alone.

He looked at the letter once more.

Your Krystyna.

CHAPTER EIGHTEEN

Julia was staying at the Moscow Kempinski. She was planning an exhibition in London and was trying to arrange the loan of a coach that King James I had once given to Boris Godunov. She texted Douglas to tell him that the negotiations were taking longer than she had thought. If he wanted to come he would just have to fly over and wait. She did not seem concerned that he might have other work or plans.

255

'I'll take my chance,' he replied.

She texted back to say that her hotel room had a view over the river to St Basil's Cathedral and Red Square with the Kremlin away to the west. *They do the best breakfasts in Moscow.*

I'm not really coming for the breakfasts, wrote Douglas.

He managed to persuade his production company to pay for his flights, convincing them that the foundation of the Moscow Hospital School by Peter the Great in 1707 was an integral part of the film he was making. The painter Kandinsky had studied anatomy in the city, the artist Pavel Tchelitchew had produced a panorama of freaks and mutants in the 1930s, and there was even a contemporary exhibition of anatomical drawings by Yevgeny Chubarov of half-man, half-machine.

Douglas took the overnight flight with Aeroflot and a taxi from the airport. It was a battered Zhiguli with an icon attached to the rear-view mirror. The driver played music that sounded vaguely Armenian. He spoke a little English and said that he had only ever had three car crashes in his life. Jesus had saved him every time.

Despite the car heating Douglas could smell the oil and sulphur through the windows. The Soviet factories on the road from Sheremetyevo looked as if they were still struggling to keep up with one of Stalin's five-year plans.

Douglas wished he had taken the time to learn the Cyrillic alphabet. Then he could name the places he needed to get to. He did not want to look a fool in front of Julia. There were only so many times he could say *privet*, *spasiba* and *do svidaniya*.

He noticed the lights of a helicopter dousing a burning building in the distance. The smoke from the fire rose into the dark grey of the sky. Douglas could not imagine what it might be like to live in that building or to be part of that fire. He could not concentrate on anything other than his life with Julia.

The car pulled up at the hotel and Douglas felt for his roubles. He was going to have to tip everyone. The taxi driver wanted paying, his luggage was unloaded, and the doorman, receptionist and bellboy were waiting.

After he had checked in he was given an envelope. It was a note from Julia. She had enclosed her spare key-card. *Welcome to Moscow— Room 514*. It was five-thirty in the morning.

Douglas took his bag to his room. He showered, shaved and cleaned his teeth. He had to smell good. Even though he was tired, he wanted to be at the top of his game.

He took the lift down to Julia's floor and walked along the corridor, passing trays of discarded room service and bags of newly cleaned shoes. He hesitated, unsure whether to knock on her door or just let himself in. He worried how he might explain himself if he found himself in the wrong room; if the whole encounter was an elaborate joke.

He put the card in the slot and opened the door. There was just enough street-light through the blinds to see Julia sleeping on her side.

Douglas took off his clothes and got into bed. He kissed her gently on the shoulder. Julia sighed. He lifted her hair and kissed the back of her neck.

I hope that's who I think it is. I'm here. Still sleepy.

257

It's all right. Perhaps I'm dreaming. No. I'm here.

This was all that he wanted.

Are you glad you've come? You cannot imagine. I can try. I forget how different it feels to be with you, I feel alive again. So you're dead without me. Pretty much.

They held each other, half waking, half sleeping.

'I have to work this morning,' Julia said. 'Do you want to sleep and join me later? We could have lunch.'

'That would be good.'

'I'll meet you in Red Square. You could have a look at Lenin.'

'Is he still there?'

'Of course. It's like a shrine; they replaced one religion with another.'

'And people still go?'

'There'll be a huge queue.'

'I've got nothing else to do.'

'We can't just spend all day in bed.'

'Why not?'

'Because some of us have to earn a living.'

Julia swivelled out of bed and walked into the bathroom. Douglas closed his eyes and listened to her turn on the shower. He even thought he could hear her humming to herself. *I've got it bad and that ain't good.*

He lay back and tried to decide if he should stay in her bed or return to his room. He was less tired than he had first thought. He imagined going into the bathroom and doing it in the shower. Soon he could not think of anything else.

'Fuck it,' he decided.

He got out of bed and knocked on the bathroom door. He wasn't sure Julia could hear.

'What do you want?'

He opened the door.

'Again?' she asked.

At lunchtime Julia picked him up in Red Square and they took a car through the streets of Moscow. As they approached the restaurant Douglas could see black Hummers dropping off middle-aged men with improbably tanned girlfriends. Bodyguards stood by the cars, checking each new arrival, smoking cigarettes to their butts.

'They're all armed,' Julia said. 'Bunch of gangsters.'

'Then I hope they don't understand what you've just said.'

'If a woman is well dressed she can say what she likes. You'll be the one thrown in jail.'

An old man in a frock coat opened the door to the restaurant. He had long white hair and a matching moustache that made him look like a footman in an opera. Douglas and Julia handed in their coats and were shown to the bar. Julia asked for a Bellini and insisted that the barman made it with freshly squeezed peaches rather than tinned juice. Douglas ordered a white wine and was already worrying how much it was going to cost and how long he could keep up the pretence that it didn't matter. His friend Paul had once told him that affairs only lasted until either you were discovered or the money ran out. Somehow he was managing to do both.

The restaurant looked like a nineteenth-century nobleman's house, with a white-stuccoed ceiling and floor-to-ceiling bookshelves.

'It's all fake,' said Julia. 'It was built in the 1990s.'

They were handed menus that had been designed to look like old Russian newspapers: *Pelmeni stuffed with chicken giblets and calf brains, Sturgeon solianka soup, Braised cockscombs.*

'I thought a cockscomb was a type of fool . . .' said Douglas.

'It's probably very stringy chicken's neck. I'd have the blinis. We can have the cheaper red caviar . . .'

'No, have the black, if you like. I don't mind. I don't care about anything when I'm with you.'

'You say that now. If we saw each other all the time you'd soon tire.'

'I don't think so.'

'What do you think then?'

'Sometimes, Julia, it seems I hardly know you at all.'

'Well, I think it's important to retain an air of mystery. If you knew what I thought what would be the point of asking me any questions?'

'I want to know everything about you,' Douglas said. 'I want to know more than anyone has ever known, I want you to tell me more than you have ever told anyone.' He leaned forward. 'I want to touch parts of you that no one has ever touched before.'

'And it's only lunchtime,' said Julia. 'I'm not sure I can keep up with all of this. Let's order.'

'Don't you?' he asked.

'What?'

'Don't you want the same?'

'Of course I do. I just choose not to express it like that.'

'I'm not sure I believe you.'

'We don't need to say everything at once,

Douglas. Every time we see each other you speak to me as if you've been saving everything up. I think we should go a little more slowly.'

'We've been going slowly for six months.'

'Life is longer than you think, Douglas. Don't ruin the present by thinking how little time there is. If you spend all your time worrying about that then there's no time to enjoy anything.'

'I just want to feel I'm living.'

'We can't live like this all the time. We'll go mad.'

'I want to go mad.'

'You can't live your life at a hundred miles an hour all the time.'

'Why not?'

'Because then you crash and burn.'

'Then what a way to go.'

'I have kids, Douglas. I don't want to crash and burn. Let's talk about something else.'

Julia started to tell him how her best friend had asked her to a party where everyone had to dress up as characters from *Gone with the Wind*. As she spoke, Douglas began to doubt. How had he got himself into this relationship with a woman who seemed so oblivious to his feelings and so wary of sharing any serious thoughts she might have about the future?

Did he know what she thought about politics, global warming, children, education, morality and the future? And if he did, would he like her? He could not picture the future at all. Were they just going to drift on, meeting intermittently for bursts of passion and then returning to their day jobs as if nothing had happened?

'You're very quiet,' Julia said.

261

'I'm just taking it all in.'

'I hope you're not going to get serious again. This is supposed to be fun, you know.'

'I know.'

'Then lighten up.'

The waiter stood between them with his pen poised. Julia asked for the blinis followed by rabbit in puff pastry.

'Rabbit always makes me think of *Watership Down*,' said Douglas.

'That's why I order it. I hate that book. Eating rabbit is a form of revenge. Would you like some more wine?'

'I can see most people are drinking beer. Or brandy.'

'Georgian wine was always the safest bet but now they've banned it. You know this is supposed to be the best restaurant in Moscow?'

'I can see.'

'Well, we need a treat. We can't just sit here eating borscht and drinking tap water.'

'I know.'

'So let's order some Russian champagne and be done with it.'

Douglas realised that Julia was beginning to irritate him. He even thought she might be doing it deliberately.

'Am I your first indiscretion?' she asked.

'Of course. Am I yours?' Douglas had never dared ask before.

'I've had my admirers.'

'I'm sure you have. But that doesn't answer my question.'

The champagne arrived.

'Oh Douglas, what does it matter? Relax. Why

262

can't we just have a good time? Don't start worrying about the past or analysing everything.'

'I can't help it.'

She didn't understand. Douglas emptied his glass of champagne, no longer caring how much it cost.

'Really, Douglas, there's no need to get upset.'

'I'm not upset.'

'You are upset. Tell me about it.'

'Does all this mean nothing?'

'I'm here, aren't I? What else do you expect me to do?'

'I don't know. Just acknowledge what has happened.'

'But it's still happening. I don't know what's going on. I can't acknowledge it. I'm too busy living. I thought you were too.'

'You don't understand.'

'I do understand.'

'You don't.'

'Then let me . . . I don't know . . .'

They couldn't go on like this.

'I've left my wife,' said Douglas.

'Oh.'

'I should have told you earlier.'

'When did this happen?'

'A few months ago.'

'She found out?'

'I told her.'

'Are you crazy?'

'I couldn't live with it any more.'

'And so she kicked you out?'

'More or less.'

'I don't suppose there's any "less" about it.'

Douglas found Julia's reply so annoying that he

wanted to walk out.

'It was horrible.'

'I'm sure it was.'

Douglas thought of Emma and how easily they used to speak to each other even when they were arguing.

'You don't seem to care about any of this at all,' he said.

'Oh I do, Douglas. It's just that it hasn't got anything to do with me.'

'It has.'

'It's your marriage,' said Julia.

'You don't understand.'

'I do, Douglas, but there's no point talking if you're going to get upset.'

'That's exactly when we should be talking.'

Douglas's mobile phone rang. He hadn't expected it to work in Moscow and he didn't want to answer but he could see that it was his mother. As soon as he answered he could tell that something had happened.

'What's wrong?'

'It's your father.'

'What is it?'

'He's very ill.'

'I know.'

'Where are you?'

'I'm in Moscow.'

Julia pushed back her chair and mouthed a question. Did he want her to leave? No, he did not.

'What are you doing in Moscow?'

'I'm doing some work. You know, the anatomy project.'

'I never know what you are doing.'

He had told her. He had told his entire family

264

but they never listened.

'Can you come home?'

'When?'

'Now.'

'It's that bad?'

'Yes,' said Elizabeth. 'It's that bad.'

'I'll come as soon as I can.'

'No, Douglas. I want you to come now. I know your father will want to see you.'

Will he? Douglas thought. I'm hardly the favourite.

'What time is it over there?' she asked. 'Can you get a flight this evening?'

'I'll find out.'

'Just come, Douglas.'

He turned off his phone.

'Bad news?' Julia asked.

'It's my father.'

'I see.'

'I have to go.'

'I'll pay,' said Julia. 'Don't worry. Just go.'

'You want to get rid of me?'

'Of course I don't.'

'I'm sorry.'

'Don't be angry.'

'I'm not angry. It's just that you don't seem to care very much about us—about the future.'

Julia put down her glass of wine.

'Do you want to stop?' she asked.

'What?'

'I said do you want to stop?'

'I don't know.' Douglas realised what was happening. It wasn't the best of times to end an affair but then, he supposed, there could hardly be a good time. 'Do you?' he asked.

'We don't have to decide anything now,' said Julia.

'That means you do.'

'I'm not saying that.'

'You are.'

Douglas was almost relieved.

'You have to go now,' said Julia.

'I know.'

'Then go. We can talk about this another time.'

'All right then.'

'Go on . . .'

'I'm going . . .'

Douglas didn't even kiss her goodbye. He left the restaurant and stepped out into the street, past the chauffeur-driven cars, the security guards and the escort girls, and hailed a cab back to the hotel and then the airport. He would buy the first ticket he could and damn the cost.

He was already thinking of his father.

Tell me good things, he always asked when Douglas came home. He did not know how he was going to answer or if his father would be sufficiently conscious to hear him.

He had no idea what he was doing any more. He realised that he no longer knew the route back to who he really was or if there was any of his old self left. He tried not to think about the mistakes he had made or the shame he felt: the selfishness that had led to this misery.

'Shit, bugger, fuck, wank,' he said in the taxi.

'Excuse me?' the driver asked.

'It's nothing,' said Douglas.

CHAPTER NINETEEN

Ian Henderson was eighty-four, 'not a bad knock', Angus could almost hear him saying. He wondered how many people would start to tell him that his father 'had had a good innings'.

Elizabeth sat by her husband but could not settle, anxious about his breathing and if he was comfortable, depressed by his diminishing consciousness and by her own powerlessness.

Jack wanted to find something to read aloud, some Shakespeare sonnets or Scots metrical psalms. Douglas arrived, sat with his barely conscious father for an hour and a half, and then went downstairs to find a consoling whisky. It was only when he was back in the family home that he realised how much he had to suspend his life and wait for the end.

Part of Ian had already left them.

'I feel I am about to discover the great secret,' he said with his eyes closed.

'More water?' Elizabeth asked. Her husband was easing into sleep.

The family fell into an informal and disorganised shift system, climbing the stairs with water and tea and food, their lives reduced to the simplest of rituals.

Sometimes it felt that the moment would never come but any activity other than waiting was an irresponsibility, a form of neglect, a betrayal.

Ian was almost impatient with his family, irritated by their continual coming and going and their questions about his comfort. He became confused as to who they were, increasingly unwilling or unable to answer their questions, annoyed about his condition, impatient with death for taking so long. It was the kind of intolerance that was usually displayed when they all took too long to prepare for an outing.

Well, come on, if you're coming.

Death was like a recalcitrant child, refusing to leave the beach at the end of a long summer day.

Oh for God's sake.

He died in the middle of the afternoon when everyone was out of the room. Jack was in Edinburgh, Douglas and Angus were watching the first of the Six Nations rugby games: Scotland against France.

Elizabeth had returned to the bedroom to check on her husband.

Angus heard her cry out just as Chris Paterson was taking a penalty to put Scotland ahead. It was unlike any sound he had ever known. At first he thought it might have been a bird.

Then he heard his own name.

'Angus . . . Douglas. Come up . . .'

Chris Paterson struck the ball and the commentator's voice sang out: *'That's a beauty.'*

Douglas reached for the remote and turned off the television.

'I'll come with you.'

Angus climbed the stairs two at a time. Douglas followed. Their father's head had fallen away to the side. There was less colour to the flesh. He made no sound.

'I don't think he's breathing,' said Elizabeth.

Angus felt for a pulse. He listened against his father's chest and touched his upper neck by the right ear. He cupped his hand against the cheek. Then he looked at his mother. He did not need to speak.

Elizabeth felt the steadiness leave her. She sat down on the edge of the bed and held her husband's hand. Then she leant forward and kissed him, first on the forehead, then on the lips.

Angus reached out his hand to touch his mother but changed his mind and withdrew.

Elizabeth looked up at her sons and then at her husband.

'I've always dreaded this moment,' she said. 'And now here it is.'

Douglas sat down on the chair of the dressing table and began to cry. His father's death had been as calm as anyone could have hoped but he had not expected it to be so simple.

Angus put his hand on his brother's shoulder.

The afternoon divided into a series of disconnected fragments as each member of the family tried to find an activity that was helpful. Angus offered to make his mother a cup of tea but realised that he had spoken too soon. She did not even appear to hear him.

'Will you telephone for the undertakers?' she said at last. 'Make sure they take care. I'd like to think of him as he was; when he was younger, not as he is now. I'd like to be able to bring him back, to pretend he's still with me.'

'Take your time, Mother. There's no rush . . .'

'Then perhaps I'd like to pick some flowers,' his mother said. 'If I can find any . . .'

'Do you need any help?'

It was half-past three in the afternoon. The light had gone.

269

'I'll go,' said Douglas.

'I think I'd like to be alone,' Elizabeth said. 'Do you mind?'

'Of course not.'

'I could never imagine this day. Will one of you tell Jack and the girls? I think he's coming this evening. Where's Tessa?'

'She's on her way.'

'When everyone is here I think we should have champagne,' Elizabeth said. 'I don't like to think of everyone in a state.'

'That's something I can do,' said Douglas.

'And will you tell Emma? Ian was always fond of her . . .'

Douglas could not think how he was going to achieve this. He would have to ask Tessa. At least he knew how to open a bottle.

He went down to the wine cellar. The last time he had drunk champagne had been with Julia. She hadn't phoned. He didn't know what they would say to each other.

He could hear the doorbell and footsteps in the hall and Angus telling his wife what had happened and what he thought she should say.

'I'll deal with it in my own way,' Tessa said, and then, 'Oh Elizabeth.'

Douglas could feel the cold from outside. He remembered his father's irritation whenever anyone left the front door open. It took so long for the house to warm up again. He remembered him shouting, *For God's sake, will somebody please close the door?*

'I'll phone the undertakers,' he heard Angus say. 'You two have a moment. I'm not sure what Douglas is doing.'

He was sitting on the steps down to the cellar.

'It's so cold outside,' Elizabeth was saying.

Tessa fetched her coat and offered to help gather the flowers.

'I know there are snowdrops under the chestnut tree. There might even be a crocus or two.'

Douglas could still recall the preparations for the last play. He imagined his father's voice again. *My masters, are you mad? Or what are you? Have you no wit, manners, or honesty, but to gabble like tinkers at this time of night?*

By the time Jack arrived Elizabeth was ironing her husband's pyjamas. He wanted to stop her. He even thought to offer to take her place, or ask what use they would have for his father's pyjamas now.

'What can I do?' he asked.

He did not know if he wanted to see his father's body.

'Ask Angus,' Elizabeth replied. 'He's in charge.'

Jack wondered which of the brothers would become most like their father in old age, and how much of his life or spirit would be preserved through the generations. There were still a few mannerisms, reminders of a life: the movement of hands, a laugh here and there, the pronunciation of certain words.

*   *   *

The boys divided the tasks between them. Angus would deal with the undertakers and arrange the funeral. Jack would make the phone calls to inform their friends and colleagues. Douglas agreed to register the death and put a notice in the papers.

They were children once more. Their father was

271

back in control of their lives, commanding them from a parental afterlife, insisting that proprieties were observed, standards upheld.

Each family member concentrated on their allotted duties, doing what they had to do, making lists and ticking off achievements. Elizabeth and Tessa went to the kirk, decided on the flowers, and briefed the Minister about the funeral.

Jack was working through his father's address book. He had reached the letter M and realised that it was the longest entry in the book: all those Macdonalds and Macleans.

Then Douglas returned from the Registrar of Births, Marriages and Deaths.

'Did you know Father had been married before?'

'I thought we all knew that,' said Angus. 'It only lasted a few years. He didn't like to make a fuss about it.'

'Who was she?'

'Some kind of showgirl, I think,' said Angus. 'Louvain.'

'What?'

'That was her name.'

'And what happened? Did they divorce?' Douglas remembered his father's disapproval when his marriage had failed.

'She died,' said Angus. 'Father said she was always frail. I think it was TB.'

'Does Mother know?'

'It's "your father's sorrow", she used to say.'

'Not to me.'

Douglas walked over to the decanter and poured himself a whisky.

'So am I the only one who didn't know?'

'We thought you did,' said Angus.

'When did you find out?'

'Years ago. It's one of the reasons Father always liked Emma.'

'I wonder if she knew.'

'I think he told her,' said Jack. 'After you'd split up. She came to see him.'

'That's a bit bloody rich,' said Douglas.

He thought back over all the Shakespearean roles Emma had played in the garden: Rosalind, Viola, Helena and Mistress Quickly. She'd even been Lady Macbeth, for God's sake. Perhaps she looked like Louvain.

'It's best not to dwell on these things,' said Angus.

'Easy for you to say.'

'I don't think he felt they had to tell us anything,' said Jack, sitting back down on the sofa. 'Father was a great believer in discretion.'

'What do you mean? He told you. He was only being discreet with me.'

'Perhaps he assumed we'd tell you. Or it didn't really matter.'

'But it does matter,' Douglas said. 'Every member of the family knew something that I did not. That makes a difference.'

Angus reminded his brother of the family mantra. *You should always speak the truth but the truth need not always be spoken.*

'Yes, but life doesn't always work out like that,' said Douglas. 'Sometimes the truth comes out at the wrong time and you can't do anything about it and then you're completely fucked.'

'Of course.'

'Believe me, I know,' said Douglas.

273

'We know you know,' said Jack.

*   *   *

The funeral was held a week later. It was the beginning of Lent. Confetti remained from weddings conducted long ago, spattered across the paths, blown amidst the graves, frozen in puddles round the kirk.

The whole family came, even those who had left. Emma stood to one side in a tight black dress, thin and veiled, the most elegant member of the congregation. She had only come on condition that no one expected her to speak to her husband.

Maggie arrived with Guy, and Jack even shook his hand, feeling nothing, unable to quite believe that he had ever been married. It made him think about Krystyna. He wished she was with him but he had done nothing about her letter. Perhaps he would just drive up and surprise her.

Tessa wore the dress in which she had played Olivia. At first, Angus had questioned her choice, but his wife said that she could not think of anything more appropriate. It was an acknowledgement of the world Ian had created; a house preserved, principles followed, values known.

'He would have smiled,' she said. 'He would have understood my appreciation of him.'

She could still hear his voice, *the fair Olivia*, greeting her as she stepped out into the garden in the black widow's dress. It had been what Tessa had appreciated most about him, the fact that he was always pleased to see her.

It was the gift of affirmation. So few people had

274

it, she thought.

The Henderson family wanted music and readings and tributes with jokes; enough, each son hoped, to acknowledge their father's vitality.

Say not the struggle naught availeth.

The singing of the first hymn, 'Amazing Grace', began timidly but Tessa, and then Maggie, encouraged the others to lose their reserve and sing out in tribute to a man who had always liked a performance.

As the service progressed Jack realised that he could be at almost any time or place in history. So many had stood in his place, uttered the same words, said the same psalms.

Elizabeth had hired a professional tenor to sing 'Ae Fond Kiss' and a piper to play 'The Flowers of the Forest' as the coffin was carried out of the kirk.

She did not cry.

It was only when the piper walked away and out down the lane, when the ceremony was over and the grave still lay open, that the tears of the rest of the family flowed: Douglas with his mother; Tessa with Angus, Imogen, Sarah and Gavin; Jack with his daughters.

Three black saloon cars took the family back to the house. Douglas could not stop crying.

'Oh for goodness' sake,' Elizabeth snapped. 'That's enough.'

Tessa handed him a paper handkerchief. Emma had already left.

Back at the house the Edinburgh friends assembled, suited and kilted survivors, respectful and appreciative, grateful for any moment of humour to leaven the gathering: anecdotes, memories, and light conversation about golf handicaps, holiday caravans, and the renewed potential of the Scottish rugby team.

'Beating France, who'd have thought it?'

Angus had persuaded as many of his father's surviving friends as he could to come, laying on lifts, providing whisky and smoked salmon. They stood around, talking about funerals they had been to in the past, playing down both their ailments and their impending mortality, seeking out chairs when they were tired.

'I much prefer funerals to weddings,' a man was saying. 'Weddings tend to go on for ever these days.'

Angus could hear his mother talking to friends and acquaintances about his father as they offered condolences, telling them again and again that Ian was a good man.

'That he was.'

'Few like him.'

Tessa handed round the canapés as Angus saw guests to and from their cars in a procession of greeting and farewell; all of them anxious to get home before the evening freeze.

Mr Maclean was asking Jack, 'Where's that nice girlfriend of yours?' and Angus could hear his brother being defensive.

'I think she's in the Highlands.'

'All going well?'

'Hard to tell.'

'You don't want to lose her. She's a fine-looking girl.'

As the cars drove away Angus watched the rooks over the fields behind the beehives. He remembered the summer, his father gathering honey, adding smoke to push the bees back, drifting it across the top bars of the frames before inspecting the combs, holding them up against the sun, a glow of gold against the light. He did not know how to continue his legacy.

It was his turn now; his mother had made that clear. He had to hold the family together. She appeared to have forgotten about Italy and his plans for a new life.

*   *   *

'We'll have to have a bit of a clear-out,' Elizabeth said, a few weeks later. 'I'm all for memories but I don't want to be surrounded by them.'

They began to sort through books, clothes, furniture and possessions; all the accoutrements that had once been so essential to a life.

Angus was persuaded to keep his father's coat and dress shoes and Jack and Douglas were offered a choice of suits, even though they recognised that they would never wear them. Of course they would have to give away Ian's professional clothing: the short bench wig for working in court, the long wig for ceremonial occasions, his gowns, tailcoats, white bow ties, and the long scarf-like falls.

There were old golfing trophies, out-of-date legal textbooks, and souvenirs of journeys made when Ian and his wife were young: a miniature gondola made out of matchsticks, a set of wooden elephants, a real ivory tusk that their father had been sent after defending a corrupt Nigerian. What on earth were they going to do with that? Angus thought. It was probably a criminal offence just to own it.

No matter how much the house was decluttered it always reminded Angus of his childhood. He could still see his father standing under the goalposts, watching him take a series of place kicks, fifteen from the right, fifteen from the centre, and fifteen from the left, working his way along a muddy twenty-five-yard line. His father punted the ball back each time so that Angus could practise his catching in the same session. Scotland B. He had waved to his mother and father in the West Stand. Even though the game had been at Murrayfield Angus could tell that the achievement had never been quite enough for his parents. He had never won a full cap.

Elizabeth had not been keen on rugby from the start. She worried that her son would succumb to injury or damage his hands in one of the rucks. 'Give blood—play rugby,' Douglas had joked but she had never thought it funny.

Angus thought of his mother before she was old, having tea on the table at ten past six, stirring the family into action as soon as her husband walked through the door. He could still smell the baking, shortbread and Victoria sponge, and hear his mother asking him to lay the table.

In those days they only had wine at Sunday lunch or when visitors came. Now they drank it all the time.

He remembered an American coming to stay, preparing one of his mother's stronger concoctions, and whispering, *This would kill me*.'

He tried to think how long it would be until he was an orphan and how much of his own life he had left. If he died at the same age as his father he would have thirty years.

He knew his mother would be upset, and that in many ways it was wrong to leave so soon after his father's death; but he was convinced that he and Tessa had to move away as soon as they could.

If they did not go now they would never go. Angus would never discover what his life could become.

*   *   *

Jack read aloud to his mother. Elizabeth tired in the evenings and she found his voice soothing. It reminded her of her husband.

She chose not fiction but guidebooks to places she had visited in the past: Germany after the war, Paris in the 1950s, the Italian lakes of her honeymoon.

Elizabeth interrupted her son with memories and contradictions, telling him that the guidebook had it wrong, that it wasn't like that at all. It failed to mention the atmosphere of each city, the taste of the food and the quality of the cocktails.

Jack's reading became an early-evening routine. His mother had done the same every night when he was a child; now the roles were reversed.

One evening she brought in an old shoebox and handed it to Jack. In the top corner, written in pencil, in Ian's handwriting, was one word: *Louvain*.

'I haven't ever opened this,' Elizabeth said. 'Do you think I should?'

'I don't know, Mother.'

'You know what it is?'

'I think so.'

'It contains her letters.'

'Perhaps you'd rather not know . . .'

He thought about his mother censoring the love letters of soldiers during the war: eighteen-year-old boys being trained for mobile units abroad, all of them fearing their letters might be their last.

'Could you read them for me?' she asked.

'I don't want to upset you.'

'I never knew what he thought about her; if there was ever any regret. There was a sadness about him sometimes. He thought I never noticed. Perhaps he was thinking what might have been, had she lived.'

'Are you sure you want me to do this?'

Jack did not know what he would do if what he found was bad. Would his mother be strong enough for the truth or would he have to make up a story?

'I'll leave you now,' she said. 'Then I'll come back and you must tell me what you think I need to know. After that I think you should burn them.'

Elizabeth left the room, stretching out her right arm to balance herself on the armchair. Jack had noticed how much more quickly she tired these days.

'I'll be in the kitchen with my gin.'

He opened the box, put the lid to one side, and pulled out a small pile of letters and playbills tied together with an old piece of string. On the top was a small signed photograph of a girl in a dancing costume and a feather boa, *Always your Louvain*.

She had probably given it to Ian before they were married. Jack untied the string. It was almost impossible to imagine Ian with a showgirl but there he was, in another photograph, in a restaurant with indoor palms, smoking a pipe, sitting with a proprietorial arm on her chair. There was a menu underneath: onion soup, *coq au vin*, *oeufs à la neige*. Jack supposed it was from his father's wedding day.

Underneath the two photographs lay a pale-lavender envelope with his father's name written in pencil. Inside was a sheet of paper filled with one word, in tiny writing, repeated again and again, filling both sides. *Come.*

Then Jack found a postcard of Notre-Dame. The same writing covered the back. *Never leave me again, never leave me, never, never, never.*

There was a birthday card, *Bon Anniversaire*, a lock of hair and a death certificate: *Françoise Louvain Henderson née Lusignan, 13 July 1947. Cause of death: heart failure.*

She had been twenty-three years old.

Jack sifted through the papers and the photographs, looking without reading, unable to concentrate. Did he want to know any of this?

He stacked the documents together, retied the piece of string, and put everything back in the box. He picked up the lid and pressed it down, giving it a tap with his knuckles that he hoped would keep it safe in some way. He left the box on the table by the fire and went to find his mother.

Elizabeth was sitting at the kitchen table. A soup was simmering on the hob.

'Anything?' she asked.

'She sounds a bit mad.'

'Yes, I think she did go mad.'

'Didn't Father say she had TB?'

'I think he found that easier to deal with.'

Easier than a broken heart, thought Jack. *Heart failure.*

281

'And she was French?'

'Her mother was French.' Jack realised that his mother knew far more than she was telling him. 'So there's nothing of note?'

'It's just a few letters that don't make very much sense.'

'Ian said she was almost illiterate. She must have been very beautiful to make up for it.'

'There's a photograph . . .'

'I always wondered what she looked like . . .'

Jack wished he had not said the word 'photograph'. He thought of Louvain smiling into the camera; feathers everywhere.

'I don't think I need to see it . . .'

'She wasn't as beautiful as you . . .'

'I was quite glamorous, I suppose. In my day.'

Jack remembered how his mother had once defined her marriage. *From mink to sink.*

'Your father once told me that my eyes were so piercing that they could open an oyster a hundred yards away. "Only a hundred?" I said.'

Her son topped up her drink.

'I never knew how much he looked at her letters; if he ever read them late at night or when I was out of the house.'

'I doubt it, Mother. I don't think anyone's looked at them for years. Perhaps Father couldn't throw them away at the time and then forgot all about them.'

'I don't like to think of him thinking of her. People are always more changed by love than they think they are.'

'I'm sure he didn't. And even if he did it was such a long time ago. He was far better off with you.'

'I hope so.' Elizabeth still sounded anxious. 'We lasted long enough.'

'And you were happy.' Jack tried to make his words sound like a statement rather than a question.

'Blissfully happy,' said Elizabeth.

Jack admired the way his father never appeared to have any doubts about the decisions he had made in his life. He just did what he took to be the decent thing and never said a word.

'By the way,' his mother asked. 'Are we ever going to see Krystyna again? I rather liked her, even if she did disappear.'

'She's a bit too young really . . .'

'After the war older men found younger women all the time. Their wives had either died or run off or gone mad— just like Louvain—and I always felt sorry for them until up they'd pop with a nineteen-year-old beauty and start all over again. And it was often the ugly men that got them.'

'Thanks.'

'I don't mean you.'

It took Jack a long time to mention the baby. Even when he did so, telling his mother immediately that the boy was Sandy's, Elizabeth knew that she could not ask if Jack had ever thought of having a child with Krystyna himself.

'She could have said something when she was with me,' Jack was saying.

'She told you all about Sandy.'

'You mean I should have guessed?'

Jack thought again how foolish he had been not to have known; to have gone through so much; to have harboured such hopes.

Elizabeth tried not to sound knowing.

283

'One thing was probably hard enough. And she's so far from home.'

'I offered her a home.'

'I know; but perhaps it wasn't the kind of home she had in mind. Perhaps it still belonged to other people.'

Elizabeth tried to imagine what her husband would have said. Perhaps Jack would have been more open with his father.

'I don't know what to do,' her son was saying. 'I don't suppose I'll ever live with anyone ever again . . .'

'I'm sure you'll find someone.'

'No. It's best to be on my own . . .'

'But you're not on your own. You have the girls, you have us . . .'

'You know what I mean. The whole thing with Krystyna has completely thrown me. I can't concentrate on my work. I can't concentrate on anything. I should never have asked her to stay . . .'

Elizabeth looked at her son.

'Perhaps there are different ways of seeing each other.'

'I don't know. It's hard to imagine the future.'

'It might be dull if it was easy.'

'I know that.'

'Do you remember a girl visiting us when you were young, just once, at the house?' Elizabeth said.

'What girl?'

'You must have been about ten. It was in the summer holidays. She brought you all a game of boules. She was dark and pale, and she went for a long walk with your father. When they came back she showed you all how to play the game. She was

284

French.'

'You're not going to start telling me he had a daughter?'

'No. He didn't.'

'That's a relief. As soon as you said the word "French" I thought of Louvain.'

'She was her daughter. Born before your father met her.'

'Is she still alive?'

'She lives outside Bordeaux.'

Jack sighed. He realised that it was the kind of exasperated noise his father always made.

'Her name is Christiane. After her mother died she went to stay with her grandmother. But your father always kept in touch. He wanted to know how she was. I worried that she would ask for money or make things difficult but she never did.'

'And she came here? To East Fortune?'

'Only once. She was in Edinburgh for the Festival.'

'Your generation. Honestly . . .'

'Sometimes you have to save your secrets, Jack. Ian was very private about it. I suppose he just wanted to know that a part of his first wife was still in the world. I'm only telling you because it might help you.'

'What about you? Did you mind?'

'I did at the beginning. I thought of her, of course, just as I thought of Louvain, I couldn't help it, but Ian never appeared to be troubled or distracted. It was not in his nature.'

'I sometimes think he never worried about anything.'

'He did, but he concealed it. He thought it was bad manners to appear over-anxious.'

'Does Christiane know?'

'I wrote to her to say that your father had died and she sent me such a kind letter back. She's around sixty now. She runs some kind of children's home.'

Jack stood up to close the shutters.

He looked out to see the snow melting under the trees and the first signs of spring on the branches. He could not remember a young French girl coming to the house at all. Perhaps it had never happened. Perhaps his mother was making the whole thing up in order to provide some kind of consolation. But he did think of his father, dressed as 'the madly used Malvolio', striding on to the stage with his yellow stockings and his cross-garters, smiling beneficently, *Please one, and please all*.

'Sometimes people want everything to be clear and final,' Elizabeth was saying, 'but I've always believed that one of the greatest blessings in life is the opportunity to see things through. Most things come back to you eventually. I suppose that's what makes everything so interesting.'

Jack wondered if 'interesting' was the right word.

He needed to think about all that had happened. He wanted to be on his own again. He told his mother that he had to get back.

'Will you be all right?' he asked.

'Oh, I'll be perfectly happy,' she said. 'You don't need to worry about me.'

Jack tried to imagine what it must have been like when Elizabeth had first met her future husband; a man living in the aftermath of another marriage. He wondered how much she had asked his father about his past, or if his mother had secrets of her own: lost possibilities. Perhaps they had decided to maintain the grace of silence, finding it safer not to ask too many questions, only telling each other what needed to be known.

His mother and father seemed always to have known that the truth did not always reveal the most about a life. Perhaps they had recognised that it was not so much their lives as the stories they made of them that mattered.

* * *

Douglas knew that he should return to London and get on with his work but he was enjoying the reassurance of family company. He told his mother that, in return for her hospitality, he would tend to his father's bees and check that the hives were ready for the spring.

He walked into the scullery, took off his jacket, and began to collect everything his father had taught him that he needed for the manipulation of the bees: the hive tool, the queen excluders, supers and the smoker. Then he changed into his overalls, making sure that his trousers were tucked into his boots. He remembered helping his father for the first time when he was a child. It was the only activity they had in common. Angus had his rugby, Jack was the scholar, and Douglas was left with the bees.

He was surprised how easily he returned to the routine. It was as familiar as a childhood country lane. He filled the smoker with a ball of newspaper, corrugated paper, sacking and dried grass. He lit it, put on his father's veil and gloves, and began to smoke the entrance to the hive.

He thought of Julia. She had sent him one of her minimalist texts. *Let me know*. Douglas replied, *Father dead. Miss you*. He thought that covered everything. His brother Jack would have been proud of such concision.

He let the heat drift in, allowing the bees to fill themselves up from the honey store. He recalled his father's wisdom: *A full bee never starts a fight*. Then he removed the roof and laid it gently on the ground. He took out the crown board and added more smoke to push the bees back, drifting it across the top bars of the frames until they had gone down into the bee ways between the combs. Some of them came out to try and defend the colony, following Douglas's movements with their front legs in the air.

Julia's texting became terse. *Call me*.

Douglas checked the colony had sufficient room. He tried to find the queen and made sure that the hive was free of disease and abnormality.

Even if he wanted to continue with Julia he was not sure that he could afford to do so. She was probably out of his league, he thought, and then asked himself whether he was in any league at all. If he were a football team what would he be? St Mirren? Queen of the South? He could almost hear rival fans taunting him: *You're shit and you know you are*.

He could see the queen's cell, suspended from the bottom strut. He made sure that there was a sufficient reserve of pollen and sugar syrup. The colony was prepared, as his father would have wanted, for the spring.

That, at least, was one good thing he could tell

his mother.

He put the lid back on the hive and returned to find Elizabeth and Angus in the living room.

'Job done. I think I'll have a shower.'

'Then you can join us for drinks,' said Elizabeth. 'When are you going back to London?'

'I'm not sure.'

Another text arrived from Julia. *Call.*

'Are you still staying with those friends of yours?' Angus asked.

'I am.'

'And you've not got work up here?'

'It's mostly London . . .'

Julia again. *Now.* He really should reply.

'So we'll see less of you,' said Elizabeth.

'Not necessarily, Mother.'

'I was thinking you might even be able to live here. Then you wouldn't have to pay any rent.'

Douglas was irritated that she had suggested this in front of his brother.

'I know, Mother. That's very kind. But it's not very practical.'

'You could even have your father's car.'

Douglas thought what it might be like. It would be a true sign of failure: the international television producer, accustomed to travelling all over Europe and eating in expensive restaurants, now living at home with his mother and driving his dad's old car.

He was supposed to be the one with the bright future, who would live in a comfortable home on the outskirts of Los Angeles with two or three beautiful children. What was he doing, childless and alone, trying to convince his mother that he still had prospects?

Soon it would be dark.

The last of the light showed the dust on the piano and side tables. Douglas looked at the windows and noticed that the shutters needed repainting. He thought he should say something, offer to help, and guessed that his mother was already worried but hadn't liked to ask. He would have to talk to Angus. It was yet another piece of maintenance; preserving the building as their father would have wanted.

'I'll go and have my shower.'

'Well, don't dilly-dally.'

Douglas knew that his mother was trying her best. She was far better at concealing disappointment than his father. That, at least, was one good thing about his death, Douglas decided. He would not have to face up to all those expectations any more.

He tried to imagine what his father would think of him now. He was almost relieved that he was dead.

*   *   *

Elizabeth knew she could not keep her boys together in the house but she wished they could stay longer or visit more often. The rooms contained so many memories of them that they felt complete when her sons were with her and empty when they were not. It never ceased to surprise her; how presence could alter the mood of a room.

Sometimes it helped to imagine that her husband was still with them, that he had only gone off to make a cup of tea and would soon return and settle down with his feet on a footstool and holes

290

in his socks. He would read *Wisden*, or the latest political biography, and the two dogs would lie asleep at his feet after their afternoon walk, muddied and satisfied.

She could even hear Ian's voice, apologising for dying first.

Selfish of me, I know . . .

You can't help it.

At least the stronger of us survives.

I don't think so.

You know I'd be hopeless without you. Everything is hopeless without you.

Elizabeth began to fall asleep. The rest of the family smiled as her head nodded down on to her chest but when she woke she looked afraid that she had been caught out.

'*Liebe kennt der allein, der ohne Hoffnung liebt.*'

'What?' Jack asked.

'It's nothing.'

'I didn't know you could speak German, Mother.'

'You'd be surprised what you don't know.'

'Perhaps you should go to bed,' said Angus.

'I think I will.'

Angus held out his arm and pulled his mother up from the chair.

'Take your time.'

Elizabeth took a moment to steady herself.

'There,' she said, 'I'll be all right in a minute. Everything takes so much longer these days.'

She stopped to look at her family. They had all stood up to say goodnight: Angus and Tessa, Douglas and Jack.

The grandfather clock in the hall struck half past eleven. She had not realised that it was so late.

She bade her nightly farewells, kissing Tessa and her sons.

'I've been so very blessed.'

She made her way up the stairs, holding on to the banister. She knew that she was getting frailer and her balance was less certain. If she stumbled she would no longer be able to say, 'It's all right, I just tripped.' She would have 'had a fall'.

In her room she listened to the sounds of the house at night: the wind in the joists and her family slowly preparing for bed; the locking of the front door, the bathroom pull-lights going on and off, footsteps in corridors, little laughs and temporary farewells. She could hear a brandy glass fall—*Shit*—Douglas, no doubt—and Tessa fetching a dustpan and brush.

She sat in front of her dressing table and unwound her hair, brushing it free. For a moment she could almost see her mother sitting in the same chair, and then herself as a child with black, velvet ribbons, preparing for a birthday party. The sofa she had hidden behind was still in the living room.

She thought back to the formality of the parties she had known in her youth: the black-tie dinners, the reels and strathspeys. She could still envisage all the giggling and the retouching of hair and make-up in the bathrooms upstairs as the men drank whisky and port in the smoking room below.

Sometimes guests would come over from other parties and there could be as many as fourteen couples dancing in the house: the Dashing White Sergeant and the Military Two Step, the Canadian Barn Dance and the Palais Glide.

They would stay on for an early breakfast, of kedgeree or scrambled eggs and bacon, before leaving for home at three in the morning, exhilarated and appreciative, and Elizabeth would walk back upstairs, look out of her bedroom window, and wait for the light of dawn.

It never ceased to surprise her how she had lived so long, become so old, or how much her sons had changed. She had not thought it possible. It seemed almost unjust.

Outside it began to rain. Looking at the darkened window, Elizabeth could only see her reflection. She noticed that her natural expression had gained a sense of mild amusement recently, quizzicality, a renewed interest in what might happen next.

She thought of Ian dead-heading the roses. He had always been fastidious about his tasks in the garden but sometimes he cut them too soon. They might have been blowsy and far-gone but they still had life in them. It was one of the few things about her husband that had always irritated her, getting things done, staying ahead of the game, cutting things off when there was still a way to go yet.

She remembered teasing him, telling him that he had a bark that was fiercer than any animal, and that he really should try to speak to his sons without giving them orders. They found it difficult enough as it was to live up to his expectations.

She could hear his voice, answering her thoughts: *What absolute rot.*

And she felt guilty for suggesting how it must have been hard for the boys to be the sons of such loving parents.

So, Elizabeth, if we'd been miserable they would have been happier? Is that what you are saying?

She remembered the last time she had been out

293

for a walk with her husband. They had driven to one of their favourite views, looking over the Borders from Soutra Summit. They had hardly said anything at all. Ian had reached for her hand and it had been enough.

Elizabeth could never have imagined that her life would turn out as it had: that she would have the boys and that they would marry, have children, face disappointments, and that two out of the three would separate.

The rest of the family had so much on their minds; so many anxieties. Elizabeth did not know what they still wanted out of life or what she could do to help them. Happiness was always so transitory, she thought, so elusive, and yet sometimes it did come, even out of darkness.

She remembered the words of the Minister at her husband's funeral and hoped that she was strong enough to believe them: *Suffering produces perseverance; perseverance, character; and character, hope.*

She knew that she had made her mistakes. She had expected too much of Angus, she had taken Jack for granted, she had spoiled Douglas; and it had taken each one of them a lifetime to leave home.

But they had survived, and Elizabeth had loved them throughout their lives. She had even learned not to show that love too strongly; just in case it alarmed them.

CHAPTER TWENTY

In early March Jack hired a car for the first time since the accident. He drove over the Erskine Bridge and up Loch Lomond, hill on one side, loch on the other, following the contours of the landscape, imagining what it must have been like to build these roads.

He remembered holidays in the Highlands when the girls were young; Annie and Kirsty on a beach, dancing by rock pools, splashing sand and water up against their legs.

Happy feet happy feet happy feet, they sang, *happy feet happy feet happy feet*.

He had watched the way the water filled their footprints, washing away the memory of dancing. He thought how he had never really known how to tell them that he loved them or discover what more he could do to make them happy.

After Tarbert he was off on to windier, more dangerous stretches of road with single tracks, passing-places, and steeper hills climbing to their peaks.

The little light that was left in the day darkened as the snow thickened. Jack was nothing more than a man travelling, following the road, negotiating each corner, concentrating on the darkness ahead.

It was all he could think to do; to drive on, no longer questioning the purpose or the duration of the journey. It filled his mind, the driving and the oncoming snow, separating him from the world.

A song came on the radio. It had been one of Krystyna's favourites. 'Mr Brightside'. She had played it loudly whenever she had thought Jack was out of the house.

On the Corran Ferry he asked for directions from a man whose car sticker read, *Caution: driver asleep*. He had the same song going.

Jack drove on through the darkness, following the edge of another loch. The miles always felt longer in the countryside. Signs warned of ice and narrow bends and of deer that could appear at any minute. He bumped and skittered over cattle grids. Sheep stumbled in the darkness ahead and in the distance. He flashed his lights and sounded his horn but sometimes the animals forced him to stop, making him wait.

It had taken him five hours to reach the edge of the Morven Peninsula; five hours before he recognised that he was running out of road.

He stopped at a pub to ask directions. Jack expected it to be quiet, occupied only by seasoned drinkers, but it was quiz night. A man with a handlebar moustache was asking for the year of Archie Gemmill's World Cup goal. Each question was repeated three times; which Pope had excommunicated Elizabeth I, how many of James VI's tutors were murdered, which part of Scotland was still at war with Russia, and could the teams name the members of the band Wet Wet Wet (one point for each).

The locals sat round wooden tables, the men with beer and whisky chasers, the women with lagers and shorts.

As he left the quizmaster was asking how to spell 'ptarmigan', who lived in the pink house at Balamory, and what was the average length of the human intestine.

Jack returned to his car. The roads were heavy with a snow that showed no sign of relenting. He passed a disused quarry. Then he turned off down a rutted track that led to a series of small cottages. He stopped at a distance, uncertain which house was Krystyna's, and parked the car in a recess, noticing how it dropped sharply away into a ditch.

Jack got out of the car, put on his coat, and slammed the car door shut. A dog began barking in a house up to the right of him.

He looked through the first of the lit windows. Inside a boy in a Rangers shirt was jumping up and down on his bed. Next door, an elderly couple were making their tea in the kitchen.

There were sheep brushing against garden fences, bleating against the weather.

A modern bungalow revealed a man being nursed by a female companion. She was giving him soup, spoonful by spoonful. It reminded Jack of his father.

The snow increased in intensity. He knew he should ring a doorbell, any bell, and ask which house was hers. But he wasn't sure if he was ready, despite the length of the journey.

A Land-Rover passed him on the road and the driver stopped to ask if he was lost. Perhaps his car was stuck in the drifts.

'A fearful night,' the man said. 'You don't want to be out in this for long.'

'I won't.'

Jack could see lights in the harbour, the pier stretching away, fishing boats and ferries berthed for the night. In the morning he could go anywhere, out to the islands or on to the North Atlantic.

297

Then he saw Krystyna come out of the doorway of a croft in the distance, just before the track curved away into darkness. He could see her in the light of a porch, brushing back her hair and looking out to sea before turning and closing the door.

The light in the porch went out.

Jack hoped she would come into sight again, through the lit windows, but she was already drawing the curtains. She stopped for a moment, distracted, and looked down.

He moved closer to the house, turning his body sideways against the wind and the snow. He could feel the cold and the damp in his feet. His hair was wet against his face.

For a time he could not see her. She had stooped away from his view but then she rose again, gathering a curtain with one hand, and Jack could now see briefly, but clearly, that she was holding a child.

Adam.

He walked up to the croft. There was a string with a small bell attached. Perhaps she would not hear it for the wind and the night. He pulled the string and waited. Then he knocked; his cold hand against hard damp wood. He expected the curtains to move, that she would check to see who it was, but the light in the porch came on once more. He was surprised by its brightness.

Krystyna opened the door. She was paler than he had remembered. Perhaps it was the winter.

'Oh,' she said. 'You are here. I was not sure . . .'

'I wasn't sure either.' His voice sounded weaker than he had intended.

She stepped aside.

298

'You must come in.'

Jack stamped the snow off his shoes. He thought he should have brought something; wine or flowers.

Krystyna closed the door.

'Let me help you with your coat,' she said. 'You look like you have walked all the way.'

'No,' he said, 'I drove.'

'I was making a joke. I'm sorry. I am nervous. *Kto ucieka, winnym sie staje.*'

'What is that?'

'Running away makes you guilty.'

The croft had one room with a kitchen off to the side and a ladder up to a raised sleeping platform. Instructions and memos were pinned to the wall. *There is no extra charge for peat, but please keep a note of the amount of coal that is used on the fire.*

Jack looked over to the cot.

'Would you like to see him?' Krystyna asked.

'Yes.'

The boy was pinker than Jack had anticipated with thick hair and dark eyelashes. He stooped over the edge of the cot to look, recalling the births of his own children, Annie and Kirsty: the long-forgotten smell of baby.

'You got my letter?'

'He's beautiful.'

'He is my brave boy,' said Krystyna and then stopped. 'I am sorry . . .'

'I could have helped you.'

'I had destroyed one life already. I did not want to ruin yours.'

Jack had not expected to speak so intensely so soon.

'You would not have ruined it.'

299

'I did not want to take that chance.'

'It would have been fine.'

'Sit down,' said Krystyna. 'I will make you some tea. You must be cold.'

The snow came again, changing direction as it fell. It began to sound like rain, taunting in the roofs and in the gutters, caught in the low repeating wind. Jack watched Krystyna, leaning over the child, hushing him gently, unconcerned by the presence of another, singing almost under her breath. *Aaa, Kotki dwa, szare, bure obydwa . . .*

He listened to the wind in the silences between them; the wood on the fire; the child sighing in his sleep.

'I suppose if Sandy had known it would have been different,' Jack said. He still did not like saying the name—Sandy—aloud.

'What do you mean?'

'If he had waited.'

'But he did not wait. And then it happened and then we met and then there was fate.'

Jack could hardly remember what his life had been like before all this had happened; before the drive through the night, the face in the darkness, the bright lights of the police station and the stark presence of Krystyna before him at the funeral.

She adjusted the bedding around the child. The croft was warm for such a cold night. Jack realised that he was hungry. He wanted to ask if Krystyna had any soup.

'I should have known,' he said instead. 'I should have guessed.'

'I should have told you.'

She knelt down and put more coal on the fire, picking out individual pieces with her fingers so as

300

not to disturb the child with the noise of the scuttle. She placed peat on the surface and watched it spit and smoulder. Then she rinsed her hands.

Jack watched the child. He remembered how he had first felt as a father; the fierceness and the fear in his love.

Krystyna realised that she had forgotten to make the tea.

'It's all right,' said Jack.

'I will do it now.'

'Had you always decided to keep the child?'

'I think it began in your parents' house. It was the day of the play. It was when the little girl fell into the swimming pool. No one had noticed. It was very slow when it happened, when I was watching, and then it was all so fast. I was there, and then I was in the water with the little girl and she lived when she could have died.'

'Tessa told me.'

'I gave back a life by accident. It was crazy but it was enough to make me stop: a piece of fortune to make up for the luck that had gone before. And then, having brought back a life by chance, I could not ignore what was inside me.'

'And then?'

'Then I don't know or I cannot remember. Sometimes I think I did not know what I was doing or thinking. Feelings I thought I did not have arrived without warning; emotions I did not understand.'

'New extremes.'

'Do you think that is normal?'

'I do not know.'

Krystyna handed Jack a mug of tea.

'But tell me your news,' she said. 'You can see what has happened to me. What about you?'

'Oh, I don't know.'

'Tell me . . .'

Jack began to talk about his father. He could have kept to the facts, making the story as simple as possible, but he found that he needed to talk at greater length. Perhaps it was a way of avoiding talking about Sandy or the child that lay beside them.

He told Krystyna how he could not stop dreaming about his father; fragments from the past kept recurring but they seemed altered and uncertain, as if he had either misremembered them all or they had never happened.

'I am sorry. He was a good man.'

Jack told her how he could still see his father in his floppy white hat, tending his bees, pruning the roses, and looking up to greet him from the end of the garden. He could still hear his voice: *Good to see you, son*.

He missed him. He missed Krystyna.

'What would he think about this?' she asked.

'He would want you to be happy. He was very fond of you.'

'I am glad.'

'And how do you live?' Jack wished he had not spoken so much about himself.

'I have a little money. People are kind. What I do is simple. And I do it as well as I can. I look after Adam. I make a big goulash that can last almost a week.'

'And how long will you stay here?' he asked.

'I do not know if I am ready to do anything different. Were you worried when you had your

302

girls? Of bad things happening?'

'All the time.'

'I am frightened of making a mistake, of not loving him enough, of neglecting him or putting him in danger. I do not want to sound neurotic. Is that the word? I cannot have more disasters in my life.'

'Sometimes children are more resilient than we think.'

'I cannot take that chance.'

Jack could hear a car starting up in the distance, a farmer probably, beginning another day. He had lost all sense of time.

'Shall I make a bed?' Krystyna asked. 'There is a sleeping platform. I do not know if it is comfortable.'

'It's all right,' Jack said. 'I should go.'

'You have come all this way . . .'

All he had wanted to do was to make things better; to atone for what had happened.

'Perhaps it wouldn't be right to stay.'

'No, you must.'

'I just wanted to see you. I liked it: how we were in the summer.'

'But it could not go on. Not with a child.'

'I don't know,' Jack said. 'Perhaps it could.'

He surprised himself with his words. He had not expected to make such an offer.

'I am too young. You have your daughters . . .'

'I'm not sure I do any more.'

'You will always have them.'

'They don't seem to be particularly keen on me.'

'They will come back. Everything comes back in the end.'

Jack tried to smile. It seemed a lot to ask.

'I am sure they love you,' Krystyna said.

Jack remembered sitting on the edge of the bed and reading to his daughters when they were small, kissing their foreheads and tucking them in. He used to look in on them when they were sleeping, listen to their slow, even breaths, and imagine what they were dreaming.

'Please,' Krystyna was saying. 'You must stay. Let me make up the bed.'

Jack could hear the sharpness of the wind circling the croft. He listened to the sea returning with the tide.

For a moment he thought that he could be a man at any time in any history, sheltering from the storm with a girl and her child.

How many people had stood in this same croft before them? How many had been born or bereaved in this very place, or had their lives changed so that when the wind abated and the snow melted they would leave knowing that nothing could ever be the same?

They talked through the night.

Jack lay on the sleeping platform. It had been cut into the rafters and there was a small window to one side. They spoke without seeing each other in the darkness. Sometimes they would drift into a half-sleep, sometimes the child would need to be fed or comforted.

Jack remembered his daughters when they were young, coming into the bed with their cold feet, warming them on their mother's back, sleeping between them.

He and Maggie had taken it in turns to get up and walk the floor with them. Sometimes he would hold the two of them together, one in each arm

304

against his chest. He had woken between two and four in the morning ever since.

Perhaps it could happen again, he thought. Perhaps he could restart his life, no longer worrying about the expectation of his parents, the rivalry with his brothers, the distance and inevitable separation from his daughters. He could leave his former life behind.

He tried to think what the future might mean.

Adam.

He thought how the recent past had changed him: the suicide of Sandy, the death of his father, the meeting with Krystyna, the birth of her child. If so much could happen in a year, how much more could happen in a life?

He looked up into the wooden rafters above him. He could not imagine sleeping. He did not know how long it would be until it was light.

He spoke again to Krystyna.

'Are you still awake?' he asked.

'What are you thinking?'

'I was wondering what it would be like to stay here.'

There was silence.

First Jack waited; then he thought that Krystyna had fallen asleep.

He was about to turn away and try to sleep once more when he heard her reply.

'You are already here.'

'I meant for longer than a night.'

'Stay as long as you like,' she said. 'It is your turn.'

'I suppose it is.'

'And then, perhaps, when we are ready, we can return together. Or go somewhere new, somewhere neither of us have ever been; as if we have no past.'

Before he had met Krystyna Jack had thought that his life was going to be little more than a slow decline towards oblivion; but he knew now that to be calm was to be removed, alone, and he wanted its opposite: to be involved, to be with another, to sell his life upon adventure.

At first he had mistaken the signs, thinking of Krystyna's absence and departure as a betrayal, but now he recognised it for what it was: an opportunity to come to terms with the possible, a chance, perhaps, to gather energy for a renewed assault on love and on death and on fear. It was the beginning of hope.

'What is stopping you?' Krystyna asked.

Jack looked out of the dark window.

'Nothing is stopping me,' he said.

Still the snow fell.

ACKNOWLEDGEMENTS

East Fortune is a real place, twenty miles east of Edinburgh, but the Henderson family home, the kirk and the river are all fictional.

I am grateful to the Meiklejohn, Stuart-Smith, Raven, and Balfour families for their inspiration.

I would like to thank early readers, friends, and colleagues: Georgina Brown, Magdalena Buchan, Douglas Cairns, Peter Chalmers, Pip Clothier, David Godwin, Erica Jarnes, Neville Kidd, Anna Ledgard, Rona Lewis, Allan Little, Joanna MacGregor, Juliette Mead, Henry and Merric McKenzie-Johnston, Mary Morris, Alex Nicholson, Kathryn Patrick, Sarah Peat, Luisa Pretolani, Alexandra Pringle, Marie Lou Shoenmakers, Gillian Stern, Mary Tomlinson, Pip Torrens, Jo Willett.

I have relied on the Loeb Classical Library version of the *De Rerum Natura* by Lucretius (*On the Nature of Things*, Harvard, 1975) and the translation by the American poet Rolfe Humphries (*The Way Things Are*, Indiana University Press, 1968).

A NOTE ON THE AUTHOR

James Runcie is the author of three novels, *The Discovery of Chocolate*, *The Colour of Heaven* and *Canvey Island*. He is also an award-winning film-maker. Recently he directed a documentary following a year in the life of J.K. Rowling. James Runcie lives in Edinburgh with his wife and two daughters.

CHIVERS
LARGE PRINT
PRINT
–direct–

If you have enjoyed this Large Print book and would like to build up your own collection of Large Print books, please contact

Chivers Large Print Direct

Chivers Large Print Direct offers you a full service:

• Prompt mail order service

• Easy-to-read type

• The very best authors

• Special low prices

For further details either call Customer Services on (01225) 336552 or write to us at Chivers Large Print Direct, **FREEPOST**, Bath BA1 3ZZ

Telephone Orders: **FREEPHONE** 08081 72 74 75